Alonzo B. Cornell

Biography of Ezra Cornell

Alonzo B. Cornell

Biography of Ezra Cornell

ISBN/EAN: 9783337030971

Printed in Europe, USA, Canada, Australia, Japan

Cover: Foto ©Raphael Reischuk / pixelio.de

More available books at **www.hansebooks.com**

"TRUE AND FIRM."

BIOGRAPHY

OF

EZRA CORNELL,

FOUNDER OF THE

CORNELL UNIVERSITY.

A Filial Tribute.

NEW YORK:
A. S. BARNES & COMPANY.
1884.

PREFACE.

FOR several years it has been the author's desire that a suitable biography of the FOUNDER OF THE CORNELL UNIVERSITY should be prepared by another, whose cultured pen would invest the work with that degree of interest to which the subject is so worthily entitled. Exacting duties have, however, delayed such an undertaking, and still prevent any reasonable promise of its early consummation. Mainly for the purpose of placing the material in form for safe preservation for future use, this simple record of the leading incidents of his earnest life and untiring labors has been prepared, which, it is hoped, may hereafter serve as a text-book of facts requisite for the more interesting treatment of the subject by other and abler hands. Prepared originally for private use, it is realized that the work is deficient of any literary merit which would justify its publication, and that

course has finally been taken only at the urgent
solicitation of interested friends.

Time has already largely depleted the ranks of
those familiar with the early history of the telegraph enterprise in America, and but few now remain with us who participated in the pioneer work
with which the subject of this sketch was so intimately associated. Viewed from the standpoint
of the wonderful development of the telegraph at
the present day, the many interesting incidents
which attended the earlier efforts to place this
novel invention on a substantial foundation, possess much of the interest of romance. The admirable and intelligent foresight, the energetic
labors, the untiring perseverance, and the unwavering faith which distinguished the efforts of this
courageous pioneer, contending with the vigorous
antagonisms of rival interests, afford a lesson well
calculated to encourage the endeavors of others,
who find themselves confronted and embarrassed
by obstacles which endanger the success of cherished ambitions or objects.

Personal incidents and characteristics have been
made the subject of more detailed reference than
may perhaps interest the general reader. Considering the nature of the work as planned in its

original design, it was deemed best, however, to canvass these features more definitely, to enable future students of the Founder's unselfish labors the better to appreciate the true character of the man. Whatever may hereafter be written of him will, with entire propriety, deal more particularly with reference to his great services in the cause of education. It has seemed better, therefore, that the present effort should treat of his individuality with all necessary completeness, especially in view of the fact that the writer is more thoroughly familiar with his whole career than others can be, who are likely to take part in future contributions to the subject.

Much space, relatively, has been given in these pages to the subject of the Cornell Library, from the fact that it is believed to have been the influence of this undertaking on the mind of the Founder, as the work progressed, which in large measure prepared the way for his subsequent course. Wider interest will doubtless incline to the greater project which engrossed so much of his philanthropic efforts. His great endeavors to establish on the most enduring basis the great educational institution which has already attained such eminence, cannot fail to interest all who contemplate

PREFACE.

them.   The limit of this work has, necessarily, confined treatment of the University to the merest outline of the circumstances leading to its endowment and organization, with a brief reference to its subsequent development.   This deficiency, however, is of less importance, from the fact that information respecting the institution is readily available to all who may have occasion to desire it.

A. B. C.

New York, January, 1884.

CONTENTS.

CHAPTER IV.

EARLY MANHOOD.

CHAPTER V.

MARRIAGE.

CHAPTER VI.

SEEKING BUSINESS.

CHAPTER IX.

THE WESTERN UNION TELEGRAPH COMPANY.

CHAPTER X.

AGRICULTURAL TASTES.

CHAPTER XI.

PUBLIC LIFE.

CHAPTER XII.

THE CIVIL WAR.

CONTENTS. xiii

EZRA CORNELL.

CHAPTER I.

ANCESTRY.

THE opportunities afforded by Republican institutions, for the development and elevation of individual character, illustrate more, perhaps, than
anything else, the wisdom of our forefathers, in
establishing a government so aptly described by
the martyred LINCOLN, as "of the people, by
the people, for the people." In no other country is it possible for the youth of humble birth to
achieve results which are constantly occurring in
our history. Here we have numberless examples
of men, born and reared in the deepest poverty

2

and obscurity, attaining the most eminent positions in public life. Dignitaries of the highest rank have in many instances ascended from the most humble and unpromising origin; while many of the greatest fortunes in the land, have been acquired by men, who began life with empty hands, and without the aid of friends or patrons. So, too, some of the most important and valuable inventions and discoveries, have been made by persons, springing from the most obscure walks of life. The learned professions furnish innumerable illustrations of like character, and it may be stated almost as a rule, that the grandest successes in the intellectual activities of our country, have been accomplished by those, who may truthfully be classed as self-made men, and have arisen, unsupported, by means of their own talents and efforts.

The career of the subject of this sketch, Ezra Cornell, the founder of the Cornell University, presents a notable example of the achievement of unaided effort. The child of humble parentage, reared in a new country, beyond the reach of advanced educational facilities, with only such rudimentary training as the district school of a frontier region afforded, by the inherent force of his native talents, he successfully gained a great fortune, that, in the desire to elevate his fellow-man,

he devoted to the establishment of a noble educational institution, which, though only now in the
second decade of its existence, has already attained a prominent position among the oldest and
most celebrated universities of the country.

A complete history of the unceasing labors and
indomitable energy, devoted to the acquisition of
his fortune; of the obstacles encountered and surmounted; of the admirable foresight with which
he planned, and the unwavering faith, by which
he was sustained to final success, through a wilderness of difficulties and discouragements, would
read almost like a romance; while the generosity
and self-sacrifice with which he dedicated the
fruits of success to the intellectual advancement
of his race, afford a striking illustration of the
real greatness of the man.

The ancestry of Mr. Cornell, both paternal and
maternal, was of Puritan origin, descending from
the original settlement at Plymouth, so celebrated
in the early history of civilization, on the American continent. For many generations, they had
been members of the religious denomination, or
sect, of Friends, more commonly called Quakers,
a class of people well-known for sturdy uprightness of character, and for their domestic virtues.
With them, industry, sobriety and frugality were
dominant characteristics, while they were espe-

cially noted for benevolence, and charitable acts. Domestic in their ways of life, marriage was with them a holy tie, and the family circle was considered a sacred precinct, which should be exempt from indecorous or trifling invasion. In those days there was but little wealth in the country, and the possession of an independent competence was, indeed, rare. Labor was, therefore, the rule, and idleness the exception. Then as now, however, industry and economy were certain to bring their reward. While some misfortune might often bring want, real poverty was but little known, but if caused by unavoidable circumstances, it was not regarded as discreditable, and was always certain to find quick relief.

Mr. Cornell's father, ELIJAH CORNELL, was born in the town of Swansea, Bristol County, Mass., October 17, 1771, and was consequently four and a half years of age when the Declaration of Independence was promulgated by the Continental Congress. He was the son of Elijah Cornell, who was married, December 4, 1769, to Sarah, daughter of Benjamin and Mehetabel Miller. Both of Mr. Cornell's parents were descended from families, who had, for many generations, been reared in the near vicinity of his place of nativity. From his parentage, he inherited the modest and unpretending simplicity of character, that so particularly distinguished the race of people from which he was descended. His father died while young Elijah was still in infancy, leaving his mother, with two young children dependent upon her, and with very slender means of support. She was afterward, August 11, 1777, married to Benjamin Chase, an estimable man in every sense of the term, who became, indeed, a father to the fatherless. Under his fostering care, Elijah and his elder brother, were brought up on an equal footing with a considerable family of children, the issue of the second marriage of their mother.

That they were fairly educated, considering the primitive times in which they lived, is attested by the fact that Elijah was frequently employed in teaching school, both before and after his marriage. Elijah, at the age of nineteen, was indentured by his mother to Asa Chase, of Somer- set, Bristol County, Mass., to learn the potter's trade. The letters of indenture, which bear date January 28, 1791, are still extant and in the possession of his descendants. The mother of Ezra Cornell, Eunice, daughter of Captain Reuben Barnard and Phebe Coleman, was born at Nine Partners, Dutchess County, N. Y., May 11, 1788. Her father was formerly a sea captain, engaged in whale fishery from New Bedford, who, in his earlier years, had made many voyages around Cape Horn to the Pacific Ocean, in the prosecution of his calling, sometimes being away on a single cruise two or three years, without tidings from home during the entire voyage. Tiring of the monotony and dangers of a sea-faring life, and especially, of the prolonged absence from his family incident thereto, he withdrew from it, and, attracted by the reported prosperity of former neighbors who had emigrated to Columbia and Dutchess Counties, N. Y., he was induced to follow them, and with his family removed to his new home, not many years prior to the birth of his daughter named above.

Elijah Cornell and Eunice Barnard were united in marriage in the "Friends' Meeting," at New Britain, July 4, 1805.* In harmony with their

---

* MARRIAGE CERTIFICATE.

Whereas Elijah Cornell, son of Elijah Cornell and Sarah his wife, of the county of Bristol, in the State of Massachusetts, and Eunice Barnard, daughter of Reuben Barnard and Phœbe his wife, of the county of Columbia, and State of New York, having declared their intention of marrying with each other, before the Monthly Meetings of the people called Quakers, held at Hudson and New Britain in the State last named, they having consent of parents and parties concerned, and nothing appearing to obstruct their said proposal, were allowed of by the Meeting. Now, these are to certify all whom it may concern, that for the full accomplishment of their said intentions, this fourth day of Seventh Month, in the year 1805, they, the said Elijah Cornell and early training, both were professing members of the religious denomination, to which their families had been attached, and throughout their prolonged and useful lives, they continued humble, consistent, and devoted Christians, careful in observing every requirement of their faith,

---

Eunice Barnard, appeared in a public meeting of said people, at New Britain, and he, the said Elijah Cornell, taking the said Eunice Barnard by the hand, did in a solemn manner, openly declare that he took her to be his wife, promising, through Divine assistance, to be unto her a faithful and loving husband, until death separate them, or words to that effect. And then the said Eunice Barnard, did in like manner declare that she took the said Elijah Cornell, to be her husband, promising, through Divine assistance, to be unto him a faithful and loving wife until death separate them, or words to that purport; and moreover they, the said Elijah Cornell and Eunice Barnard, she, according to the custom of marriage assuming the name of her husband, as a further confirmation, did there to these presents set their hands.

ELIJAH CORNELL.
EUNICE CORNELL.

And we, whose names have hereunto subscribed, being present at the solemnization of said marriage and subscription, have as witnesses hereunto set our hands, the day and year first above written.

REUBEN BARNARD.	SIMEON MACY.
SHADRACH WILBUR.	GIDEON SWAIN.
DAVID REYNOLDS.	PHEBE MACY.
PHILIP CORNELL.	ELIZABETH BARNARD.
FRANCIS BARNARD.	MARY BARNARD.
BENJAMIN CHASE.	ANNA GARDNER.
ELIAKIM MOSHER.	ANN PECKHAM.
URIEL COFFIN.	LIDIA SWAIN.

following in both speech and dress the peculiarities of their sect. Although Elijah Cornell was nearly thirty-four years of age, when he
entered into the wedded state, he lived to see
all of his eleven children grow to maturity,
married and settled in life, the youngest being,
at the time of his death, more than thirty
years of age. He resided in Westchester County, N. Y., at the date of his marriage, and for
about two years thereafter, at Westchester Landing, a hamlet at the head of tide-water navigation, on the Bronx River. Here Mr. Cornell
and his brother, who had learned the trade of
ship carpentry, joined as partners in building a
vessel for the Atlantic coasting trade, which unfortunately was lost on its first voyage, and being
uninsured, proved a serious loss to its owners, who
had invested the greater portion of their savings
in its construction. Discouraged by this experience, Mr. Cornell abandoned further ventures in
navigation, and determined to change his residence
to what was then the Far West, and in 1807 removed to the town of De Ruyter, Madison County, N. Y. Here he purchased and settled on a
farm, on what is now known as Crum Hill, about
three miles east of De Ruyter village.

It is not at all improbable, that in selecting
the location of his new home, Mr. Cornell was

influenced, to a considerable degree, by the fact
that within a short distance was an extensive
neighborhood of "Friends," numerous enough to
maintain a religious society of their own peculiar
faith. This portion of the town of De Ruyter,
acquired the designation of "Quaker Basin,"
from the circumstance that nearly all of the residents of that beautiful valley were Friends, and
although their numerical predominance in the
vicinity long since ceased, Quaker Basin still continues as a local geographical name.

Certain it is that the locality proved more satisfactory, on account of its social and religious
associations, than as a profitable field of labor, for
after an experience of two years in pioneer life,
Mr. Cornell was induced to return to Westchester
County, and resume work at his trade. He entered the employment of William Young & Co.,
at Westchester village, as foreman of their pottery in April, 1810, at a compensation of $10 per
week, and his family joined him a few months
later. The following year he located at Tarry-
town, on the Hudson River, and was interested
in the same kind of business about four years,
after which he changed to West Farms, where he
was also employed at the potter's trade. In 1817
he removed to the State of New Jersey and settled in Bergen County, and soon engaged in the

manufacture of earthenware on his own account, at what was then called the English Neighborhood, not very far from the present beautiful and thriving village of Englewood. Here he continued about three years, but owing to the depressed condition of affairs after the close of the war with England, and the severe competition in his line of business, from the importation of English manufactures, he sold out his pottery and determined once more to try his fortunes in De Ruyter, whither he returned with his family late in the autumn of 1819.

CHAPTER II.

PIONEER LIFE.

THOSE of our own generation, familiar only with existing modes of travel, can but faintly realize the hardships encountered by families emigrating to any considerable distance, with their household effects, in that, to us, remote period. At the present day, the journey from New York City to Madison County, may be made in ten hours time, with all the comforts and luxuries of the drawing-room car by day, and the sleeping car by night. It would have been utterly impossible for the pioneers of our then frontier region, to contemplate with any degree of intelligence, even had they been foretold by the most minute revelation, the wonders of the modern development of railway facilities.

At the period of the occurrence of incidents related in this chapter, the means of transit, in the
State of New York were very meagre.   On the
Hudson River, steam navigation was in its infancy,
and the only mode of public conveyance through
the western portion of the State, was by stage-
coach across the older counties bordering on the
Mohawk Valley, and thence to Buffalo, a village of moderate size, at the foot of Lake Erie.
The southern tier of counties, adjacent to Pennsylvania, were but sparsely populated, and no ac-
commodation for travel, had as yet been established through them.   The original Erie Canal,
was only then in course of construction, and was
not opened for traffic until several years later, while
the first railway in the State, was not yet even
projected.   In removing his family from New Jersey to Madison County, Mr. Cornell was obliged,
for want of other transportation, to make the
journey with his own teams, carrying also his
personal effects, household goods and provisions,
as well as many farming utensils, and implements
of his mechanical trade.   Their course was, of
necessity, much of the way, through an almost
uninhabited wilderness, over the rudest and sometimes nearly impassable roads, frequently interrupted by unbridged streams.

With so many obstacles to overcome, and at

the slow pace of animals drawing lumber wag-
ons, loaded with the persons and possessions of
a family seeking a new home, it would indeed be
difficult for us to realize the tedium and positive
discomforts of such a journey. The route followed, was along the Ramapo Valley, and, by
way of Goshen, through Orange County; across
the Shawungunk range of mountains near the
present town of Otisville on the Erie Railway,
and over the Navesink River at the little hamlet of Cuddebackville, about eight miles above the
site of the now prosperous village of Port Jervis,
which was then covered with a dense forest.
Thence through the great beech woods of Sul-
livan and Delaware Counties, crossing the Chenango Valley at Oxford, and over the bleak hills
of Chenango County, to the place of destination.

The travelling party consisted of Mr. Cornell,
his wife, and six children, the oldest only twelve
years old and the youngest an infant in its mother's arms, and these, with their domestic goods,
constituted the burden of two ordinary teams.
For a portion of the distance, they were so fortunate as to obtain entertainment over night, at public inns or farm-houses, while through the more
secluded regions, they were obliged to content
themselves with the shelter of their own covered
vehicles, and the cheering hospitality of a camp-

fire in the woods.   In the cold, short, wintry days,
the journey thus made, covering a distance of
about two hundred and fifty miles, occupied something more than two weeks, a period of time sufficient at the present day, to permit emigrants to
be conveyed from Great Britain, or the Continental ports of Europe, to Iowa and Minnesota, or
the frontier regions of the United States.

The contrast between the modes of travel in
1819, and those which we now enjoy, striking as
it may seem, is not greater than the difference
between the condition of pioneer farmers of the
former period, and those of the times with which
we are familiar.   While through the older settled
portions of the country, the stage-coach furnished
means for the transit of passengers, there were
no public facilities for the conveyance of freight,
except over such natural water-courses as were
navigable.   To find purchasers for surplus farm
products, the producer had necessarily to convey
them to a point of shipment, however distant it
might be.

Beyond the ordinary home consumption of such
articles, no market existed short of localities favored with water navigation.   For the very meagre growth which could be realized from the cold
and sterile hills of De Ruyter, there was no demand which could be relied upon, more acces-

sible than at Albany, one hundred and fifty miles distant, to which place the farmers of Madison County, were often obliged to convey their grain by teams. It may readily be imagined, therefore, that the net avails of the small surplus of agricultural products, after paying the expense of transportation, were limited indeed. Mr. Cornell determined to establish an earthenware pottery on his farm, to enable him to furnish an article, which would command a home market. The wares of foreign· potteries, had not yet penetrated the wilds of Madison and adjoining counties, and the pioneer was fortunate enough to find ready sale for the goods of his manufacture, thereby very profitably supplementing the operations of the farm. In the work of the shop, as well as that of the field, he utilized the labor of his growing sons, thus rearing them to habits of industry, and preparing them for careers of usefulness and prosperity, when they should venture forth from the paternal home.

Gradually the introduction of the celebrated Amboy clay, from New Jersey, by water transportation, enabled potteries located on the line of the canal to produce stoneware at prices which proved injurious to the sale of earthenware; and owing to the isolated location of De Ruyter, it was found impossible to compete successfully with manufactories more favorably situated. Several of his children having previously settled at Ithaca, and desiring their parents to locate near them, Mr. Cornell, in 1841, changed his residence to that place, where he established a new pottery, for the production of both earthen and stoneware.

This change was found advantageous, not only on account of the added variety of product, but also from the more extended market, which the new location allowed him to supply. He continued the manufacture of both kinds of ware at Ithaca, for about ten years, when, owing to advanced age, he was induced to dispose of his property, and retire finally from active business pursuits. The pottery thus inaugurated by him at Ithaca, has been carried on by his successors in business, and still remains one of the useful and prosperous industries of the village, affording remunerative employment for a considerable number of persons.

He continued to live at Ithaca until 1855, when, with his wife and youngest daughter, the only one of his children remaining at home, he removed to Albion, Mich., where several of his daughters were then residing near each other. Here the declining years of their long and useful lives, were spent in the enjoyment of the loyal and grateful devotion of their thoughtful and affectionate children.

In all that constitutes sturdy and upright manhood, Elijah Cornell was a worthy example. Beginning life empty-handed, by industry and frugality he was able to maintain in comfort and contentment, a family of eleven children, giving them the best opportunities for education which the locality of his residence afforded, and training them by precept and example, to habits of sobriety and thrift, under the influence of which they became prosperous and useful members of society. He was a man of singular frankness and simplicity of character; of unquestioned integrity, and faithful in the discharge of every duty and obligation.

His house was ever the seat of graceful hospitality, and the needy never went from his door, without a generous response to all reasonable appeals for assistance. Mr. Cornell's marriage was, perhaps, the most fortunate event of his life. His wife was a woman of a remarkable character; gentle and benevolent in disposition, with a peculiar sweetness of manner, which won the admiration and esteem of all with whom she became associated. Domestic in her tastes and habits; amiable, patient, and cheerful at all times and under all circumstances; devoted to the dis-

3

charge of home duties, she was in every respect
a model wife and mother, enjoying in the fullest
sense, the affection of her husband, and the love
and veneration of her children. An humble and
earnest Christian, she never tired in the service
of her Master.

To the sick, the poor, and the unfortunate, it was
her pleasure to minister with the kindness and
patience of a good Samaritan, and no worthy
call failed to receive her sympathetic attention.
After fifty-two years of happy married life, through
the whole course of which hers was the presiding
spirit of a peaceful, Christian home, she was called
to her rest, lamented and revered by a large circle
of loving and appreciative friends.

Her husband survived her five years, and died
March 27, 1862, having attained the remarkable
age, of ninety-one years, in the full possession
of his mental and physical faculties. Seldom, indeed, is it given to man to pass such number of
years, so absolutely free from enmities or antagonisms, and so universally respected and esteemed
by all who knew him.

It is, of course, impossible at this late day, to
place on record, more than a very brief outline of
the career of Elijah Cornell, which covered the
whole period of our national existence, down to
the second year of the late civil war. Born prior

to the revolution, he was a voter at the second election of Washington, as President of the United States, and was in the full maturity of manhood at the beginning of the present century. Like the generality of members of his religious faith, he took but little active part in the direction of public affairs, and therefore no public record affords intelligence respecting him. A quiet, unpretending, law-abiding citizen, engrossed in the care and maintenance of a large family, he left no written account of his daily walk and labors, beyond that found in his family register.

The only source of information, therefore, available at the present day, especially in reference to the earlier portion of his life, consists of such traditions of the family, as those now living, have from time to time, incidentally acquired, and treasured in their memories. From the sketch herewith presented, it will be observed that his children must have been reared in the path of virtue and rectitude, and it is gratifying to record, that, in subsequent life, they justified the expectation, which such training would naturally inspire.

The descendants of this worthy couple, at the present time, number about one hundred and fifty, already extending to the fifth generation, and it can be truthfully stated that the family, in all branches, are free from discredit, in all that pertains to good citizenship, and independent self-maintenance. It is also, a matter of especial congratulation, that they are exempt, in a remarkable degree, from the blight of intemperance, that abominable curse, which has brought misfortune and sorrow to so many families, that would otherwise have been prosperous and happy.

Earnest and painstaking in the pursuit of knowledge, they have shown commendable zeal in improving every opportunity for education. Quite a number have devoted themselves to teaching, and several are members of the professions of law, medicine, divinity, and the sciences. Whereas but few of them have acquired large wealth, many have become possessed of considerable estates, and the rest are in thrifty and comfortable circumstances, occupying creditable standing in the communities in which they reside; while several have attained prominent and influential positions in public life, and in the business affairs of the country.

Although never in the enjoyment of any large surplus of worldly wealth, Elijah Cornell was an industrious and prosperous man, whose financial condition, was quite equal to the average of his neighbors. He was always able to maintain a comfortable and cheerful home, from which his children, ever reluctantly, went forth to establish themselves in independent life, but to which they often returned, with feelings of gladness, certain of being received with a cordial and affectionate parental greeting. In the several places of their residence, the family were highly respected and esteemed for their uprightness and genial neighborly qualities.

CHAPTER III.

BIRTH, CHILDHOOD AND YOUTH.

Birth of Ezra Cornell, 1807.—Vigorous Constitution.—Obedient
Childhood.—Active and Studious.—Anxiety to attend School.
—Superior Scholarship.—Meagre Educational Advantages.—
Mechanical Tastes.—Assists building Pottery.—Erecting
Dwelling.—Surprising Success.—Ambition for Self-support.—
Seeking Employment.—Syracuse a mere Hamlet.—Employ-
ment at Homer.—Visiting Home.—Decides to locate at Ithaca.
—Early Advantages of the Village.—On Foot to Ithaca.—
Worthy Ambition.

OF all the worthy people assembled in Friends'
meeting, at New Britain, on that pleasant Sabbath summer morning, July 4, 1805, probably not
a single one contemplated, even in what might
have seemed the wildest realms of imagination,
the possibility of results which, down to the present time, have actually been realized from the
marriage they were then called upon to witness,
of the staid bachelor, Elijah Cornell, already approaching middle age, and the young and gentle
maiden, Eunice Barnard.   As related in the preceding chapter, the descendants of the couple then
united in the bonds of matrimony, number at this

time, 1884, more than one hundred and fifty persons, all of whom, point with pride, to their common ancestry. The direct issue of this marriage was the birth of eleven children, six sons and five daughters, of whom all were reared to maturity, and married.

The eldest of these children, and the subject of this sketch, EZRA CORNELL, was born at Westchester Landing, Westchester County, N. Y., January 11, 1807. From his parents he inherited a superb constitution, which, with his temperate habits, enabled him to endure an unusual amount of labor, and throughout his active life, he was noted for the wonderful energy he devoted to the accomplishment of whatever undertaking, he was called upon to perform. In stature he was about six feet high, rather spare in figure, with fine muscular development. His features were rugged, with high cheek-bones and prominent forehead, indicating marked alertness of the perceptive faculties. He was remarkably industrious and never an idler, either as boy or man. While fond of the ordinary sports of youth, and a leader in those in which he engaged, his ingenious and practical mind led him, even during boyhood, to constant endeavor in an useful direction, such as repairing some damaged article or devising a new implement.

Naturally of an inquiring turn of mind, young Cornell early manifested an extraordinary desire for the acquisition of knowledge. He was a devoted student, and eagerly availed himself of every means for improvement within his reach. His privileges in this respect, however, were extremely narrow, as, owing to the inability of his parents to send him from home, in pursuit of an education, he was obliged to content himself, with the resources of the common school of the remote region of his residence, supplemented with such additional instruction, as his father's accomplishments qualified him to bestow.

As an evidence of the earnestness with which he embraced every chance to secure a good education, it may be related, that at the age of sixteen, with the sole aid of his brother, who was one year his junior, he undertook the chopping and clearing of four acres of heavy beech and maple woodland, plowing and planting it to corn, as the condition of being permitted to attend school during the winter term. This task was successfully accomplished, and the privilege thus secured utilized to complete his preparation for active life.

His peculiar faculty of observation and reflection not infrequently aided him to prosecute particular lines of study far beyond the limit of the teachers' capacity, thus placing him greatly in advance of the average scholar, who enjoyed the same facilities for instruction. The ending of school-days did not, however, as is too often the case, put a stop to farther effort for mental cultivation. On the contrary, all spare time throughout his entire life, was devoted to reading and investigation.

Endowed with rare talent for mechanics, he improved every opportunity, to pursue the studies relating thereto. No science was too intricate for his understanding, and in the years of maturity, he sustained himself creditably in association with those who had in early life enjoyed advantages of education very much superior to those afforded him. After leaving school, the following year was devoted to labor on the farm and in the pottery. The next year his father decided to build a more extensive manufactory, and engaged a carpenter for the purpose. Ezra was permitted to work on the job, and thus becoming somewhat familiar with the use of tools, he took a fancy to the carpenter's trade, as a means of livelihood.

Upon the completion of the new building, with the assistance, only, of his younger brother, he cut from the forest, the necessary timber and lumber, and erected for his father's family, a two-story frame dwelling house, which, at the

time of its construction, was the best residence
in the town of De Ruyter. Without previous
experience, or special knowledge of house building, except such as he had acquired in the
erection of the new pottery, and wholly without
instruction, or supervision by others, he planned
and framed the structure, so that every timber
went to its place without fault. When the young
builders, had so far progressed with their work,
as to be ready for putting up the frame, the customary invitation was given to the neighbors to
assist at the raising, which was responded to with
unusual alacrity, on account of the novelty of the
youthful architect. Much surprise was manifested
by the veterans in building, who were present, at
the perfection of the work, and the correctness
with which every mortise and tenon fitted to its
place.

This achievement, by a boy of seventeen was
the wonder of the neighborhood, and won for
him an enviable reputation for practical ability
and usefulness. His success as a master builder
aroused an ambition to establish himself on an independent and self-supporting basis. Work on
the farm, and in the pottery, had no further attractions for him, and under his new resolve, at
the age of eighteen, he sallied forth from the parental roof in quest of business.

He did not readily find occupation at the carpenter's trade, but, willing to try his hand at any useful work, he soon found employment in Onondaga County, where, in the vicinity of Syracuse, then but an insignificant hamlet, he was engaged nearly two years in getting out timber for shipment by canal to the city of New York. He then went to Homer, in Cortland County, where he was employed one year, in the machine shop of William Turner, in making wool-carding machinery. While engaged at Homer, which was about twenty miles from De Ruyter, he was accustomed to make frequent visits to his father's family, going home Saturday evening and returning to his work, on Monday morning following. In good weather and fair travelling, these visits were generally made on foot.

Having completed his engagement at Homer, and hearing some favorable account of the outlook for business at Ithaca, Mr. Cornell was thereby induced to proceed thither in search of employment. His mission in this respect was successful, and that place, thereafter, became the home of his life. Ithaca was then a small village, and, from its location at the head of Cayuga Lake, through which, it had already been placed in direct communication with the Erie Canal so recently completed, was just beginning to enjoy the advantages

of its position, as a shipping point for a large
range of country. No railroads had yet been constructed, and Ithaca was the most eligible point
connected with water navigation, for the southern
counties of New York, and the adjoining portion of Pennsylvania.

The whole space of country, from Binghamton to Painted Post, and as far south as Towanda,
in Pennsylvania, was thus rendered tributary to
the prosperity of Ithaca. Hundreds of teams
were constantly employed in hauling lumber and
grain to Ithaca, for shipment to eastern markets,
returning loaded with salt, plaster, and merchan-
dise for the use of the inhabitants in the extended
region above described. A small settlement, comprising some three families, had located on the
site of the present village as early as 1789,
but it continued a mere hamlet until about the
year 1800, when Ithaca was practically founded,
by the late General Simeon DeWitt, for many
years Surveyor-General of the State, who, attracted by the romantic scenery and natural beauty
of its surroundings, acquired title to a large tract of
land, which he laid out as a town site, and gave
to it the classical name which it has ever since so
worthily borne.

A post-office was established in 1804, and, under the interested patronage of General DeWitt,

through whose influence a number of prominent families were induced to locate in the embryo village, Ithaca soon became a growing place, having at the time of Mr. Cornell's advent attained a population of about two thousand, and was enjoying the benefit of a thriving trade from the large territory dependent upon it for communication with the principal markets of the country. With a spare suit of clothes, and a few dollars in his pocket, the earnings of his previous labors, Ezra Cornell entered Ithaca on foot, having walked from his father's house in De Ruyter, a distance of about forty miles. He had chosen to make the journey thus, not only for the purpose of saving the expense of riding, but also for the pleasure he enjoyed in walking. With him, pedestrianism was throughout life, one of the highest sources of enjoyment, and in any ordinary trip, he usually preferred walking to any other means of transit. He could travel forty miles per day, with perfect ease, and follow it up from day to day.

In this manner came the man who was destined to identify himself with the place of his adoption as a home, with such effect that the names of ITHACA, and CORNELL, should be made familiar to the whole civilized world. Without a single acquaintance in the village, and with no introduction or certificate of character, in any form, except such as he could offer in his own behalf, he arrived at Ithaca, with youth, courage, and ambition as capital stock, determined by his own exertions to earn a living, and establish himself on a permanent and prosperous basis. This was his purpose, and no ordinary obstacle was to be permitted to turn him from the line of action thus marked out for himself. How well he succeeded in accomplishing the task undertaken, can be gathered from the story of his subsequent career—a record which may be studied with advantage by every young man who has to conquer a place in the world by his own exertions.

CHAPTER IV.

EARLY MANHOOD.

Employment at Ithaca, 1828.—Ira Tillotson.—Bloodgood House.
—Baptist Church.—Otis Eddy.—Cotton Factory.—Repairing
Beebe's Mill.—Continued Employment with Colonel Beebe,
1829 to 1841.—Mechanical Skill.—Fall Creek Tunnel.—Beebe Dam. — Lifelong Friendship with Colonel Beebe. — Improving Schools.—Influence in Local Affairs.—Political Action.—Hard Cider Campaign.—" Tippecanoe and Tyler too."
—Death of President Harrison.—Loss of Employment.—
Looking Abroad.

ALMOST immediately after his arrival at Ithaca, in
April, 1828, Mr. Cornell succeeded in securing
engagement as a carpenter, and by good workmanship and strict attention to the interests committed to him, he was not long in gaining an
enviable repute, as an industrious and painstaking mechanic, thus insuring his continued and
satisfactory occupation. Mr. Ira Tillotson, then
a prominent and influential citizen of Ithaca, who
was a master-builder, enjoying an extensive patronage in that line of business, was his employer,
and his first labor in Ithaca was in the construction of a dwelling-house, situated at the corner

of Geneva and Clinton Streets, which has, now for many years, been the residence of the Blood-good family. He was next engaged in the erection of the Baptist Church building, fronting on the east side of the DeWitt Park, and which was afterward, about the year 1853, destroyed by fire.

Within a few weeks of his location at Ithaca he was offered a situation by Mr. Otis Eddy— the proprietor of an extensive cotton manufactory, occupying the site of the present Cascadilla Place building—who was in need of the services of a person competent to keep his mill and machinery in suitable condition for operation. Mr. Cornell's experience during the preceding year, at the Homer machine-shop, had been a valuable preparation in qualifying him to fulfil the requirements of his new position, which he was able to meet so satisfactorily as to result in his continuance in Mr. Eddy's employment for more than a year. Mr. Jeremiah S. Beebe, proprietor of the flour-ing and plaster mills at Fall Creek, near the village of Ithaca, was about this time in want of the services of a millwright, to overhaul and repair his mills; but having been unable to find an artisan skilled in that particular branch of mechanism, and hearing of Mr. Cornell as an ingenious and versatile workman, he applied to Mr. Eddy for permission to engage the young man for the purpose

named, which was granted in true neighborly
spirit.

Although Mr. Cornell was quite unfamiliar
with work of the kind which was required, his
practical intelligence aided him to successfully
accomplish the desired task; and such was the
satisfaction of his employer, that the engagement, which was of the most incidental and temporary character, as contemplated by both parties
in the beginning, proved to be permanent; and
was continued without interruption more than
twelve years, extending from 1829 to 1841, and
was only brought to a close by the retirement of
Colonel Beebe from active pursuits. Engaged
at first only as a mechanic, Mr. Cornell's duties
were gradually modified and enlarged in importance, until he finally became the confidential
agent and general manager of Colonel Beebe, in
the transaction of his extensive affairs at Fall
Creek, which involved the disbursement of hundreds of thousands of dollars annually, and for
many years the business was almost as completely under Mr. Cornell's control and discretion as it
would have been were he the proprietor of the
entire establishment.

With an especial adaptation to the science of
mechanics, both theoretically and practically, and
having rendered himself thoroughly familiar with

4

the operation of the mills, in all of its interesting details, Mr. Cornell was able to devise and introduce into successful use, many valuable mechanical improvements, and to utilize various plans for economizing the methods of manufacture. He was especially fertile and ingenious in planning and perfecting labor-saving appliances of many kinds, by which the current expenses of the establishment were very materially reduced; and his thorough system of business enabled him to realize the best results in marketing the products of the mills. Under his management, the success of the enterprise induced the proprietor to erect a new flouring mill of largely increased capacity. The mill was planned by, and built under the exclusive supervision and direction of Mr. Cornell, and, for excellence and economy of construction, the admirable character of mechanical devices and arrangements, as well as for the superiority of practical operations, it was unexcelled and perhaps unequalled in the entire State.

At the beginning of Mr. Cornell's connection with them, the Fall Creek mills—not only those of Colonel Beebe, but also the paper-mills occupying the adjoining mill-sites—were supplied with power by water brought from the head of the great falls through a wooden race-way, or flume, attached to the overhanging wall of rock, on the south side of the creek. Even under the most favorable circumstances the maintenance of such a structure is a matter of continual expense. In this instance, the annual expenditure was considerably enhanced by reason of the exposed situation and the danger to life and limb, incident to the care and repair of the flume. The liability of interruption to the flow of water by ice, was also, frequently the cause of serious annoyance in winter.

To remedy these difficulties, Mr. Cornell proposed the plan of excavating a tunnel through the solid rock, a distance of several hundred feet, so as to convey the water, by an uninterrupted flow, over a rocky bed, from the channel of the creek above the falls, directly to the mills, thus wholly dispensing with the wooden structure. The mill-owners, though at first somewhat skeptical as to the success of the project, were finally convinced of its entire practicability, and were thereby induced to provide the necessary means, with which the work should be executed. Mr. Cornell was thereupon duly installed as engineer-in-chief of the undertaking, although without previous experience and quite unacquainted with work of the character projected.

The excavation was begun and prosecuted from each end, and such was the correctness of calculations, that when the opening was made in the centre, between the two sections of the tunnel, it was found that the variation was less than two inches from an exact line. The enterprise was successfully completed at a cost considerably within the estimates originally made, and was put into practical use, to the great advantage of the mill privileges dependent upon this particular supply of water. This important improvement, finished in 1831, has for more than fifty years, admirably served the purpose for which it was designed, and still continues in operation with un-impaired usefulness, a lasting monument to the wisdom and foresight of its projector, and the enterprise of the proprietors who ventured the investment.

The tunnel has already entered upon the second half of the first century of its existence, and so far, without apparent depreciation, thus giving promise of serving future generations quite as usefully. It would be difficult, and indeed quite impossible, to make any definite estimate of the money value of this work; but aside from the material advantage of freedom from interruption in the supply of water, it cannot be doubted that the cost of opening the tunnel has been saved many times, over and again, by abandoning the wooden flume, with its constant burden of expense for maintenance and renewals.

The wild and romantic features of the gorge and cataracts of Fall Creek, have ever been a source of attraction for strangers visiting Ithaca, of whom thousands annually seek and clamber along its rugged banks. No part of the bold and weird scenery is more interesting than the "Tunnel," which, however, long since ceased to be regarded or spoken of as the work of man, but by casual visitors is considered, simply, as part of the Fall Creek wonders, and without stopping to inquire, they take it for granted that it is the work of the Great Architect who designed the adjoining cataract. Another very important step for improving the Fall Creek water-power, was the construction of a stone dam, on the stream about three-quarters of a mile above the tunnel, by which a reservoir, covering an area of some twenty acres, was created for the retention of the surplus water of the creek. This work also was constructed under the supervision of Mr. Cornell, in 1838, and has ever since been known as the Beebe Dam.

In addition to his milling interests, Colonel Beebe was the senior partner of the firm of Beebe, Munn, & Mack, merchants engaged in general trade at Ithaca, and doing an extensive business. With his time largely occupied in the conduct of his mercantile affairs, and in the care

of an invalid wife, to whom he was tenderly attached, it was quite natural that the management
of the milling business should have been left
largely to the direction of Mr. Cornell, who had
already proved himself abundantly qualified for
its successful prosecution. Colonel Beebe was a
man of peculiar temperament, impulsive but generous to a degree, and he soon learned to repose
the fullest confidence in the fidelity and wise discretion of his manager.

It is not surprising, therefore, that the earnest
and faithful manner in which Mr. Cornell devoted
himself to the interest of his employer throughout
his prolonged term of service, should have been
the means of establishing between them a cordial and sincere friendship, which was continued
without interruption until terminated by the death
of the latter, covering altogether, a period of more
than thirty years. In the later years of Colonel
Beebe's life, when he had suffered financial re-
verses and was in sore need, this friendship
served him a good purpose, as it was Mr. Cornell's
privilege to be able to furnish employment to
his former patron, and in many ways to smooth
the pathway of his declining years.

Though but just past his majority at the period of the commencement of his residence at
Fall Creek, Mr. Cornell, by intelligent and well-

directed participation in public affairs, very soon
gained an influential position in the community,
which was continually augmented as the years
passed by. Enterprising and public-spirited, he
took an active part in support of all measures,
calculated to advance the interests of the village.
He was especially active in improving the educational facilities of the place, and was largely
instrumental in placing them upon a higher and
constantly ascending grade. Through his influence, a local school was established at Fall Creek,
which, under the direction of able teachers, speedily became an important factor in the intellectual
development of the rising generation.

In the political divisions of the day, Mr. Cornell
was an ardent Whig, and in the local counsels of
that party, he exercised a potent influence. He
was a devoted friend and admirer of William H.
Seward, and in the several campaigns in which
that gentleman was the candidate of his party for
Governor, he labored zealously for the promotion
of his friend. In the celebrated hard-cider and
log-cabin campaign of 1840, he applied himself
with great earnestness to the support of "Tippecanoe and Tyler too."

The sudden and lamented death of General
Harrison, so soon after his elevation to the Presidency, and the speedy alienation of the acting

President from the great bulk of the party, which had so vigorously supported the successful candidates, were to Mr. Cornell, as to so many other active young Whigs, a terrible loss and sore disappointment, which resulted in greatly cooling his political ardor. Although continuing his association with the Whig party, and subsequently with the Republican party, he was never afterward able to arouse himself to the political enthusiasm of the great hard-cider campaign.

The withdrawal of Colonel Beebe from active business, and the conversion of the mill property into a woollen factory, left Mr. Cornell without employment, and owing to the depressed condition of financial affairs at the time, he did not readily find other occupation. While to a man of less energy and force of character, such a circumstance might prove a serious misfortune, in his case it proved to be the turning-point in his life, which, being advantageously utilized, led him to both fame and fortune. Had the milling business been continued without interruption, whether by Colonel Beebe or by others, the probability is that Mr. Cornell would have remained as its manager, and, very likely, he would have ended his life in that service.

It is a common saying, that, what seems a misfortune often proves to be really a blessing in disguise, and thus it certainly happened in this case. To be suddenly thrown out of a position to which one had long been accustomed, and particularly where a young and helpless family was dependent on the daily earnings of its head, the situation was serious. When, added to all this, was the fact that other employment could not be found, and the question of daily bread threatened soon to present itself for solution, the gravity of the case was largely enhanced.

Such were the circumstances in which Mr. Cornell found himself placed in 1841. Fortunately for him and his family, and especially fortunate for the future growth and prosperity of Ithaca, he was forced to seek elsewhere opportunity for business ; and, by a curious combination of circumstances, he was thrown into contact with the men who were just then casting about with the infant telegraph in their keeping, quite at a loss to know how to utilize the grand instrumentality, which was destined to revolutionize the social and commercial customs of the entire civilized world. Mr. Cornell's quick practical comprehension enabled him to solve the question which was puzzling these wise men as to the proper mode of constructing the telegraph lines, and he speedily made himself indispensable to the development of the new enterprise. At the age of thirty-six, he thus stepped forth from the narrow path he had previously trod, and with but little delay entered upon a career, which was not only a grand success for himself, but equally beneficial to the country at large.

CHAPTER V.

MARRIAGE.

Elijah Cornell and Benjamin Wood.—A prolonged Friendship.—
Notable Visit.—" Woodlawn."—Mary Ann Wood Born, 1811.
—Marriage Engagement.—Married, March 19, 1831.—Housekeeping.—Early Home.—Nine Children, of whom five Survive.—Quaker Discipline.—Telegraph Enterprise.—Absence
from Home.—Success in Business.—" Forest Park."—Domestic Felicity.

DURING the period of his first residence in De
Ruyter, Elijah Cornell was engaged during the
winter seasons in teaching the district school in
Quaker Basin. Among the older boys in attendance at the school in 1808, was one who, by
manly qualities and respectful deportment, as well
as by earnest efforts to improve the educational
advantages thus offered, won the especial regard
and confidence of his teacher. This favorite pupil
was Benjamin Wood, whose parents had, a few
years earlier, emigrated from the State of Rhode
Island. The acquaintance then begun between
the teacher and scholar, ripened into a mutual
friendship which was continued without interrup-

tion throughout the remainder of their lives, and it became in after years their custom to visit each other, whenever circumstances brought either of them within the vicinity of the other's place of residence.

On one occasion, when at Ithaca on a business trip, Mr. Cornell invited his son Ezra to accompany him on a visit to the home of his friend Mr. Wood, who had some years previously located in the town of Dryden, Tompkins County, distant some six miles from Ithaca. This chance visit, which occurred in the third year of his employment at Ithaca, was destined to exert an important influence in all of the future course of the young man, as it was the beginning of his acquaintance with the young lady, who was to become the partner of his domestic life. Mr. Wood's second daughter, Mary Ann, was then nineteen years of age, and it was by no means strange that an attachment of more than passing interest was soon formed between her and the son of her father's friend, which, ere long, resulted in a marriage engagement. Both families were gratified with the proposed alliance, and the old-time friendship was rendered still more cordial and intimate.

Benjamin Wood was a native of Scituate, Providence County, R. I., where he was born October

14, 1789. He was a son of Nathan Wood, and the maiden name of his mother was Amy Hammond. In youth he had been bred to the trade of reed making, and was an expert mechanic. In those days—before the advent of the great woollen and cotton factories—the weaver's reed was in demand in almost every well-regulated farmer's household, where the home-grown wool was converted into cloth and blankets for domestic use. Mr. Wood was united in marriage at De Ruyter, June 12, 1808, to Mary, daughter of Philip Bonesteel and Elizabeth Ray. She was born at Florida, Montgomery County, N. Y., October 2, 1790. The young couple continued to reside in DeRuyter some five years after their marriage, when they removed to the husband's native place in Rhode Island, and there remained two or three years.

Finding the change unsatisfactory, the family returned to the State of New York, and after spending two years in the town of Sherburne, Chenango County, they located at Willow Glen, near Dryden Village, in Tompkins County, where they also resided about two years. In 1819 Mr. Wood contracted for the purchase of a tract of land in the western portion of the town of Dryden, and determined to make it his permanent home. This land was then covered with a heavy

pine forest, which with his own hand he cleared,
and brought into cultivation a farm, that, under
his energetic and thrifty management, became one
of the most desirable homesteads in the county.
He afterward established on the place a manufactory for the production of weavers' reeds, which
proved a profitable accompaniment to his agricultural pursuits, furnishing as it did favorable occupation for the intervals of other work.

At the period of his settlement on the " Woodlawn" farm, as the estate is now widely known,
Mr. Wood's worldly possessions consisted principally of the tools of his trade, and a very moderate equipment of household furniture and
personal effects. Purchasing his land on credit,
by industry and frugality he was enabled to pay
for his property, and to support, and educate in
superior manner, a family of eleven children, and to
improve and maintain a home which, during all
of his life-time, was the pride of his family. Acting
on the maxim that a thing worth doing should be
well done, he was in all of his farming operations
enterprising and painstaking. His buildings and
fences were uniformly in good repair, and his fields
demonstrated excellent tillage.

In every relation of life—as a citizen, as a neighbor, and also in his family—Benjamin Wood was
universally esteemed. It is entirely within bounds

to state that no man ever lived in the town of
Dryden, who was more generally respected, or
more completely enjoyed the confidence and good
will of the community. In business affairs he
was prudent, orderly, and thoroughly reliable,
while with all with whom he had dealings his
word was equal to his bond. He was the best of
husbands, and no father was ever more devotedly
loved and reverenced by a family of children. Mr.
Wood after only a very brief illness, entered his
final rest at Woodlawn, May 16, 1858, at the age
of sixty-eight years and seven months. His wife
survived him nearly twenty years, ten of which
she continued to reside at Woodlawn. During
the last ten years of her life, she made her home
with her youngest daughter, at Ithaca, where she
died, February 20, 1878, at the mature age of
eighty-seven. Eminently domestic in her tastes
and habits, she was regarded with tenderest affection by her husband and family.

Children to the number of eleven, of whom
seven were daughters and four sons, resulted from
the matrimonial union of Benjamin and Mary
Wood. All of them lived to reach the age of maturity. The second daughter, Mary Ann, was
born at De Ruyter, Madison County, N. Y., April
25, 1811. She was eight years of age when her
parents located at Woodlawn, and although she

had taken lessons both at Sherburne and at Willow Glen, the most of her education was acquired at the district school in the Snyder neighborhood. It was during her attendance at this place, that the now venerable-appearing octagonal brick school-house was erected and first occupied. For several years she and her elder sister, Almira, were permitted to attend school only on alternate weeks—one of them being required to assist their mother in the discharge of her domestic duties.

In conformity with their engagement, the marriage of Ezra Cornell and Mary Ann Wood was celebrated at "Woodlawn," the homestead of Benjamin Wood in the town of Dryden, Tompkins County, N. Y., March 19, 1831. Mr. Cornell was then in the second year of his employment with Colonel Beebe at the Fall Creek mills. The wedded pair boarded a few months at the hotel at Fall Creek, until their house was prepared for occupation. Mr. Cornell purchased a plot of several acres just north of the mills, on which he built a dwelling, where they began housekeeping during the summer after marriage. This continued to be their home for more than twenty years, and it was here that their nine children were born. Of these, three sons died in infancy, and the eldest daughter, a beautiful and interesting girl, died at the age of fifteen. Three sons and two daughters were raised to mature years.

Until his marriage, Ezra Cornell, both from his own inclination and the influence of his parents, always identified himself with the religious associations of his ancestry, and was a regular attendant at the Friends' meetings when in their vicinity. There was no organization of this kind at Ithaca, but ever on his return to De Ruyter, he was prompt in attendance. Having married a wife who was not a member, his case was taken into consideration by the church society at De Ruyter, and he was by them formally excommunicated for this offence. It was, however, intimated that in case he should apologize for having thus offended, and express proper regret therefor, he would receive pardon and be reinstated. This he declined to do, and therefore continued under the ban of condemnation. He had been too well grounded in the faith of his fathers, to be thus cast away, and so was always firm in his belief and sympathy. In intercourse with his parents and with members of the sect, he was careful at all times to use the phrases of address customary with Friends, and though he seldom conversed on the subject, it was in many ways manifest that he remained throughout his entire life, a faithful and consistent disciple of the Friends'

5

religious creed. He believed that it was a question between him and his Heavenly Father, and that no body of men and women, could say that he should not commune with his Maker in accordance with his convictions.

The first ten years of married life with the young people, passed without unusual incident. Mr. Cornell continued in the service of Colonel Beebe, and took much interest at leisure intervals in improving his home, and by the cultivation of choice fruit. The diversion of Fall Creek mills to other uses in 1841, deprived Mr. Cornell of his vocation, and on account of the dull times then prevailing, he was unable to find satisfactory employment at home. He was therefore obliged to seek business abroad, in which, after some serious discouragements, he was successful beyond all expectation.

He became interested in the introduction and development of the Magnetic Telegraph, which for the dozen years following, required him to be absent from home a large portion of the time. His family retained their residence at their original homestead until 1852, when they removed into the village of Ithaca, and there resided until 1857. In the latter year, Mr. Cornell, having withdrawn from the active management of his telegraph interests, purchased the " Forest Park " property, and here established a new homestead. He acquired nearly three hundred acres of land adjoining, and for several years took great pleasure in the building up of a fine herd of short-horn cattle. A few years later, upon the organization of the Cornell University, he donated the principal portion of this beautiful farm to that institution, retaining only some twenty-five acres for his own use.

The dwelling-house at Forest Park not fully meeting the demands of modern times, Mr. Cornell determined to erect a new one as a permanent family residence. Pending the construction of this edifice, he found it convenient to reside in the village of Ithaca, occupying the large brick dwelling at the corner of Tioga and Seneca Streets, opposite the Cornell Library. This was his home from the spring of 1869, until his death, which occurred in this house in December, 1874.

Rarely does it happen to man to find more perfect satisfaction in his marital relations, than Mr. Cornell enjoyed, during the more than forty years of his married life. Often and again he has been heard to attribute his prosperity in life, to the assistance and encouragement which he received from his wife. In the early days, she was the companion of his joys and sorrows, while in the years of his great struggle with fortune, she was the inspiring spirit at home, in the care of his young family, ever faithful, ever patient and cheerful, with firm confidence in his final and complete success.   Thus sustained at home, with high hope he labored on, until after long toil and struggle, he was enabled to triumph over obstacles which sometimes seemed almost insurmountable, and finally to retire from active business with a fortune far greater than he had ever hoped for.   Nor was he more loyally supported by his wife, in the building up of his great fortune, than in the devotion of a large proportion of it to the noble institutions of learning he founded, which will carry his name with undiminished lustre, to a long line of future generations.

CHAPTER VI.

SEEKING BUSINESS.

THE great monetary crisis of 1836–37, will long
be remembered in consequence of the wide-spread
disaster visited upon commercial activities throughout the entire country. While the violence of
the financial storm gradually subsided, it was followed by a paralysis of industrial interests, which
continued for several years. Labor was in slight
demand, and consequently every avenue to employment was crowded with applicants. Such
was the condition of affairs in 1841, when, by the
retirement of Colonel Beebe from milling operations at Fall Creek, Mr. Cornell found himself
without occupation.

For some months he endeavored to find new business, but without satisfactory results, and, as an alternative, he purchased from his neighbors, Messrs. Barnaby & Mooers, the patent rights for the States of Maine and Georgia, of an improved plow which they had recently invented, and determined to visit those States, for the purpose of selling the interests thus acquired. Mr. Cornell, therefore, in 1842, proceeded to Maine, with the object of introducing the new invention to the farmers of that State, and, as a preliminary, sought the acquaintance of the editor of the *Maine Farmer,* an agricultural paper of considerable influence, then published at Portland, presuming that favorable notice therein would be his best introduction to the more intelligent citizens. The editor and publisher of this paper proved to be the Hon. Francis O. J. Smith, then a member of Congress from the Portland district, and a man of much influence in the State of Maine. Convinced of its merits, Mr. Smith became a ready advocate of the new plow, and strongly commended it to the attention of his readers. Very cordial relations were speedily established between Mr. Cornell, and the editor of the *Maine Farmer*, and the office of that paper, became the headquarters of the stranger, during the several months of his tarry in the State.

In the autumn of the same year, Mr. Cornell, went to Georgia, with the purpose of interesting the agriculturists of that State in the use of the new plow. At that time the facilities for travel in the Southern States, were very meagre, there being no railroads and the stages were quite primitive. From Washington to Augusta, Ga., he proceeded on foot, making an average of forty miles each day. He travelled in like manner, largely through Georgia, and as far as Washington on his return, making a distance of about fifteen hundred miles. He had a threefold object in determining upon this mode of travelling; first, economy; second, that he could choose his own route; and third, that walking was ever to him a pleasure and privilege. He was not much encouraged by the reception that was accorded to his presentation of the plow in the South, and returned home without having accomplished anything satisfactory in that region.

After spending a few months at home with his family, Mr. Cornell, in July, 1843, proceeded again to Maine, to close up the plow interests in that State, which he had left uncompleted the preceding year. This journey also, was made on foot from Ithaca to Albany, covering the distance of one hundred and sixty miles in four days. From Albany he travelled by railway to Boston, thence on foot

to Portland, one hundred miles in two and a half
days.   In writing of this trip he said: "Travelling
on foot has always been a source of great enjoyment to me.   If I had the time to spend in pleasure travel, I should prefer to walk if I could make
satisfactory arrangement for the transit of my
baggage.   Nature can in no way be so rationally
enjoyed, as through the opportunities afforded the
pedestrian."

On arrival at Portland, he lost no time in calling
at the office of the *Maine Farmer*, to renew his
acquaintance with the Hon. F. O. J. Smith.   As
the circumstances which followed this visit, resulted in establishing Mr. Cornell's permanent
connection with the telegraph enterprise, it will
be interesting to quote from his own description
of the interview, which he afterward wrote in his
memorandum book.   He says: "I found Smith
on his knees in the middle of his office floor with
a piece of chalk in his hand, the mold-board of a
plow lying by his side, and with various chalk-
marks on the floor before him.   He was earnestly
engaged in trying to explain some plan or idea of
his own to a plow manufacturer, who stood looking on with his good-natured face enveloped in a
broad grin that denoted his skepticism in reference to Smith's plans.   On my entrance, Mr.
Smith arose, and grasping me cordially by the

hand, said: 'Cornell, you are the very man I wanted to see. I have been trying to explain to neighbor Robertson, a machine that I want made, but I cannot make him understand it,' and proceeding, he explained that he wanted 'a kind of scraper, or machine for digging a ditch, that will leave the dirt deposited on each side, convenient to be used for filling the ditch by means of another machine. It is for laying our telegraph pipe underground. The ditch must be two feet deep, and wide enough to enable us to lay the pipe in the bottom, and then cover it with the earth. Congress has appropriated $30,000 to enable Professor Morse to test the practicability of his telegraph on a line between Washington and Baltimore. I have taken the contract to lay the pipe at $100 per mile, and must have some kind of a machine to enable me to do the work at any such price.'

"An examination of a specimen of the pipe to be laid, which Mr. Smith showed us, and a little reflection, convinced me that he did not want two machines, as he said, one to excavate, and the other to fill the trench after the pipe was deposited. I, therefore, with my pencil sketched a rough diagram of a machine that seemed to me adapted to his necessities. It provided that the pipe, with the wires enclosed therein, was to be coiled around a drum or reel, from whence it was to pass down through a hollow standard, protected by shives, directly in the rear of a coulter or cutter, which was so arranged as to cut a furrow two and a half feet deep and one and one-fourth inch wide. Arranged something like a plow, it was to be drawn by a powerful team, and to deposit the pipe in the bottom of the furrow, as it moved along. The furrow being so narrow would soon close itself and conceal the pipe from view.

" Mr. Smith examined the diagram and listened to my explanation, but could not see how it would work. I was entirely convinced of the practical working of the plan and so insisted. The day was spent in discussing the various objections raised by Mr. Smith, and we finally separated for the night, with his doubts as firm as ever. Upon coming together again in the morning, he was still more an unbeliever, while my confidence had greatly increased, as the result of my reflection. He finally, however, without much confidence or hope of success, proposed that I should construct a machine in accordance with my plan. He said: ' I will pay the expense, whether successful or not, and if successful, I will pay you $50, or $100, or any other price you may name. The price is a matter of no consequence if the machine is successful.'

" I finally engaged to build the proposed machine, and commenced work at once in a machine-shop in which Smith obtained permission for me to work. I made the patterns for the necessary castings, and while these and the other iron work were being made, I employed my time in making the wood-work for the frame. As the work progressed, Smith's confidence in its success rose to a point which induced him to write to Professor Morse in New York, and invite him to witness the trial of the machine. The invitation was accepted, and the Professor arrived about the time we had completed our work. He visited the shop and inspected the machine, and expressed satisfaction with its appearance. This was the beginning of my personal acquaintance with Professor Morse.

" The machine was finally completed on the 17th of August, 1843, and, on the 19th, we made a successful trial of it on the homestead farm of Mr. Smith, at Westbrook, a few miles north of Portland. The trial was made with a team consisting of four yoke of oxen, brought together for the occasion, and quite unused to work together. They were under the direction of a ' son of sweet Erin,' whose lingo was Greek to their ears. He flourished the gad vigorously, and soon produced the most violent disorder with the cattle. This state of affairs threw Smith into a condition of great nervous excitement. Soon, however, the Irishman and the oxen effected a compromise, when the latter started with a rush, for a distance somewhat greater than the length of pipe we had on the drum of the machine. The consequence was that when the driver brought his team to a halt, the pipe had disappeared, which being discovered by Smith, caused him anxiously to inquire if we had forgotten to put the pipe in the machine. Professor Morse was equally bewildered by the turbulent movements of the animals and their driver, and hence had paid as little attention to the action of the machine as Mr. Smith had, and he also was anxious to know what had become of the pipe. I assured them that the pipe was where we intended it should be, namely, about eighteen inches beneath the surface of the ground. With an expression of doubt Smith directed the driver to get a spade and dig for the pipe, for which he proved more competent than driving oxen. An hour's work uncovered the pipe, which we again coiled on the drum of the machine, which was then gauged for two feet depth, and the team started for a second trial. Both team and driver worked more kindly this time, which gave a better opportunity to observe the operation of the machine in depositing the pipe in the earth, and both Professor Morse, and Mr. Smith, expressed their admiration of the manner in which the work was accomplished. This experiment removed all doubt from their minds as to the practicability of laying the telegraph conductors in a perfect manner at a minimum cost. The more important question of insulation not being fully understood or appreciated at that time, Professor Morse could see nothing in the way of immediate success for his great enterprise, and left Portland for New York in the best of spirits.

" The complete success of my machine, and the prompt manner of making the invention the moment circumstances demanded its use, inspired Mr. Smith with great confidence in my ability, both as a mechanic and a practical man. He, therefore, urged me to go to Baltimore with the machine and take charge of laying the pipe between that city and Washington. As this proposition involved the abandonment of the business which I had come to Maine to look after, it was with some hesitation that I entertained it. A little reflection, however, convinced me that the telegraph was to become a grand enterprise, and this seemed a particularly advantageous opportunity for me to identify myself with it. Finally, convinced that it would surely lead me on the road

to fortune, I acceded to Mr. Smith's urgent solicitation and engaged to undertake the work, on
condition that I should first devote a little time
to the settlement of my business in Maine.   This
was accomplished in about six weeks, and early
in October, I left Portland for Baltimore, via
Boston and New York.

"On arriving in New York, I called on Professor Morse to ascertain how soon a supply of pipe
might be expected at Baltimore.   He accompanied
me to the factory of Mr. Serrell, where the pipe
was being manufactured.   The process of manufacture was briefly as follows: The lead was
first cast in ingots eighteen inches in length, containing sufficient metal for about three hundred
feet of pipe, leaving a hole through the ingot of
proper size for the interior of the pipe, say five-
eighths of an inch.   The ingots were then passed
between rollers, by which they were drawn to
the proper size, the four electrical wires being
drawn into the pipe through a hollow mandrel
during the passage of the ingots through the rollers.   These were No. 16 copper wires covered
with cotton yarn saturated with shellac, each wire
being covered with different colored yarn, in order
to be identified at the opposite ends of the pipe.   To
insure the proper insulation, it was of course necessary that the pipe should be water-tight, and

thus exclude dampness. To be assured of this, when completed each section of pipe was subjected to test by an air-pump, and if it would sustain a vacuum it was passed as perfect. The ends were then soldered to hold the wires in place, and the pipe placed on reels ready for shipment. This branch of the work was under the immediate supervision of Dr. Fisher, who was the principal assistant of Professor Morse. Professor Leonard D. Gale was also employed as a scientific assistant, and Alfred Vail as mechanical assistant. They were each employed at the rate of $1,500 per annum.

"I had not been long in the factory before my attention was called to the process of casting the ingots, from which the pipe was drawn when cold. I thought I could detect air-bubbles in the ingots, from which I reasoned that the pressure of the rollers must of necessity enlarge these defects, and thus leave the pipe imperfect. I called Professor Morse's attention to the subject, and asked him if there was not danger that the pipe would leak when placed in the ground. He replied, 'Oh, no; we test each piece of pipe with the air-pump. That is Dr. Fisher's especial duty, and if a piece fails to sustain a vacuum on the air-pump, it is rejected as defective.' I told him I thought this test deceptive, and suggested that a force-pump would be more likely to expose defects from the cause apprehended. My warning proved of no avail, however, at the time, as no change was made in the mode of testing; but my opinion was fully vindicated by subsequent events."

CHAPTER VII.

EARLY DAYS OF THE TELEGRAPH.

FINDING that the pipe would not be ready for
shipment as early as had been anticipated, Mr.
Cornell remained for several days in New York,
devoting much time to the fair of the American
Institute, which greatly interested him. On October 17, 1843, he proceeded to Baltimore,
where he was soon after met by Mr. Smith to
make the necessary arrangements to commence
laying the pipe. Continuing the narrative in Mr.
Cornell's own language, he proceeds thus : " After
a survey of the locality, it was determined that
the most eligible place for laying the pipe was on

6

the line of the Baltimore & Ohio Railroad, between
the double tracks. In selecting a team to draw
the plow, Mr. Smith secured a large and elegant
span of spirited horses, with a view of sending
them to his residence near Portland, as a carriage
team, after the work was completed. The first
day's trial, however, convinced us that they could
not be safely or usefully employed where so many
trains were passing. The horses were accordingly rejected and their places supplied by an eight
mule team, which answered the purpose admirably.

"The work of laying the pipe was commenced in
due time and proceeded satisfactorily; the machine worked perfectly, and we were enabled to
lay from half a mile to a mile each day. My duties were simply to direct the laying of the pipe,
leaving the connections between each length to be
made by men under the direction of Mr. Vail,
who also tested the wires as to their working qualities. My work proceeded much faster than his,
so that when I had three miles laid, only one mile
had been connected through. By this time I had become convinced of the defects in the pipe suggested to Professor Morse, and I made inquiries as
to the character of the tests which were being
used. Mr. Vail was not disposed to be communi-
cative, but from Mr. Avery, who had charge of
the battery, I learned that they were accustomed

to attach the black and red wires to the battery
and then apply the galvanometer to the same
wires at the opposite end. Finding the current
satisfactory, the same test was then applied to the
other two wires. I told Mr. Avery that this test
did not prove the wires to be properly insulated,
and suggested that a test should be made by attaching the black and red wires to the battery and
then to connect the green and yellow wires with
the galvanometer. He, however, declined to offer
any suggestions to Mr. Vail, who appeared very
jealous of any interference, and had already intimated to Mr. Avery that he should confine himself to his own duties. I then suggested to Mr.
Avery that we should make the test for our own
satisfaction that evening, which after considerable
hesitation he agreed to, on condition that we
should wait until midnight in order to avoid
any possible observation. Accordingly, at twelve
o'clock we left the hotel where we were boarding,
and went to the place where the battery was kept,
and attached it to the black and red wires. We
then proceeded to the other end, a mile distant,
and attached the green and yellow wires to the
galvanometer. This gave us a strong current,
proving conclusively that imperfect insulation allowed the current to escape from one wire to another. This was the first positive evidence of the

coming failure, and on our return hence, I urged
upon Mr. Avery the importance of advising Professor Morse of the discovery; but he dared not
do so, and I accordingly went on with my part of
the work, expecting every day to receive orders
to suspend laying the pipe. Thus matters proceeded until we had completed the laying of pipe
as far as the Relay House, about ten miles from
Baltimore, when about five o'clock one afternoon,
as a train arrived, Professor Morse alighted and
walking along the track to where we were at
work, said he desired to speak with me aside.
Withdrawing a little distance from the men engaged with me, he said: ' Mr. Cornell, can you
not contrive to stop this work for a few days in
some manner, so the papers will not know that it
has been purposely interrupted? I want to make
some experiments before any more pipe is laid.'
This was a summons which I had been expecting
for several days, and was not, therefore, surprised
by it. Replying to Professor Morse that I would
comply with his request, I stepped back to the
machine and said: ' Hurrah, boys, whip up your
mules, we must lay another length of pipe before
we quit for night.' The teamsters cracked their
whips, and the animals started at a lively pace, as
I grasped the handles of the plow, and watching
an opportunity, I canted it over so as to catch into

a point of rock, breaking the machine into a complete wreck. The following morning's papers
gave a graphic account of the accident which had
befallen the machine, and stated that, as a consequence, the work would be interrupted a week or
two, until the necessary repairs could be made.

" Professor Morse, Mr. Vail, and Mr. Smith had
various consultations during the few days following, which resulted in the condemnation of the cold
ingot pipe, and the determination to substitute
pipe made by the 'hot process.' My opinion
was not sought, and my only duty was to prolong
the machine repairs until the new pipe was ready
for use. When this came, we resumed work and
laid a mile of the new pipe, when we were ordered
to suspend further laying, until it could be
thoroughly tested. It was soon discovered that
the insulation was defective, and this time the fault
was charged to the undue heating of the hollow
mandrels through which the wire passed into the
pipe. This, it was claimed by Mr. Vail, had charred
the cotton covering of the wire, and destroyed its
insulating properties. At this crisis a council assembled at the Relay House, consisting of Professor Morse, Dr. Fisher, Professor Gale, Mr. Vail,
and Mr. Smith. They spent several days in secret session discussing the difficulties encountered
and the various remedies proposed. I was not

present, nor was my opinion sought, but I was privately informed, day by day, of the progress of the discussion, by one of the parties present. It was decided that the wires were useless as electrical conductors on account of deficient insulation, but it was not so easy to determine a practical remedy.

" The situation was extremely critical, as already $23,000 of the appropriation had been expended, leaving only $7,000 on hand, while Smith claimed $4,000 of that amount to satisfy his contract for laying the pipe from Baltimore to Washington. He claimed his right to this sum whether the pipe was laid or not, as he stood ready to perform his part of the contract. Mr. Smith regarded the enterprise as a practical failure, and insisted on his legal rights under the contract, in order to reimburse himself for expenditures made in promoting the scheme. This was the beginning of the differences between Morse and Smith, which afterward became an open quarrel, and their relations were never friendly thereafter. The remnant of the appropriation was fast melting away by the payment of salaries; viz.: Professor Morse, $2,500; Professor Gale and Dr. Fisher, $1,500 each; and Mr. Vail, $1,000. It was estimated that to re-insulate the wire, and complete the work, would require $25,000, and it was concluded, therefore, that the work must be suspended until another appropriation could be obtained.

" While these conclusions were being reached, I made some experiments which satisfied me that the wires could be re-insulated at a very small expense, and so reported to Professor Morse. Mr. Vail insisted that the wires could not be taken out of the pipe except by melting the latter ; but I explained my plan to the satisfaction of Professor Morse, and he finally decided that I should undertake it. The services of Gale and Fisher were dispensed with in order to reduce expenses, but Mr. Vail refused to retire. Professor Morse had me appointed Mechanical Assistant, by the Secretary of the Treasury, and directed me to proceed with the work of removing the wires from the pipe and re-insulating them. We obtained permission to do this work in the basement of the Patent Office at Washington, where we were soon engaged in active operation.

" Realizing the importance of more definite information in electrical science, I decided to utilize the long winter evenings in study. To this end, I applied to Professor Page, an examiner in the Patent Office, to furnish me a list of works on the subject, which would be useful. The Commissioner of Patents, Mr. Ellsworth, kindly gave me an order to take these books from the Patent Office Li-

brary to my lodgings ; but on applying for them
the following day, the Librarian reported them all
out.   Repeated applications only served to obtain
the same response, and further inquiry led to the
discovery that Mr. Vail had drawn these books
the very day of my interview with the Commissioner.   Finally, becoming satisfied that he was
keeping the works to prevent my examination of
them, I explained the circumstance to Mr. Smith
who, thereupon, introduced me to the Librarian of
the Congressional Library, from whom I had no
difficulty in obtaining the desired books.

" The reading of these works soon revealed the
fact that the same difficulties which we had encountered, had also been experienced in England,
where Cooke and Wheatstone had undertaken the
same experiments and met with the same failures,
and that they had finally adopted the plan of placing their wires on poles.   It was not long before
it became apparent that somebody was reading the
books which Mr. Vail had obtained from the Patent
Office Library, and that to a very good purpose,
as Professor Morse said to me quietly, one day,
that he might conclude to change his plans.   This
announcement satisfied me that light was breaking in an important quarter, and while I pressed on
with removing the wires from the pipes, I did not
hasten the re-insulation, as I was confident that

the order would soon come to erect the wires on poles. In this I was not disappointed, for before the end of March, Professor Morse informed me that he had decided to put the wires on poles, and gave me directions to make the necessary arrangements accordingly.

" The question as to what mode of insulation should be adopted in fastening the wires to the poles was one of the first that confronted us. After a little reflection I submitted to Professor Morse a plan for this purpose, which was condemned by Mr. Vail, who proposed another kind of fixture. Professor Morse finally decided in favor of Mr. Vail's plan, and started for New York to have the necessary fixtures manufactured. At the end of a week Professor Morse returned to Washington, and said he had concluded to use my plan of insulation. At my expression of surprise at his change of mind, he said: ' On my way to New York I stopped over at Princeton to see my old friend Professor Henry, to whom I explained our change from underground to pole line, and showed him the model of Mr. Vail's insulating fixture. Professor Henry examined it carefully and soon satisfied me that it would not answer our purpose, as it would only bring a repetition of the troubles which we have suffered in our underground wires. I then explained your

plan to him and he approved it entirely. I have,
therefore, returned for the purpose of putting
your plan in use.' The last difficulty having thus
been removed, the work of erecting the line on
poles went rapidly forward, and about May 1, 1844,
we had the line completed and in operation between Washington and Baltimore. This was accomplished so far within the $7,000 remaining of
the appropriation, as to still leave a sufficient balance to continue Professor Morse's and Mr. Vail's
salaries for the remainder of the year."

Shortly after the completion of this line, the
National Democratic convention assembled in Baltimore, which nominated Polk and Dallas for President and Vice-President. Brief reports of the
proceedings of the convention were telegraphed
to Washington, and caused great excitement
among the members of Congress, who crowded
the telegraph office in the basement of the Capi-
tol. While much had been heard about the telegraph for several years, it was regarded by most
people as an idle dream, and the sudden discovery of the fact that an event of such public interest as a presidential convention could be reported
by telegraph, took almost everybody completely
by surprise.

CHAPTER VIII.

TELEGRAPH DEVELOPMENT.

THE operation of the telegraph between Washington and Baltimore, despite the frail character of the line and the crudity of the instruments, was quite successful, and afforded satisfactory evidence of its practicability for the purpose of conveying intelligence between distant places. It substantially fulfilled the claims of Professor Morse and his friends as to its capacity and usefulness for the object designed. This having been demonstrated, the next question to be solved was, what should be done with it? In default of any other demand for it, the owners of the patent first offered it to the Government, placing upon it the nominal price of $100,000. but they would have been glad, at that time, to have realized a considerably smaller sum for their interest. This proposition was, by Congress, referred to the Post-Office Department, for consideration and recommendation as to the probable value of the invention. The Hon. Cave Johnson, then Postmaster-General, made a report in response to this reference, advising against the proposed purchase by Government. The following quotation from his report shows the estimate in which the telegraph was then held as an instrumentality of practical usefulness: " Although the invention is an agent vastly superior to any other ever devised by the genius of man . . . . . yet the operation of the telegraph between this city (Washington) and Baltimore has not satisfied me, that under any rate of postage that can be adopted, its revenues can be made to cover its expenditures." Under the influence of this report, it was not strange that Congress declined the offer of the patentees, and the telegraph was consequently left to seek development by the aid of private capital. This, however, proved to be a very slow and tedious process. Those familiar with the almost universal use into which the telegraph has now come, will find it difficult to realize the utter indifference with which it was regarded in the days of its infancy.

That the new medium of communication was especially adapted to the necessities of commercial business, and that its utilization for public use would command profitable patronage, Mr. Cornell had become thoroughly convinced. He, consequently, determined to devote himself to the development of the telegraph as a business enterprise, and accordingly spent several weeks at Washington in familiarizing himself with its practical workings. After a brief visit to his home and family, from whom he had been absent nearly a year, he proceeded to Boston for the purpose of introducing the telegraph to the personal attention of business men, in accordance with an understanding previously made with the Hon. F. O. J. Smith. After some consideration as to the best mode of accomplishing this object, it was finally decided to build a line of telegraph for public demonstration. A line was, accordingly, erected by Mr. Cornell, extending from Milk Street to School Street, which he opened for that purpose. He spent the summer and autumn of 1844 in this work, with the view of enlisting capital to build a line of telegraph between Boston and New York. The result of these efforts was, however, very unsatisfactory, as but few persons were attracted by the novelty, and, as a general rule, they were not of a class who had means for investment in new enterprises. It was, therefore, decided to transfer the exhibition to New York, in the hope of arousing in that city a more active interest in the proposed undertaking.

Proceeding thence to the city of New York in conformity with this policy, Mr. Cornell constructed a line of telegraph, extending from No. 112 Broadway, opposite Trinity Church, to a place on Broadway, near the site of the present Metropolitan Hotel, and it was put into actual operation late in the fall of 1844. Here the display attracted even less attention than it had in Boston. Owing to the low state of finances in which the promoters of the telegraph found themselves, a fee of twenty-five cents was charged for admission, in the hope that the exhibition might be made self-sustaining. This, however, proved almost a failure, as the receipts were quite insignificant and not adequate to defray the extremely moderate expenses which were incurred. The *Tribune* and the *Express* gave the enterprise favorable notice, but the *Herald* carefully avoided any reference to the subject, and ignored even the existence of the telegraph. On one occasion, the proprietor of the *Herald* was solicited to give some friendly attention to the exhibition, when he frankly replied that he was opposed to the success of the telegraph, and should do nothing to promote it. He said he was then able, by special couriers, to beat his rivals in procuring early news, whereas, if the telegraph was generally established, it would deprive him of his present advantage. This narrow-minded policy was pursued by him until two years later, when, by the transmission of the Governor's message by telegraph, the *Herald* was badly beaten in its efforts to obtain an advanced copy of the same by special messenger. Mr. Cornell spent the entire winter in the attempt to secure public attention to the subject of the telegraph, but almost without success.

By dint of much personal effort, however, a few individuals were finally induced to venture small amounts for the erection of telegraph lines. The parties who thus gave early vitality to the enterprise were not capitalists or men of wealth, but, on the contrary, were generally of quite moderate financial resources. Two classes of persons, who were notably conspicuous as early promoters of the telegraph enterprise, were those formerly engaged as proprietors of stage transportation, who so lately had seen their occupation superseded by the railroads, and that other body of enterprising pioneers—peculiar to the material development of the American continent—who had recently es-

tablished the express system on a firm and successful basis. The "Magnetic Telegraph Company" was the first incorporated company that
was organized for the prosecution of the proposed
business. The object of this organization was
the erection and operation of a line of telegraph
between the cities of New York, Philadelphia,
Baltimore, and Washington. The section of line
between Fort Lee, opposite New York, and Philadelphia, was constructed under the superintend-
ence of Mr. Cornell, in the summer of 1845. He
was engaged in this service at a compensation of
one thousand dollars per annum, and demonstrated
his faith in the financial success of the scheme
by subscribing five hundred dollars to the capital
stock of the company, which he paid out of his
meagre salary.

No means of insulating electric wires for submarine crossings had, at that period, been discovered. There had not yet been devised any mode
of utilizing rubber for purposes of insulation,
while gutta-percha had not then become an article of commerce. The only practical way for the
crossing of navigable waters by telegraph conductors, available to the intelligence of man, was by
the suspension of wires from points on either
side of the stream, high enough to clear passing vessels. For the establishment of telegraphic

intercourse between New York and Philadelphia, the crossing of the Hudson River was accomplished by the use of masts, erected at Fort Washington and on the Palisades opposite. In opening communication between Philadelphia and Fort Lee, prior to the completion of the river crossing, an attempt was made to utilize, for temporary use, the telegraph instruments which had originally been employed on the line between Washington and Baltimore. They proved unavailable for the purpose, however, as, after several days' trial, they were found unsuited for use on a line of this length, owing to crudity and imperfection of construction. Other relay magnets were thereupon devised by Mr. Cornell on a new plan, that worked admirably, and were continued in use until supplemented by a new style of relay, designed and constructed by a French electrician, which Professor Morse brought home with him from France. These instruments were found well suited to the purpose, and came into general use in this country.

A company was also formed for the erection of lines of telegraph between New York and Boston in 1845 ; and still another was organized to construct a line from New York to Buffalo, of which the section between Albany and Buffalo was built the same year. That portion of the line

7

between New York and Albany was erected by
Mr. Cornell, on a contract, for the New York,
Albany & Buffalo Telegraph Company, and was
successfully completed in the autumn of 1846.
This contract was the first enterprise that Mr.
Cornell had been able to conduct for his own advantage, and from it he realized a profit of about
six thousand dollars, despite the embarrassment
of having been prostrated by severe illness
several weeks during the progress of the work.
He also built a considerable extent of telegraph
line below Quebec, for the account of a Canadian
company, and the following year he erected a line
of telegraph from Troy through the State of Vermont to Montreal, under contract with the Troy
& Canada Junction Telegraph Company. These
several transactions proved highly remunerative
to the enterprising contractor, and from the profits
thus realized, he found himself strong enough,
financially, to undertake more pretentious adven-
tures on his own account.

With a view of extending his operations into
a wider field of usefulness, and enabling himself
to become more distinctly master of his business,
Mr. Cornell, in 1847, organized the Erie & Michigan Telegraph Company, designed to provide a
line of telegraph between Buffalo and Milwaukee,
by way of Cleveland, Detroit, and Chicago. It

was his hope and expectation to obtain, from residents of the several cities and towns along the route, subscriptions to the capital stock of the company, sufficient, with what he himself was able to invest, to complete the line. In this, however, he was almost wholly disappointed, as, beyond a few thousand dollars contributed by citizens of Detroit, Kalamazoo, South Bend, Racine, and Milwaukee, scarcely anything was provided by those residing on the line. At Chicago, it was found impossible to raise a dollar of subscription, owing to the poverty and indifference of the people. The marvellous change which has come over that city, which in 1847 was unable or unwilling to take a share of telegraph stock, is strikingly illustrated by the fact that in this year of the Lord, 1884, the citizens of Chicago are paying at least three thousand dollars per day for their telegraph service. A thorough canvass of the territory interested, resulted in failure to secure anything like the necessary capital, and but for Mr. Cornell's boldness in obligating himself for a large amount, beyond the investment of his entire available means, the enterprise must have been abandoned. Confident, however, of the great ultimate value of the proposed line, he pushed it forward with his characteristic energy to a successful completion, which was accomplished in 1848, to the gratification of all interested.

Desiring to furnish a direct and independent connection for the Erie & Michigan Telegraph system with the city of New York, Mr. Cornell also organized the New York & Erie Telegraph Company, for the purpose of building a line of telegraph from New York to Dunkirk, through the southern tier of counties of the State of New York, which was completed in the year 1849. The glass insulators then in common use were so delicately made as to be easily broken, subjecting the lines to frequent interruption from this cause. To avoid this embarrassment, and insure a permanent and reliable structure, an insulator was especially designed for this new work, consisting of an iron shield filled with brimstone as its insulating substance. When first completed, the line was very perfect in operation, but in a few weeks it began to work badly, and in the course of some months its usefulness was substantially destroyed. Many weary months of experiment and investigation finally disclosed the fact that, whereas brimstone in its ordinary state was a perfect insulator, exposure, for a few weeks, to the atmosphere in connection with the iron produced a chemical change which converted it into a positive conductor of the electric current. Thus the theoretical results of the scientific laboratory misled the company into a fatal error, which, for the time being, completely prevented the operation of the line. The only alternative, therefore, was to provide for re-insulating the entire structure with glass.

In all of the struggles incident to Mr. Cornell's laborious career, nothing compared with the obstacles which continually obstructed the progress and prosperity of the New York & Erie Telegraph Company. He had induced many personal friends to invest their means in the stock of the company, and he felt more than an usual degree of personal responsibility and anxiety to make it successful. The ignorance of the chemical experts, as to the change in the insulating qualities of brimstone after exposure to the atmosphere for a brief time was the principal cause of the long-continued misfortune which attended this enterprise, and finally ended its career in insolvency.

Another cause of annoyance was the difficulty of crossing the Hudson River with the wires. At that period there was no substance available for submarine insulation, and suspension of the conductor over the channel of the river was the only mode of crossing. For this line, a wire was suspended from the opposite cliffs of the Highlands, just above Cold Spring. This, however, was frequently destroyed as the result of heavy sleet storms in winter, and many hardships were experienced in maintaining the frail structure. Mr. Cornell often personally participated in the difficult and dangerous feats of replacing the conductor when thus prostrated.

On one occasion, while travelling over the Erie Railway, in the service of this unfortunate enterprise, Mr. Cornell met with a singular accident, which is worthy of record in this relation. Proceeding east over the road on a bitter cold night in February, when near Callicoon, about three o'clock, a broken rail threw the last car from the track and severed its connection with the train. Going at high speed, the car struck and completely demolished a telegraph pole, the shock of which tore the roof from the car, and it finally landed in the Delaware River. The occupants, of whom there were some twenty or thirty, men, women, and children, were plunged into the water waist deep. The river was running full of anchor ice, and by the time the passengers had scrambled out of the water, their garments were frozen stiff. None of the victims were seriously injured, but they all suffered intensely in the cold night air while waiting for the return of the train, which had gone on several miles before missing the lost car. They were taken forward to Narrowsburgh where the best provision possible was made for their comfort.

The Erie & Michigan Company proved a successful venture, and became the trunk line of a
considerable system. Lines were erected to connect with it, extending from Cleveland to Pittsburgh ; Cleveland to Zanesville and Wheeling ;
Cleveland to Columbus and Cincinnati, and thence
to St. Louis. The Ohio, Indiana, & Illinois Telegraph Company also came under the control of
the managers of the Erie & Michigan. Throughout nearly all of the territory west of Buffalo
telegraph lines were established before the railways. The Michigan Central, the Little Miami,
and one or two other minor roads were par-
tially built before electricity was introduced, but
with these exceptions, the telegraph was the pioneer, and was generously welcomed by the people
in all parts of the West. The tedious delay in
the transmission of the mails in those early days,
made the new medium of communication especially acceptable to the vigorous and enterprising
men of the then frontier region ; and there can be
little doubt that the telegraph was in no small
degree entitled to credit for the prodigious development of the Western States, which occurred in
the decade preceding the great rebellion. In this
connection it may also, without impropriety, be
stated, that the assertion has often been made by
those extremely competent to form an opinion,

that the success of the Government in subduing the rebellion and restoring the Union was due more to the service of the telegraph than to any other one cause. But for its use, it would have been impossible to move or supply the enormous armies which were found requisite to overcome the rebel forces.

It was a slow and difficult process to interest people in the telegraph business in the beginning. Indeed, nothing but the most abiding faith in final success could have kept up the courage of the pioneers of the enterprise in the first years of their struggles. It was not strange, however, that the average business man could not see the practical utility of the new invention; the mails then served every purpose of ordinary intercourse, and it required the sanguine anticipation of a thorough convert to realize what it was to accomplish. As soon, however, as the ultimate success of the enterprise had been demonstrated by the experience of the early lines, there were plenty of people ready to embark in the business, and within three years all of the principal cities of the country were placed in telegraphic communication with each other. Despite the protection the original companies fancied they were to enjoy from the patent rights which they had acquired from the inventor and patentees, duplicate lines soon began to invade their territory, and they found themselves power-less to prevent a ruinous competition. Many of the early companies were driven to bankruptcy from this cause, and their lines sold by sheriffs under executions of judgments. This condition of things continued for several years, until nearly every important line in the country was paralleled.

The summer of 1854 was a season of bitter and relentless rivalry among the various telegraph organizations in the Western States. The most extraordinary efforts were constantly being made to gain some advantage, until, indeed, the rivalry became almost a state of open warfare, often in-cluding legal controversies over the title and pos-session of lines which had been the subject of forced sales. In the midst of this trying period, when his active attention was more than ever es-sential to the protection of his many interests, Mr. Cornell met with a painful accident, which kept him a prisoner in his room for several weeks. In travelling by rail from Lafayette to Indianapolis, his arm, resting on the sill of the open car-window, was caught by the frame of a bridge. The arm was drawn out of the window and pounded against the timbers, through the entire length of the bridge, fracturing the bones twice above and three times below the elbow, besides breaking three fingers. The flesh of the hand and arm was terribly lacerated, and the injury was extremely painful. Fortunately, it was not found necessary to amputate the limb, and it was restored to a condition of usefulness, though the fingers were ever after stiff, and awkward for many purposes. It happened, at the time of the accident, that Mr. Cornell was accompanied by friends, who cared for him to the best advantage. He was taken to Indianapolis for medical treatment and care. Mrs. Cornell was summoned from her home, by telegraph, and hastened to attend him in the long and tedious confinement which awaited him. A subsequent investigation as to the cause of the accident demonstrated that it was in consequence of the fact that the car, in which he was riding, was much larger and wider than those ordinarily used on the road, and almost filled the space in the bridge.

It was several weeks before Mr. Cornell was permitted to leave his room, and many months before he was able to travel without much pain and discomfort. His telegraph interests suffered materially in consequence of this circumstance, notwithstanding his associates did all in their power to make good the interruption of his active attention to them. Advantage was taken by some of his business rivals of the opportunity

afforded by his prostration, to discredit and em-
barrass him, by spreading false reports as to
his solvency. In one instance this enmity proceeded so far as the purchase of one of his un-
adjusted obligations, by some of his telegraph
opponents, for the sole purpose of prosecution,
while he was still confined to his house by this
accident. The unexampled brutality which would
induce such a proceeding as this, illustrates the
extreme hostility to which the telegraph war had
been pushed in the West. Mr. Cornell was, however, enabled to provide for his outstanding liabilities ; and those who were engaged in the dis-
reputable attempt to ruin a competitor at a time
when he was disabled by a cruel accident, had
the mortification afterward of witnessing him triumph over all obstacles, and by the wise and
beneficent use of his fortune, establish a name
and fame for himself, which will brighten in future
ages when even the names of his petty tormen-
tors shall be forgotten.

CHAPTER IX.

THE WESTERN UNION TELEGRAPH COMPANY.

THE newly settled and rapidly developing
Western States were, from the beginning, the
very El Dorado of the telegraph business. The
new system of communication seemed peculiarly
adapted to the necessities of the wide-awake business men of that region. In the older States, telegraph offices could be sustained only in the large
villages and cities, but in the Western States,
every little hamlet demanded telegraphic facilities,
and often it was found that places quite insignificant in numbers of population proved to be rich
placers for the new enterprise. This was true
especially of points at which any considerable
amount of agricultural produce was gathered for

shipment to the Eastern markets. Dealers in grain were the earliest and most profitable patrons of the telegraph. The necessity of keeping themselves promptly advised of fluctuations in the market prices of their commodities, at the great trade centres, made them extremely liberal in their patronage. Those engaged in other branches of business were not slow to avail themselves of the facilities of quick communication thus brought within their reach, and the telegraph business increased with unexampled rapidity. The inevitable consequence of this vigorous development, was the introduction of rival lines, and the opening of competing offices in almost every community, frequently three or four in towns of any considerable importance. In many places the competition was sharp and often bitter. Thus profits were consumed by an extraordinary burden of expenses, and an advantageous field for a single line was converted into an absolutely unprofitable region by the duplication of lines, while the companies owning these lines were drifting on to inevitable bankruptcy.

This alarming condition of affairs convinced the managers and proprietors that the salvation of their property from absolute ruin required immediate and radical change of policy. Various attempts were made, looking to the mitigation of

the evil, but nothing was accomplished to afford
any substantial relief until 1855, when, by the co-
operation of Mr. Cornell and some of the other
principal owners of telegraph property in the
Northwestern States, a consolidation of interests
was effected, which resulted in the organization of
the Western Union Telegraph Company. This
new company was formed by a combination of the
lines of the New York & Mississippi Valley Telegraph Company; Erie & Michigan; Cleveland
& Cincinnati; Cleveland & Pittsburgh; Cincinnati & St. Louis; Ohio, Indiana, & Illinois; Lake
Erie & Ohio; and a few other minor companies, embracing substantially all interests then
existing in the States of Ohio, Indiana, Michigan, Wisconsin, and a portion of Illinois.

By this course a valuable territory for telegraph business was immediately relieved from the
evils of competition, and the lines converted from
an impecunious condition to one of great prosperity. The managers realized that, to save the
advantages which their experiment at consolidation had so strikingly demonstrated, they must
continue to develop the policy so auspiciously
commenced. They wisely determined, therefore,
to use their rapidly accumulating profits in establishing their own system over a more extended
range of operations. This they did by purchasing

such lines as could be advantageously acquired, and by building new ones wherever a profitable field of business appeared within their reach. Old lines which could not otherwise be secured were leased in perpetuity, and thus brought under the management of the new company, rendering their position more complete and impregnable.

Primarily, therefore, the great and crowning triumph of the telegraph enterprise in America grew out of the ruinous competition which so speedily extended through the Western States, and reduced that prolific field of telegraph patronage to a condition of absolute loss, and, in many instances hopeless insolvency As indicated by the peculiar style of its name, the Western Union Telegraph Company was originally organized as a *Western* company, with no definite idea on the part of its active projectors, in the beginning, that it would become anything more than a local organization, and thus a part only of the telegraph system of the country. The evils of competition were first and most seriously realized in the Western States, and the necessity for consolidation of interests was there soonest appreciated. The success of the new policy, however, became so quickly apparent to the managers of the company, that they were speedily induced to push their advantage into new territory. Within a few

years they had so far advanced in their successful career, that the continent of America became
the only limit recognized by them as the extent
of their operations.

Early in the progress of the new company it
inaugurated a system of co-operation with the
railway companies, which has proved of inestimable value in the rapid, economical, and permanent
development of the enterprise. Contracts were
entered into for the erection of lines of telegraph
along the railroads, with one or more wires for
railway use and additional wires for the general
commercial business of the telegraph company.
These contracts generally covered a period of
twenty or thirty years, and, in most cases, provided for the furnishing of poles and wire by the
Western Union Company, while the railway companies supplied the labor for erecting the lines
and keeping them in repair. Railway depôts
were generally utilized for telegraph offices, and,
in many of the smaller towns, the railway agents
performed also the duty of telegraph operators,
thus providing for the economical maintenance of
telegraph facilities in many places where limited
patronage would not justify a separate establishment. This plan of co-operation has been extended until the Western Union Company has
become thoroughly identified with almost every

considerable railway company in the United States and Canada. Under this policy the railways have been provided with superior means for telegraphic service, while the telegraph company has been enabled to secure for itself an extended system of lines far cheaper than they could have been built independently, besides the enormous advantage of acquiring the entire volume of commercial business as its exclusive right.

Steadily and with much wisdom, from the commencement of its organization to the present time, the Western Union Telegraph Company has pursued the policy of extending its jurisdiction, by the building of new lines and the acquisition, by purchase or lease, of those already in existence. The extraordinary success of the company must be attributed, in great measure, to the wisdom, courage, and vigor of its early management. While it cannot be denied that some errors were committed, these were so insignificant in comparison to the general results accomplished, that they are quite unworthy of serious comment.

Following the policy adopted and so ably pursued, the company has now become practically invincible, and has attained an eminence in the telegraph business unrivalled in the whole civilized world. Its lines now cover every State and Territory in the United States and all of the

8

Provinces of the Dominion of Canada, supplemented by cables to Europe and the West Indies, while it maintains offices in every city and prominent town within the jurisdiction of the United States and Canada, together with several thousand offices in villages and hamlets of very insignificant importance. At the present time (1884), the Western Union Telegraph system embraces 142,-459 miles of line, consisting of 422,382 miles of wire. The company maintains 12,386 telegraph offices, and its employees number more than twenty thousand persons. During the past year the volume of its business amounted to more than forty-one millions of messages, while for the last fiscal year its gross earnings were $19,454,803; expenses, $11,794,533, and net profits $7,660,350.

With the extension of its plant and the increase of facilities the Western Union management has pursued the policy of reducing its tariff of charges, and it is now, by far, the cheapest system of telegraphic communication in the world. Some idea of the reduction in tolls on telegraph messages which has been effected by the Western Union Company may be realized by the fact that in 1867 the average rate of charge for each message over its lines was $1.09, while in 1883 the average rate was only 35 cents; expense per message in 1867, 68 cents, and in 1883, 23 cents;

profits per message in 1867, 41 cents, and in 1883, 12 cents. Compared with the rate of charges for telegraph service throughout the entire continent of Europe, the Western Union service averages considerably less than one half in price per message, notwithstanding the fact that the compensation of operators is very materially higher in the United States and Canada than in Europe.

One of the principal elements of strength, and that which, probably more than anything else, insured the final and substantial domination of the Western Union Company, was the enterprising spirit which animated its executive management. From the first consolidation of rival lines into one compact and vigorous organization, it proceeded with unceasing activity to strengthen its position by reaching out and covering new territory. The vigor with which it pushed its lines across the continent in advance of civilization and brought the Pacific coast into instant communication with the Eastern States was a marvel in its day. After the failure of the first Atlantic Cable in 1858, the Western Union Company undertook the building of overland lines through the British possessions, to connect with cable across Behring Strait, and thence by land lines over the continent of Asia, to provide for telegraphic correspondence

between America and Europe. Four millions of
dollars were expended by the Company in the
extension of its lines to accomplish this purpose,
when, in 1866, the Atlantic Cable was finally completed and successfully opened for business. It
was obvious that the expense of maintaining the
overland lines through the vast and uninhabited
wilderness, without intermediate business to contribute to their support, would render it impossible to successfully compete with the direct ocean
cables in the transmission of Transatlantic business. As soon, therefore, as the permanence of
the cable was assured, the overland system was
abandoned, to the complete sacrifice of the entire amount invested therein.

Convinced at an early period of the imperative
and increasing necessity of harmonious action
between existing telegraph organizations to save
them from bankruptcy and ruin, Mr. Cornell was
one of the originators of the Western Union
Telegraph Company. He was one of the earliest
directors of the company, and in that capacity
was identified with its management for a period
of twenty years. His large experience in telegraph matters, together with his mature judgment and practical wisdom, rendered his counsel
of infinite value in shaping the policy of the company in its earlier years. He understood the

nature of difficulties to be overcome and the dangers to be avoided, which enabled him to exercise a potent and guiding influence with associates who had come into the business at later stages of its history. He was emphatically, and in every sense of the term, one of the pioneers of the telegraph enterprise, and no other person contributed more valuable service toward securing its early and successful establishment. He was present at the birth of the infant as a practical business project; he helped to give it vitality and strength in the days of its weakness; and he had the great satisfaction of witnessing its extraordinary growth and development to the proportions of a veritable giant. From the beginning of active operations his faith was absolutely unwavering in the ultimate and complete success of the telegraph as a profitable enterprise, and he realized very substantial compensation as the result of his early and correct judgment.

For more than fifteen years Mr. Cornell was the largest individual stockholder of the Western Union Telegraph Company, and in addition to his interests in that company, he was a large stockholder in the Illinois & Mississippi Telegraph Company and also in the Northwestern Telegraph Company. These organizations for many years occupied most of the territory west and north of Chicago and St. Louis, and were conducted on terms of amity and co-operation with the Western Union system, but were at last absorbed by the greater company under permanent leases, and their lines now constitute a portion of the property of the Western Union Company. From the commencement of his career in the telegraph enterprise, Mr. Cornell demonstrated his faith in its complete success by investing every dollar of his earnings in the business, and steadfastly declined to part with his holdings of telegraph stocks, until his plans for the building up of the great University at Ithaca, rendered such a course necessary to provide means therefor.

The wisdom of his policy was abundantly vindicated by the fact that he was enabled to realize for his telegraph interests in the aggregate probably more than two millions of dollars. He was not possessed of any considerable amount of capital at the beginning of his operations, and this large accumulation was the result simply of the investment in telegraph property of earnings and profits realized from the construction of lines. It is a remarkable fact that Mr. Cornell thus gained from the fruits of his labors in the telegraph enterprise, a sum larger than all of the owners of the original patents of the telegraph realized for themselves from their entire interests. It is also true that nearly all of those who accumulated large fortunes from the profits of the telegraph development, were men who engaged in the business without much capital, or other advantage than their superior perception in anticipating the results which were to be attained in the business.

CHAPTER X.

AGRICULTURAL TASTES.

Rural Tendencies.—Resuming Agricultural Pursuits.—Improved Breeds of Animals.—The Forest Park Herd.—Farmers' Club. —Agricultural Societies.—President of State Society.—Delegate to London Exposition.—European Travel.—State Fair. —Embarrassments of the Agricultural College.—Proposition to Endow an Institution for Agricultural Education.—Donating a Farm.—Neglected Facilities.

ALTHOUGH reared on a farm from his eighth year, the rugged hills of De Ruyter did not offer sufficient attractions to induce the youth, Ezra Cornell, to choose the farmer's life as his vocation. Whether, if his lot had been cast in a more attractive agricultural region, he would as readily have forsaken the farm to enter upon the laborious occupation of a carpenter, cannot be stated with any satisfactory assurance. Affectionately attached to his parents and family, every influence of consanguinity would seem to have been favorable to his remaining at home. Perhaps the natural ambition of youth, which too often assists in the planning of "air castles," would have induced a change under any circumstances. Certain it is, however, that in all of his mature years, Mr. Cornell had an inextinguishable longing for farm life, and whenever other duties permitted him to follow the bent of his own real pleasure he was drawn irresistibly to rural affairs. In selecting a homestead after his marriage, instead of choosing an ordinary village lot convenient to business, he went outside the village and secured a plot of several acres, upon which he built his home. Here he spent much of his leisure time in the planting and cultivation of fruit, and within a few years possessed the choicest orchard to be found in the whole region about. He was a close observer, and speedily became an accomplished pomologist and an excellent authority on the character and habits of insects injurious to the orchard.

Agricultural periodicals and publications relating to farming, fruit culture, and stock raising were ever favorite reading for him, and he was a frequent contributor to many of the leading journals on all of these subjects. He was especially interested in improved methods of cultivation, the introduction of labor-saving implements and machinery, and in the improvement of the breeds of domestic animals. He was one of the original founders of the Tompkins County Agricultural and Horticultural Society, and devoted much time and labor to the success of its exhibitions during the early years of its existence. As early as 1840, Mr. Cornell purchased at the cattle show of the American Institute, a superior thoroughbred, short-horn bull, named "Arab;" a number of pure bred South-down sheep, and a pair of Berkshire pigs, which he brought to Ithaca for the improvement of the domestic stock of the Tompkins County farmers. These were the first pure bred animals which were ever brought into that county, and were greatly admired by all lovers of fine stock. "Arab" proved an extremely valuable sire, and the result of his breeding with the native stock was such as to make his name remembered for many years after he had passed away; and not a few of the most celebrated milking families of cows, which at this time are so numerous in that excellent dairy region, are indebted to him for their good qualities. The benefit of the new blood on the sheep and swine of the locality was also of marked character, but of course it did not attract so much attention as in the case of the cattle.

Constantly engrossing occupation in the telegraph field, covering a period of about a dozen years, kept Mr. Cornell so continually engaged as to prohibit any considerable attention to agricultural affairs. When, however, by the successful organization of the Western Union Company, he was relieved in large measure from personal responsibility, and enabled to withdraw somewhat from the direct supervision of his telegraph interests, he resumed his rural habits with all of the enthusiasm of a novice.

Governed by an impulse never before fully satisfied, in the spring of 1857 he purchased a superior farm of about three hundred acres, adjoining the village of Ithaca, upon which he established the residence of his family. Here he planted extensive orchards, and conducted many experiments in agricultural science for the purpose of demonstrating various theories which were advocated by progressive minds. He gathered here, also, a magnificent herd of Short Horn cattle, which attracted visitors and customers from every section of the United States. It embraced representatives of the most valuable families of this celebrated breed, many of them acquired at prices which would have been deemed fabulous by persons not familiar with the current value of such animals.

He imported Short Horns, and also South-down sheep, from England, besides making extensive purchases from the best herds in New York and Kentucky. The " Forest Park " cattle were for many years prominent in the exhibition rings of the

New York State Agricultural Fairs, and animals of Mr. Cornell's raising were sold to breeders in at least twenty different States, some, indeed, going to England—many single animals selling at prices ranging all the way from $1,000 to $10,000 each. This celebrated herd of cattle, which had attained an enviable repute, was finally dispersed, some years after the death of its owner, on account of the principal part of the homestead farm going into the possession of the University as a portion of his munificent endowment.

The Farmers' Club at Ithaca owed its existence and much of its prosperity to Mr. Cornell's active support and generous patronage. It was organized at a meeting of the leading farmers and fruit-growers of that and the adjoining towns, which was convened upon his invitation. At his own expense he maintained a club and reading-room, which was provided with an excellent collection of literature appropriate to the subjects of consideration, including most of the agricultural journals of America and some of European publication. Meetings were held weekly, at which subjects of especial interest were discussed, and not unfrequently carefully prepared papers were read by members of the club. Mr. Cornell was a regular attendant on those occasions, and took an active part in the discussions with his neighbors.   In erecting the Cornell Library building, he arranged a large and handsome room, which he dedicated to the use of the Farmers' Club, suitable for its gatherings, and also for library and museum purposes.

In 1858 Mr. Cornell was elected to the presidency of the Tompkins County Agricultural and Horticultural Society, and, by earnest efforts, he succeeded in enlisting a renewed participation in the affairs of the society among the farmers of the county.   The annual fairs, which were held under his administration, were the most successful in the history of the organization, thus placing its financial affairs in a highly prosperous condition. Mr. Cornell was for many years a life member of the New York State Agricultural Society, and was accustomed to devote much time and attention to the duties of its Executive Committee, of which he was for a number of years a member. He contributed much to the success of the annual exhibitions, and it was his usual practice to be in attendance throughout these interesting occasions. In 1862 he was chosen President of the society, and in that capacity attended the great International Exposition at London, as the official representative of the New York State Agricultural Society, where he was the recipient of marked attention and courtesies.

This was the first, and, as it proved, the only
visit to Europe which it was Mr. Cornell's good
fortune to make, and, as may well be imagined,
it was to him an occasion of the most absorbing
interest. With his wide practical knowledge and
useful habits of observation, he saw and appreciated much that would have escaped the attention of travellers, who fail to utilize their opportunities. Sailing from New York in May, 1862,
by the Inman steamship City of Baltimore, he
was accompanied by Mrs. Cornell and the Secretary of the State Agricultural Society. After an
extremely rough passage, considering the season
of the year, he arrived in Liverpool early in June,
and proceeded immediately to the discharge of
his official duties in connection with the Exposition, devoting several weeks to these labors. He
next visited a number of the noted Short Horn
herds of England, and made some purchases of
choice representatives of this popular breed of
animals for his herd at Forest Park, as well also
as some South-down sheep. He travelled extensively throughout England, Wales, Scotland, and
Ireland, occupying for this purpose nearly a
month of his valuable time.

After having visited the most accessible points
of attraction in the British islands, Mr. Cornell, accompanied by his wife and other friends, proceeded

to the Continent of Europe, and devoted several weeks to a hurried trip through France, Switzerland, Holland, Germany, and Austria, visiting such places of special interest as the limited time at their command would permit. He was an enthusiastic admirer of the architectural wonders of the European cities, and greatly enjoyed the opportunity of inspecting many of the grand Cathedrals within the range of his journey. The necessity of returning to London to complete his official engagement in connection with the Exposition, obliged him to curtail his continental travel much within the limit of his desires, and he was unable to resume it, owing to the necessity of his returning home in time to give personal supervision to the annual fair of the State Society in September. This exhibition occurred in the darkest year of the war for the suppression of the great rebellion, and although the country was in the very depths of gloom, the·fair was, considering all circumstances, a grand success.

As President of the State Agricultural Society, Mr. Cornell was, *ex officio*, a trustee of the New York State Agricultural College, then located on the site of the present Willard Asylum for the Insane, at Ovid, Seneca County. This institution owed its existence to the efforts of leading agriculturists of the State, to provide for furnishing instruction in the various sciences relating to agriculture and its kindred pursuits. Substantially all of the funds so generously provided for the college had been expended in the purchase of a magnificent estate of several hundred acres, and in the erection of a large and imposing college edifice.

The institution was quite destitute of proper equipment, and was wholly wanting in endowment to aid in its support. Its doors had been opened for the admission of students the preceding year, but the youth of the State responded in meagre numbers. Upon entering the management Mr. Cornell found the College languishing for want of an adequate income to give it vitality. The object of its organization greatly interested him, and after a thorough examination into the condition of its affairs, he proposed to the trustees that, if the institution were removed and located at Ithaca, he would endow it with a fund of $300,000 for its maintenance, in case the Legislature would donate to it one-half of the College Land Grant Fund, which had been provided by Congress for the support of agricultural and mechanical colleges.

This fund had already been appropriated in favor of an embryo college located at Havana, Schuyler County, called the People's College, but this was not regarded as a suitable disposition of it, and there was considerable dissatisfaction on this account. The controversy which ensued was diversified by a demand on the part of several colleges for a division of the fund amongst them. This sentiment became so strong that the more intelligent friends of education became alarmed for fear this princely donation from the general government, consisting of nine hundred and ninety thousand acres of the public lands, might be wholly dissipated and rendered useless by division into small portions among existing colleges.

The Legislature thereupon directed the board of Regents of the University to investigate and inquire into the condition of the People's College, and report as to the adequacy of that institution to meet the requirements of the acts by which it had been made the beneficiary of the Land Grant Fund. Their report was adverse to the pretentions of the People's College, whereupon legislation was promoted resulting in the incorporation of the Cornell University, which will be the subject of more extended observation in a subsequent chapter.

The act of incorporation of the Cornell University provided that it should be located in "the town of Ithaca," and that "the farm and grounds to be occupied by said corporation, whereon its buildings shall be erected, in such manner and to such extent as the trustees may from time to time direct and provide for, shall consist of not less than two hundred acres." Upon the organization of the University it was the unanimous voice of all concerned that Mr. Cornell's farm was beyond comparison the most eligible and advantageous site that could be selected within the "town of Ithaca," to which the authority of the trustees was confined by the charter ; and whoever may have been privileged to view the institution in its developed form, may be safely depended upon to declare that no more magnificent or appropriate location could have been selected within the broad domain of the entire State, had such a choice been authorized.

Although the board of trustees would have been entirely justified in purchasing the farm at its full value, Mr. Cornell demonstrated his entire unselfishness in dictating the location of the University at Ithaca, by presenting to the trustees a warranty deed of the property, without fee or reward of any kind, thus adding the value of the farm to his already magnificent endowment of half a million dollars. This disposition of his farm and incessant occupation in promoting the various interests of the University during all the remainder of his life, rendered it impracticable for him to devote himself further to the gratification of rural tastes.

In the charter of the Cornell University, agriculture is named first in order as one of the subjects of education, and in the arrangement of the special faculties in the general organization of the University, that of " Agriculture " is given the place of rank. This predominance, which is in proper accord with the original act of Congress creating the Land Grant Fund, was given to that particular subject in deference to the expressed wish of Mr. Cornell. Throughout the entire career of the University the faculty has been kept especially strong in its membership in all of the branches of learning related to that science, and the fact that this course has attracted less patronage from the young men of the State than any other principal department is, certainly, no fault of the University authorities. The meagre development of this branch of the University course can only be attributed to the general indifference of the farmers of the State to the education of their sons in the higher branches of agricultural science. The neglect of these valuable facilities by the farming interests was, to the generous founder, the cause of deep and sincere regret, although in every other direction the University was a complete and gratifying success.

CHAPTER XI.

PUBLIC LIFE.

Duty of Citizens.—Activity in Public Affairs.—Political Management.—Delegate to first National Republican Convention.—Fremont.—Seward.—Lincoln.—Elected to State Assembly.—Re-elected.—State Senator.—Second Term.—Declines farther Service.—Legislative Labors.—Measures Supported.—Official Fidelity.

POPULAR government, like ours, based on an extremely liberal and extended elective franchise, constantly demands the considerate attention of all classes of reputable citizens to securely protect the public interest from injury by prejudicial influences. The very liberality of the franchise, and especially the extraordinary facility for attaining citizenship, affords constant temptation for those having slight concern in the public welfare to seize every opportunity for abusing the great privileges thus generously granted them. It is the more to be regretted, therefore, that any class of intelligent and prosperous citizens should be inclined to avoid the duty of active participation in the direction and conduct of public affairs. Worthy and commendable in every other respect, as in truth it must be admitted, the Quakers are certainly disposed to evade this duty. Having large property interests at stake, and thus peculiarly exposed to the evils of improvident and unwise administration, it is particularly unfortunate that they, as a class, should not cheerfully exercise the influence in public concerns to which they are justly entitled. By no other dangers are our free institutions more seriously menaced than by the habitual and inexcusable neglect of appropriate political duties by prosperous and self-respecting citizens.

Quite in contrast with the ordinary custom and peculiarity of the Quaker people in this respect, Mr. Cornell was accustomed, from early manhood, to take an active part in public concerns. Whether this variation from the traditions and practices of the ancestry from which he descended was due to, or influenced by, the discipline administered to him as punishment for marrying out of the sect, cannot be stated with any degree of certainty. Whatever the cause may have been, it is a fact, well known to those acquainted with him, that he was, far beyond the average of men, interested in management and direction of public affairs. In the early years of his career it was customary for him to exercise a potent influence in the determination of events, not only in the school district,

but as well in the local affairs of the village, town,
and county.   He was an ardent Whig in politics,
and occupied an influential position in the counsels of that party.

Always alert and energetic in any cause in
which he enlisted, Mr. Cornell was enabled to
render valuable service to his party organization
as a member of its local committees.   For a period
of a dozen years after making his residence at
Ithaca he was accustomed to give much attention
to the details of political work.   He was neither
an office-holder nor an office-seeker, but he felt it
a patriotic duty to contribute his mite to the advancement of those political interests which represented his peculiar faith.   He had an admirable faculty for promoting systematic organization
which enabled him to forecast results and thus
more effectually to accomplish success otherwise
unattainable.   He was especially active in the
great Log Cabin campaign of 1840, which resulted in the elevation of General Harrison to the
Presidency.   The lamented death of the new
President within a month of his inauguration was
a sad blow to the partisans who had labored so
zealously for his election.

Absence from home much of the time subsequent to 1842, and the pre-occupation of his
mind consequent upon the constant and absorb-

ing labors in the development of the telegraph enterprise, diverted Mr. Cornell almost wholly from attention to local politics for many years. Although continuing his affiliation with the Whig party, and taking a lively interest in the general political questions of the State and Nation, he took no part in the direction of partisan matters at home until the organization of the Republican party.

His sympathies had always been in accord with the anti-slavery element of the Whig party, so that, when a general re-organization of the great parties resulted from conflict on the question of limiting the extension of slavery into free territory, it found him enlisted as a determined opponent of the slave power. Mr. Cornell was one of the delegates representing the State of New York in the first Republican National Convention, that assembled in Pittsburgh in February, 1856.

In the great Free Soil campaign of that year he took an extremely active part in support of John C. Fremont as the Republican candidate for the Presidency, and he was a generous contributor in support of the Republican party in all of the succeeding years, until it finally accomplished the complete success of its candidates in the general election of 1860. Mr. Cornell very earnestly favored the nomination of Governor Seward for the Presidency, in the latter year, but,

with equal earnestness supported the candidacy
of Mr. Lincoln when he was selected as the
Presidential nominee by the action of the National Convention. The Republicans of New York
were sorely disappointed by the failure to secure
the promotion of Governor Seward at Chicago,
and nothing in the political history of the country
illustrates more honorable devotion in behalf of
party organization, than the remarkably faithful
support which was accorded to Mr. Lincoln in the
Empire State in the campaign which ensued.

In the autumn of 1861 Mr. Cornell was placed
in nomination by the Republican Convention of
Tompkins County for the office of member of
Assembly of the State of New York   This action
was taken without his knowledge, and was the
spontaneous and unanimous tribute of the representative Republicans of the county, in recognition of his generous services rendered in behalf of the soldiers and their families during the
first year of the civil war. He accepted the
nomination in the spirit in which it was tendered,
and was elected by a very large majority, receiving
a vote numbering considerably in excess of his
party candidates. His services in the Assembly
proved so satisfactory to his constituents, that he
was the following year re-nominated by acclamation and re-elected by a largely increased majority.

In the second Assembly of which Mr. Cornell was a member, that of 1863, the Republican and Democratic parties were evenly divided, each having sixty-four members, and, as a natural consequence, a deadlock ensued as to the choice of Speaker and the other officers of the House. Thus a prolonged and bitter partisan struggle was inaugurated, which was continued, with constantly increasing acrimony, for a period of three weeks before an organization of the Assembly was finally effected. The extraordinary excitement, incident to the abnormal condition of the country during the progress of the war, tended to heighten the ardor which would ordinarily attend such an occasion. Few contests of this nature—certainly none in this State—have been productive of so much political feeling and asperity.

Heartily tired of service in the Assembly, especially in view of the unpleasant incidents of the Speakership contest of his second session, a very agreeable change was experienced by Mr. Cornell in his subsequent legislative career. In the fall of 1863 the Republicans of Tompkins County designated him as their choice for nomination as State Senator, for the twenty-fourth district, composed of the counties of Broome, Tioga, and Tompkins. No candidate was presented on behalf of the other counties, and he was conse-

quently nominated for that office without opposition in the district convention. At the ensuing
election he was duly chosen by a very large vote
in the aggregate, having been honored with a
handsome majority in each of the several counties comprising the district.

The Senate proved far more congenial to his
tastes and habits than the Assembly, and he took
rank in the smaller and more appreciative body,
more in conformity with his practical abilities and
large experience in affairs. His success in the
representation of the district, during the first two
years of service in the Senate, was very signal-
ly attested by the fact that, at the expiration of
the term, he was re-nominated by acclamation by
the delegates of his party from the three counties, in district convention assembled, without the
dissent of a single voice. This very complimen-
tary action of partisan friends, was in due order
ratified by the electors of the district in November following, when he received still more flattering evidences of public appreciation. Returning
with a renewed commission, Mr. Cornell found
the Senate very much changed in its *personnel*,
containing as it did twenty-five new Senators.

This circumstance was calculated to greatly
enhance the relative influence of the few old
Senators, in the disposition of business coming

before them, as well as to increase their labors.
Mr. Cornell devoted himself to Senatorial duties
with great assiduity until the close of his second
term, in 1867, when he positively declined a re-
election, which awaited him with great unanimity.
Having thus served six years continuously in the
Legislature—two years in the Assembly and four
in the Senate—he felt that he had fairly earned
exemption from further service. Besides, having taken upon himself the burden of locating
and managing the public lands for the benefit of
the University, he felt desirous of dedicating his
undivided energies to that important work.

As a member of the Legislature, Mr. Cornell
gave his earnest support to all measures which
were calculated to strengthen the cause of the
Union in the struggle for its maintenance. The
vigorous manner in which the law-making power
of the State of New York sustained the federal
authorities in their conflict with the rebellion, was
one of the most important elements of final victory.
The act extending to the New York soldiers in
the field, in distant States, the facilities of voting
for President at their homes, by sending their
votes to designated friends to be cast for them,
was very cordially supported by him.

The subjects which, next to the preservation
of the Union, occupied Mr. Cornell's attention

more especially, were those of agriculture and public education. He regarded one as the foundation of the material prosperity of the State, and the other as the safeguard of the liberties of the people, and that its general dissemination would, more than anything else, serve to perpetuate our free institutions. He therefore gave particular attention to the consideration and promotion of various questions which he deemed advantageous to these interests. The first legislation providing stringent regulations to guard against the spread of contagious diseases among cattle was due to his influence. Under it the Governor was invested with extraordinary power, through agents acting in his name and under his direction, to quarantine herds of cattle ; to kill all animals which had been exposed to or were likely to be contaminated by disease, and providing for indemnifying owners from the State treasury.

At frequent intervals, during the last few years, by the wise exercise of these arbitrary powers under executive direction, numerous very threatening outbreaks of pleuro-pneumonia have been suppressed, and devastation of the great dairy and cattle interests of the State has been safely guarded against. Mr. Cornell introduced and passed, against great opposition, a bill to prohibit the running at large of animals in the streets and highways of the State. The immediate effect of this action was to bring upon the devoted head of its author, the dire vengeance of those who deemed that they were to be deprived of the natural right of pasturing their animals in the public roadway. The manifest propriety of the provision, won the majority of people to its support, and the intolerable nuisance, once so prevalent, of cattle roaming at will in public, has been almost entirely eradicated, thus permitting the removal of fences and the adornment of lawns of many a rural village throughout the State. Though of trifling interest compared with other public measures, the effect of this reform has been marvelous, when realized, and the present situation contrasted with the old.

Many other acts were promoted by the advocacy of Mr. Cornell, but which need not receive especial mention in this connection. He was a member of the finance committee of the Senate, and devoted close attention to the consideration of financial questions. He was an uncompromising advocate of sustaining the credit of the State by payment of the principal and interest of the public debt in specie, in accordance with the true spirit of the contract under which the obligation was incurred. In providing for extraordinary expenditures incident to the pros-

ecution of the war for the suppression of the rebellion, Mr. Cornell insisted that ample provision
should be made for the creation of sinking funds
for the gradual extinction of liabilities created.

Under the salutary operation of these wisely
framed statutes the State has long since discharged every dollar of the war debt, and, indeed,
of all other State indebtedness, except a small
remnant of the Canal Fund debt, not yet matured, but for which complete provision is made
in the collection of an annual contribution to the
sinking fund for this purpose, which will entirely ex-
tinguish that obligation before its maturity, and
within a very few years from the present time.
The bill for the incorporation of the Society for
the Prevention of Cruelty to Animals was zealously supported by Mr. Cornell, and the final passage of the measure, which was vigorously resisted
by an influential lobby, was due largely to his
vigilance and persistence in its behalf. The extremely valuable results which have followed the
enactment of this measure have more than vindicated the wisdom of its promoters.

While not endowed with any considerable facility for public speaking and, therefore, taking but
little part in the formal discussions of the Assembly or Senate, Mr. Cornell was accustomed to
state his views on public questions with a brevity

and clearness of expression, which, supported by his well-merited repute for practical good sense, gave his voice more than ordinary weight of authority. He was indefatigable in attention to his duties, and rendered invaluable service in the work of the committee room. His wide range of experience and extended knowledge of many subjects gave him an enviable influence in the disposition of business before committees of which he was a member.

The truthfulness of his character and the fairness with which he was accustomed to treat all questions coming before him for consideration, gave him in general the unreserved confidence of his associates, and his position in support of, or in opposition to, a measure was almost sure to carry others with him. While he was habitually public-spirited in reference to the expenditure of State funds for meritorious purposes, he was especially pronounced in his opposition to useless or extravagant measures. In the discharge of official duty he was governed solely by his own view of the public interest. Neither the solicitation of friends nor the menace of opponents was effective in influencing him in the performance of what he believed to be his sworn duty. No more resolute and unimpeachable member of the Legislature ever sat in either house.

CHAPTER XII.

THE CIVIL WAR.

IN the long-continued and never-ending controversy over the slavery question, Mr. Cornell's sympathies were ever on the side of freedom. The first serious contention which threatened to cause forcible conflict with the Federal authority —the nullification acts of South Carolina—happened soon after he had attained his majority. From this period, in all of the various divisions of political sentiment into which the "irrepressible conflict" forced itself continuously, or at least at frequent intervals, during the thirty years which elapsed prior to its final culmination in open rebellion, he was uniformly to be found with the friends of the black race. Though never identified by political association with that small class of advanced thinkers who declared themselves abolitionists, he was nevertheless in full sympathy with their object. Extensive range of travel through several of the Southern States had given him more than ordinary opportunity for observing the evils resulting from slavery, and it was his belief that the white people themselves suffered but little less than the colored race from those evils.

He saw that civilization was apparently declining instead of advancing, and that the great States of the South were really being dwarfed by the presence of the institution which their people so jealously guarded. In his letters written while journeying in the South, he frequently contrasted the prospects of the two sections, and clearly predicted the inevitable results of the constantly increasing advance in wealth and power which the Northern States were making as compared with those of the South.

But while fully sympathizing with the general objects desired by the abolitionists, Mr. Cornell, like the great majority of the true friends of freedom, was unable to see that the final liberation of the bondmen was to be hastened by ill-ad-

vised, premature efforts. He was, therefore, in
full accord with the sentiments of the Republican
party in its declaration of opposition to the farther
extension of slavery. While there might be no
lawful means to eradicate it from its existing limits, it should not thrust itself upon other States
or Territories. Descended as he was from a long
line of Quaker ancestry, every instinct of his nature responded in sympathy with the oppressed.
The only question as to his political classifica-
tion, therefore, was governed by his judgment as
to the most completely effective way in which
ultimate freedom could be insured.

Had the slaveholders been content to accept
the basis of the non-extension of slavery into
new territory, there can be little doubt that their
favorite institution would have remained undis-
turbed within its old limits for many years. The
sentiment in the North was practically unanimous
against interference with slavery within the States
where it then existed. "Those whom GOD wishes
to destroy, He first makes mad." Never was the
significance of this declaration more apparent
than in the results which followed the repeal of
the Missouri compromise. Designed thus to provide for the introduction of slavery into Kansas
and Nebraska, as well as other new Territories,
an uproar was raised in the North which effect-

ually checked this object. These new States secured to freedom, the result of the next census of
the United States upon the apportionment of
Congressional representation, must inevitably invest the Northern States with the power to control
the Government in any contest over the vexed
question.

It was most undoubtedly this anticipation which
determined the Southern leaders to press on the
issue to final solution in advance of the re-ap-
portionment under the approaching Federal census. By many the theory is fully believed that
the Democratic National Convention of 1860 was
purposely divided and forced to make dual nomi-
nations, in order to insure the election of the Republican canditates, and thus force the issue of
secession by appealing to the bigoted resentments
of the Southern people.

Like an overwhelming proportion of the Northern people, Mr. Cornell was unable to realize the
possibility of actual war as the result of the triumph of the free-soil sentiment in the election
of Mr. Lincoln to the Presidency. The highly
extravagant declarations of Southern speakers
and the Southern press were regarded as bravado,
intended to frighten the North from its purpose
of resisting the spread of slavery. The operations
of Buchanan's War and Navy Departments, in

transferring war material from the Northern depositories to others in the South, and in dispersing the vessels of war to far-distant and inaccessible stations, were not generally appreciated until too late for remedy. Even with the perfectly undisguised preparations for war, which were so vigorously carried on in the Southern States, during all of the time intervening between the election of Mr. Lincoln in November, and his inauguration in the following March, it seemed impossible for law-abiding citizens of the free States to realize that a conflict of arms was really to come.

The teachings of those who preferred slavery to the perpetuation of the Union, which had been so generally disseminated throughout the slave States for a whole generation, had, however, done great work. The Southern people were terrorized by what they regarded as the real significance of the crisis which was approaching. With the success of the Republican cause in 1860, the limit to the extension of slavery would become a fixed fact, and the Territories would be dedicated to the cause of freedom, only to produce free States for future admission to the Union. This they construed to mean the gradual but ultimate fall of slavery, and being fully resolved that this should not come without resistance, they reasoned that they were then relatively stronger for the conflict than they ever would be again. The prodigious development of the free States would inevitably make the struggle the more desperate by any delay.

Thus the conflict was approached with full determination and equipment on the one hand, and with almost fatal blindness and lack of preparation on the other. No sooner, however, had the unmistakable signal of war been sounded —as it was by the firing of the rebel battery upon the walls of Fort Sumter—than the loyal North was aroused to instant and complete realization of the situation. Like the sudden awakening of a sleeping giant, the free States arose in the grandeur of their strength, with unquestioned determination that the integrity of the Union should be maintained and vindicated—that no star should be blotted from the flag of freedom.

The call of President Lincoln for volunteers to sustain the authority of the Government was responded to with alacrity and enthusiasm throughout the Northern States. Communities vied with each other in the promptitude with which they furnished their quotas of troops. The first necessity to promote enlistments was suitable provision for the maintenance of the families of those who should go forth to battle. In this patriotic work Mr. Cornell took the lead in the community of his

residence.   He headed a public subscription with
a generous contribution, and, by his influence, a
large sum was raised for the care of these depend-
ents.   He accepted the chairmanship of the committee of disbursement, and devoted much time
and personal labor to the painstaking distribution
of this fund to the families entitled to participate
therein, making extremely careful inquiry into
the circumstances pertaining to each family, in
order to provide for the faithful administration of
the trust, in accordance with the compact under
which the enlistments were secured.

As the war progressed, and the struggle lengthened into months and years, Mr. Cornell busied
himself in visiting the armies and the hospitals
in looking after the personal comfort of the soldiers from his locality.   He was at Washington
at the time of the first battle at Bull Run, and on
the Sunday morning of that event, he proceeded
to the scene of the conflict, in order to be of any
possible service to those who might suffer from
the casualties of the expected battle.   Many gal-
lant fellows had occasion to remember, with grateful feelings, the thoughtful kindness of Ezra Cornell, in seeking them out and ministering to their
peculiar necessities.   The fatalities of the bat-
tle-field, however, were by no means the worst
terrors which menaced the life of the soldier.

Disease claims many more victims than the bullet.

The hospitals were full of those suffering from all sorts of illnesses, and when, added to other disease, homesickness had taken possession of a victim, his case was desperate indeed. Mental depression, added to physical prostration, was almost sure to bring a fatal ending. Not a few such were found languishing for the soothing care of the loved ones at home, when with patience, and the most unselfish devotion, Mr. Cornell would follow the wearisome technicalities of the military service until he secured the necessary furlough or discharge, and then at his own expense, and under his personal care, conduct the invalids to homes and friends. Numbers were saved to future usefulness, and not unfrequently returned to the service full of renewed vigor, who, but for Mr. Cornell's considerate attention, would have early filled soldiers' graves. Until the final ending of the war, when the rebellion was conquered, and the authority of the Federal Government was once more completely restored throughout all of our broad domain, Mr. Cornell was unremitting in his devotion to the cause of the Union, in promoting enlistments, and in contributing to the comfortable maintenance of the soldiers and their families. He was, in every sense of the term, the soldier's friend, while to many of them he was, in very truth, a " good Samaritan."

The dependent families of the patriots who sacrificed their lives in the service of their country, were, to Mr. Cornell, subjects of especial interest and solicitude. He felt that the orphaned children of the martyrs of the great rebellion, were a sacred charge upon those for whose benefit their natural protectors had perilled their lives, and he was deeply interested in all measures calculated to promote the welfare and provide for the maintenance, comfort, and education of all such, who chanced to be left without adequate provision. His purse was ever open to, and his best services were always at the command of, these unfortunates. In whatever capacity their appeal reached him, whether as an individual, as a member of community, or as an official representative in the Legislature of the State, he ever had a listening ear and a responsive heart, and it may safely be asserted that no meritorious appeal of this character ever sought him in vain.

The gigantic struggle for the suppression of the rebellion, and the restoration of the authority of the Union, was brought to an entirely successful ending by the complete collapse of the rebel power. Never was a mistaken cause more obstinately defended, nor a loyal cause more gallantly

supported than in the conflict thus finished. The
grand army of the Union was, perhaps, at the
very maximum of its strength, when its usefulness
was thus suddenly arrested. Within a few weeks,
hundreds of thousands of the veterans of the war
were mustered out of service, only to meet each
other as competitors for civil employment.

Fortunately, their return to ordinary pursuits
happened at a time of remarkable prosperity in the
country, and the labor of willing hands generally
found ready employment. Many, however, by
the effect of wounds or sickness, were rendered
incapable of discharging duties with which they
were previously familiar. These were especially
the wards of Mr. Cornell. He provided many of
them with artificial limbs, and devoted much time
to aid them in securing employment suited to their
capacities. Some were furnished with the means
of educating themselves to new pursuits, while
others were provided with capital and credit to
enable them to engage in business. Many a vet-
eran of the Union cause is now in prosperous
circumstances from the help received from this
patriotic benefactor, who, but for the timely aid
thus rendered, must inevitably have suffered from
inability to pursue his ordinary vocation. Mr. Cornell was eminently practicable in his charities, as
in all other characteristics. He delighted to help

those who would profit by his aid, and it was his custom to so direct his efforts in behalf of those needing assistance, that momentum might be given toward self-support and independence. It was ever by him considered a privilege as well as a duty to serve, in any possible manner, those who served their country in the time of its great need.

CHAPTER XIII.

THE CORNELL LIBRARY.

THE too frequent result of extraordinary success in business, or in the accumulation of fortune, seems to be to create ambition for still farther achievement in the same direction. Men are seldom inclined to stop when they have acquired an ample competence and devote themselves to the higher duties of life. They press on and not unfrequently make themselves the slaves of their gigantic operations, wearing out their lives in useless toil and care. To this general rule the subject of this sketch was certainly an exception.

In the pursuit of fortune no man could have devoted himself more assiduously than Mr. Cornell did to the success of his telegraph ventures. For ten years his labors were incessant, and the tasks he accomplished would have completely discouraged a less resolute man.   Often he would spend every night of a week in travelling and occupy the intervening days in the transaction of business which constantly demanded his attention in widely separated localities.   When success was fairly reached, he retired from active participation in business and devoted himself to the more agreeable duties of agricultural experiment and study. This gave him leisure to take suitable observation of surrounding circumstances.   Ithaca had been his residence during all of his years of manhood, and though called from it much of the time for a number of years, he always returned to the home of his choice with feelings of gladness.

Thus at the age of fifty he found himself independent of further labor, and in the enjoyment of a liberal income.   He was inspired with an ambition to do something to adorn and improve the village, and at the same time to benefit the rising generation, and encourage them to endeavors for higher mental cultivation.   It is not unlikely that recollection of the meagre facilities for education, which were within reach in his younger days, had something to do with the particular direction of his benefaction.   The impediments which he had encountered at different times in trying to utilize for his own purposes the facilities of some of the great Libraries in leading cities made him desire to see such an institution free from the restraints he had met with. He therefore resolved to establish at Ithaca, a Public Library which should be free for the use of every resident of the County of Tompkins.

Having become fixed in this purpose, Mr. Cornell took occasion to call into his confidence a few leading citizens, with a view of perfecting suitable plans and arranging such an organization as would insure the most careful attention in the future administration of the trust. The gentlemen who were invited to the conference entered cordially into the merits of the proposed institution, giving much useful assistance in the initiatory work, and have continued, through the many intervening years, to render valuable service in the direction of the Library.

It was, in the first place, Mr. Cornell's idea to devote $20,000 to the erection of a Library building, and $30,000 for books. Further consideration, however, convinced him that the institution should be possessed of means of self-support, and under the advice of the associated citizens, he finally concluded to erect a building, which should contain apartments for rent sufficient to produce the desired income, and leave the books to be

provided by gradual accumulation.   He then purchased an eligible site on a prominent corner adjacent to the business centre of the village, and
in the spring of 1863 began the erection of what
is now known as the Cornell Library.

The edifice is of brick, 64 by 104 feet in size;
three stories and basement ; containing, besides
the library fitted to receive thirty thousand volumes, a fine lecture hall, 50 by 60 feet, with gallery,
and several apartments for business purposes, designed to furnish an income for the care and maintenance of the Library, which it was estimated
would amount to at least $3,000 per annum.   The
cost of the site and building was $61,676, besides
$4,000 for books, all paid for by Mr. Cornell,
conveyed by trust deed to the trustees of the
Cornell Library Association, and delivered to
them in the presence of a crowded meeting of
citizens of Ithaca and vicinity, assembled in the
Library Hall on the evening of the twentieth of
December, 1866.   During the day the building
had been decorated with flags by appreciative citizens, and the lecture room was tastefully trimmed,
with the name of the founder wrought in ever-
greens.   The weather was intensely cold, but at an
early hour every available portion of the hall was
crowded, while the firing of cannon and the exul-
tant ringing of the village bells gave voice to the

general appreciation of the generous gift to the public.

In his address of presentation Mr. Cornell said:

Ladies and Gentlemen: I have invited you to assemble this evening to witness the consummation of a long-cherished purpose —the establishment of a Public Library in the village of Ithaca, "the use of which shall be *free* to all residents of the County of Tompkins," an institution which I trust will be found useful in increasing the knowledge and elevating the moral and religious standard of the people. It may not be deemed improper on an occasion like this to refer briefly to the history of the progress of the undertaking; the motives which prompted it, controlled the plans of the edifice, and fashioned the organization to which the trust and management of the property will now be committed.

The conception of the undertaking may be traced to a settled conviction in my mind of the unwise policy, so prevalent in men of large means, of deferring until death their benevolent plans, and committing them, by their last will and testament, to the execution of unwilling heirs, indifferent executors or administrators, or selfish trustees.

The results of the noble and wise example of Peter Cooper, as contrasted with the equally well-meaning but less successful example of Stephen Girard, led me to decide in favor of the former, and to adopt a policy which might be executed, in part at least, during my lifetime, thus giving me the opportunity of aiding in the execution of my plans, and enjoying the benefits while living which may flow from them. . . .

After giving a detailed description of the edifice, the uses for which the several apartments were designed, and the particulars relating to the progress of its erection, he said:

The sums which have been collected for rents up to the present time amount to $1,965, and there will have accrued by the coming first of January the further sum of $534. These sums have been held as the property of the Library Association, and payments for maintenance to the amount of about $1,500 have been made from them, leaving about $1,000 in the treasury of the Library at the commencement of the new year, and may no future New Year's day find here an empty treasury.

Fellow citizens of Ithaca : This property belongs to you and to the other citizens of the County of Tompkins. The Board of Trustees to whom I am about to commit the trust and management of this property are your agents, and it is their duty to manage the property within the limitations fixed by law, so as to give all the residents of the County of Tompkins equal privileges and opportunities in the use and benefits to be derived from this Library.

In the organization of the Board of Trustees, it was my aim to secure a full and fair representation of the various interests in the county as far as it was practicable. The pastors of seven of your churches, the principal of the Academy, and of the public school, the chairman of the County Board of Supervisors, the President of the village of Ithaca, and the Chief Engineer of the Ithaca Fire Department are ex-officio trustees, to which are added the names of the founder and six citizens, constituting a board of nineteen members, and representing, as fully as practicable, all classes and interests.

Gentlemen of the Board of Trustees : Having thus briefly related the history and stated the present condition of the property I am about to commit to your charge, it is perhaps my duty, and I can assure you it is a very pleasant duty, to address a few words to you.

By the Act, chapter 126, of the laws of 1864 of the State of New York, you and your successors in office are created and constituted a body corporate by the name and title of the " Cornell Library Association," " the corporate existence of which shall commence when the said Ezra Cornell shall convey to it the lot of land and edifice hereinbefore mentioned, and shall continue forever."

The act on my part which is required, under the law, to give you official and legal existence as a corporation, I am now about to perform. For full instruction as to your powers and duties under the trust you are about to assume, I must refer you to the above-cited Act and the statutes of this State.

In closing, Mr. Chairman and gentlemen, I must express the hope that your administration of this trust will be so impartial, so wise, and so just that a truthful history of it, which should at all times be found on your records, will stand as a lasting monument to your honor through all time.

Mr. Chairman, I now present to you the deed of the property and the keys of the edifice, and may God bless the enterprise and make it fruitful to this people in

KNOWLEDGE, TRUTH, AND VIRTUE.

On receiving from Mr. Cornell the trust deed and the keys of the Library building, the Hon. Benjamin G. Ferris, who had been designated by his colleagues of the Board of Trustees, made the following response in their name.

ADDRESS OF THE HON. BENJAMIN G. FERRIS.

I feel profound gratification in receiving from your hand this deed and these keys. By this conveyance and these symbols of possession we become a body corporate, fully organized to carry out your views, as the donor, and discharge our duties to the public, who are the recipients of your bounty.

To simply say we thank you would too coldly express the emotions which the occasion naturally calls forth. When a private citizen like yourself steps out of the ordinary round of self-interest, within which men usually regard and regulate their private fortunes, and with a lavish hand confers great benefits on the public, language becomes too feeble to express the gratitude which is felt and which becomes due.

I know, in speaking of these things, it is not easy to confine one's self within the limits of good taste. We are apt to run into the common phrases of laudation and flattery. But at least we may be permitted to hold up such a case as *an example to be followed by others.* Our country is now full of great fortunes, but how many counties like Tompkins, how many towns like Ithaca contain the visible evidences of private munificence for public uses? There is many a man who has a large surplus beyond the necessities and luxuries of living, beyond the display of a costly residence, beyond the full gratification of a taste for fine arts, beyond the establishment of his family from the contingencies of want. What becomes of this surplus? Is it heaped up like Pelion upon Ossa, as men know how to heap up money, for the mere purposes of accumulation? We have, on an occasion like this, the right to point to this Library, to point to the magnificent structure rearing on yonder eminence and say, "GO AND DO LIKEWISE!"

You, sir, will be neither surprised nor pained to learn that your motives in making large public donations have been pretty freely canvassed. Some people have distressed themselves over the vexed questions as to whether you are influenced by an eye to future fame, or whether you are trying to undermine the institutions of your country, by building up an aristocracy in your family, or whether, as those who know you best believe, you really possess a heart which delights to promote the welfare and happiness of mankind.

We have no trouble on those points. We accept the gift; we take upon ourselves this trust; and from this moment the COR-NELL LIBRARY becomes an established institution.

Yet I can scarcely realize that a large Free Public Library, one which stands up among the great public libraries of the world, *is really founded in Ithaca.* In less than the threescore and ten years allotted to a single life, savages roamed at will through this pleasant valley, and an Indian wigwam may well have occupied the very spot on which this building now stands, and in which are assembled the beauty, fashion, and intelligence of an advanced stage of civilization, to participate in this inauguration. But history is full of contrasts, and when we reverse the historical tele-scope, and look back into remote ages, we shall see how small and feeble were the beginnings of the efforts of mankind for mental culture. Statesmen of all ages have realized the necessity of storing up the written thoughts of the wise and good for public benefit ; and this really marks the distinction between civilized and savage life. Barbarians pass along from one generation to another, with no change except that which too often indicates a lower scale of human degradation. The wigwams which here and there dotted the valley of the Cayuga, were the exact counter-parts of the wigwams which had been built here for a thousand years anterior. The Feejee Islander, who now feeds upon human flesh, but follows the custom of his ancestors for generations past. But civilization builds step by step upon the thoughts and inven-tions of each age, until the vast monuments of modern improve-ment leave us to wonder if there can be anything more to discover.

In the dim light of the past, Egypt seems to have been the cradle of the arts and sciences. One of its sovereigns, Osyman-dias, is said to have founded the first public library known to his-tory. The motto on the building was " *The Dispensary of the Soul.*" The sculpture upon the walls represented a Judge with the image of Truth suspended from his neck, and many books or rolls lying before him. The contents of the library were the sacred writings of the Egyptians in manuscript, written upon sheets prepared from the papyrus, a reed growing on the banks of the Nile, from which our word paper is derived. The length of these sheets was from one to fifty yards, according to the magnitude of the works. The manuscript, when complete, was rolled on a staff, and from this called " volumen," the source of our word volume. The ends of the staff were usually ornamented with bosses of wood or ivory, and sometimes with gold, silver, and precious stones. At an earlier period, stones and metallic substances were used for writing. The Ten Commandments, we know, were inscribed on tablets of stone. Joseph speaks of two columns, one of stone, and the other of brick, on which the children of Seth wrote their inventions and astronomical discoveries. The works of Hesiod were written on tablets of lead. Mr. Layard has exhumed from the ruins of Nineveh writings upon earthen tablets, to the number of about twenty thousand, constituting, as is supposed, the Royal Library. The Library of Alexandria, founded by one of the Ptolemean kings, was undoubtedly the largest of antiquity, and is said to have consisted at one time of seven hundred thousand rolled manuscripts, the ends protruding from the pigeon-holes, if, indeed, pigeon-holes were of that date.

There were booksellers, also, in Egypt, and subsequently in Greece and Rome, of whom the book sought to be purchased was ordered, as we now go to the tailor and order a coat, and the book was furnished as soon as it could be copied from an original. What a change! Think now of going to one of our bookstores and ordering a copy of Shakespeare, to be delivered in three months. At present prices, it would cost enough to pay the expense of the Cornell Library for well nigh a year.

All the great libraries of the old world commenced in a small way. The now mammoth library of Paris commenced with only twenty volumes. That of the University of Oxford had at first only six hundred volumes, and one of its regulations was : " Let no scholar occupy a book of the Library above one hour, or two at most, so that others may be hindered from the use of the same." During this period books were so scarce that the sale of one was attended with more formalities than are now observed in transferring the title of a thousand acres of land. This Institution, however, thanks to your princely munificence, springs suddenly into complete life, the full panoplied Minerva from the brain of Jupiter, with its organization and ample endowment for its career of usefulness.

Each age of the world fancies itself at the limit of improvement. The twenty thousand tablets of old Nineveh formed, it was thought, a perfect library. So, too, thought the Ptolemies, when proudly viewing the ends of the sticks on which were rolled their countless manuscripts. It was related of Hercules that he made a great voyage of discovery. He skirted along the shores of the Mediterranean in a row-boat, suffering almost as much danger from shipwreck as Sir John Franklin among the hummocks of the Polar regions. When he reached the Straits of Gibraltar, as the story goes, he erected a pillar on either side of the strait, on which he inscribed the words :

"NE PLUS ULTRA."

(There is no more beyond.) That to him and those of his time was the end of the world; beyond was an illimitable waste of waters. But beyond this, in time and space, lay marvelous things. Beyond was the mariner's compass in the hands of Columbus, and at the end of his voyage lay a mighty continent ; beyond was the genius of Fulton and steam navigation with voyages around the world, performed with more safety than Hercules in rowing his craft half a dozen miles ; beyond was the printing-press, an engine more powerful than the sword ; beyond, too, was the electric telegraph, by which Jupiter's thunderbolts have been changed into news-carriers, and we can hear from Mount Olympus in less time than Puck, in the play, proposed to put a girdle round the earth.

We, too, after these achievements, think we have got to the terminus. But we are grandly mistaken ; we are not yet at the half-way house. This is a material world, the world of effects upon which the inner world, the world of causes, is continually pressing further developments of the power of mind and matter. And the names of the men who have the power and the will to obey the sacred impulse will be found written with yours in the pages of history.

The formal address of dedication, which was next delivered, was listened to with deep and appreciative attention by the great audience. This admirable feature of the occasion is given in full in the succeeding chapter.

The Hon. William H. Bogart, of Aurora, who had been a citizen of Ithaca, and an intimate

personal friend of Mr. Cornell during the earlier
years of his residence there, was next introduced,
and spoke as follows:

ADDRESS OF HON. WILLIAM H. BOGART.

Mr. President: There is an adage in which the few words convey wisdom it is well to heed: "Speech is silver and Silence is
golden." A voice that has so often been heard by you as mine
has been, may wisely think of this before the golden bowl is
broken. It was a pleasant duty to comply with the invitation
which Mr. Cornell sent to me to come here to-night to take part in
the dedication of the Library. My journey hither was amid the
terrible cold of this day, but I found, as I came by the shore
of our broad and pure Cayuga, a picture all around me. I was
coming to a library. Everywhere the library of nature was un-
folded to me, as if recognizing that it had its own part to do in
all the teaching of the soul. While elsewhere the sky was
cloudless, the great chemistry of nature was busy, and the lake
was pouring upward massive clouds of vapor, that indicated its
own warmth and the cold air that was around it. This uttered
the lesson that we darken our own horizon. Our clouds are born
of ourselves. The snow was of such whiteness it seemed the very
image of purity. I knew this could endure only till it felt the
footsteps of man. It was renewing the story of Eden. The trees,
erect and gaunt and leafless, had prepared themselves thus to
meet the tempests of winter, and voices came thence to bid us, in
the chances and changes of this mortal time, to lay aside every
weight and keep no hindrance to our strength. The chill and
pain of the journey had their recompense.

Perhaps it was appropriate that I should take part in the service of dedication. Of all around me on this platform, only the
gentleman [Mr. Ferris] who has with such worthy and appropriate
remarks accepted on behalf of the trustees this gift, only himself
and myself were of the associates of the generous giver of this
Library in the days when his task in life had, it may be, in it more of

the shadow than the sun, when he was vigorously engaged in his calling of industry, perhaps even then creating in his own mind the hope, the wish, the plan, that when more genial and more prosperous influences should be about him, he would leave, with his fellowmen, good evidence that he had sought to make them happier; perhaps even then with some glimpse of the possibility of that control of the electric fluid which has been developed by the labors of himself and his associates into the very chief of all the agencies of power permitted to the custody of man. So it was fitting that I should be here to share the luxury of witnessing his reward—I do not say his triumph, his victory—these words belong to the false state of action formed out of the sorrows of the fallen.

As I came to this beautiful hall this evening I heard in the crystal air the bells ring out their clear tones, and the loud cannon in their deeper voice. I doubt not that as the sounds struck the hillside and the far valley, men rushed from their hearths to gather tidings of the cause of this wild alarm, as to them it seemed, and I can imagine with what proud look each Ithacan met the inquiry—"The Illumination?" Yes, of the mind. "The Fire?" Yes, that shall burn up Ignorance. It is kindled to-night.

But not alone in voice of bell, and cannon, and exultation is his reward. Your presence thus crowding this hall tells him that his gift is appreciated by a people who will remember the giver. Beyond all this, I have heard the ministers of religion this night invoking on him the blessing which endures when knowledge itself "shall vanish away." It is so gratifying to me to-night to see that which is so seldom seen, a work accomplished. If the curtain should fall to-night, it falls on a good, no longer a promised or an expected good, but one realized. It is something in a life such as ours is when the light of to-day but feebly interprets the darkness of the morrow; it is something to know that a good is done. Henceforth, when the State of New York shall call over its roll of men who have done the State service by increasing the happiness of the people, it must speak the name of Ezra Cornell! Sometimes our good deeds are resolved upon; often they do not get beyond an easy imagination, where the beautiful only is seen, and the stern, real gate of trial is avoided. Sometimes a good deed is only planned out. How often it is like our human nature in its infancy only, and never reaches the strength of manhood. How full the satisfaction, then, when a purpose of good has passed through all alternations of hope and fear, and is fully, gladly, joyously before us, at our side, an accomplished reality, a bestowed blessing.

Proceeding at some length to dilate upon the advantages to follow the establishment of such an institution, Mr. Bogart closed his eloquent remarks as follows :

Mr. President, Mr. Cornell has achieved his high purpose. Henceforth this Library is for the public use. Ithaca from this hour rises in value. Her lands and tenements and hereditaments count greater value. I think I predict only what calm and cool fact shall confirm, that they who seek for a genial home will be guided hither by the light of this Library, and you will find following all that belongs to Order, and Refinement, and Wisdom.

The exercises of the evening were finished with great enthusiasm by the adoption of a resolution that each member of the vast audience present should, in the coming holiday week, contribute one or more books to the Library as a Christmas gift. This action resulted in the presentation of a large number of valuable works, and in that manner made many persons feel a more direct individual interest in the Library than they would otherwise have experienced.

This noble benefaction was accepted by the citizens of Tompkins County with a gratifying appreciation of the generous impulse which prompted the founder in designing and presenting it for their use. Unfortunately, however, for the rapid increase of the facilities of the Cornell Library, it was speedily eclipsed by the act of its founder in the endowment and organization of the Cornell University, and has ever since been over-shadowed by the brilliant success of the greater institution. But for the establishment of the University in such immediate proximity, the Library would, no doubt, have achieved far greater development than it has thus far experienced. Its growth, however, if slow, has been substantial in character, and it has already attained a collection of about fifteen thousand volumes, including many extremely valuable works of reference. Its management has been prudent in all things, and its financial condition has been materially strengthened in each year of its existence.

The Library has been extensively patronized by citizens, as well as by the students of the University, who have shown a grateful appreciation of the facilities thus furnished them. Strangers visiting Ithaca inspect the Library with great interest, and are profuse in their expressions of admiration for the literary advantages with which

the residents of the locality have been so generously provided.   The superb educational facilities
established by the munificence of Mr. Cornell, at
Ithaca, have given the town an enviable repute
throughout the country, and have attracted there
many desirable residents, and a constant procession of visitors.   From the stimulus thus given the
village has more than doubled in population, and
grown to be a large and prosperous town, now
rapidly developing as a manufacturing centre of
no insignificant importance.

The Cornell Library was projected and established by Mr. Cornell as an evidence of his gratitude to the kind Providence which had vouchsafed
to him the great measure of success that had attended his onerous labors in the telegraph enterprise.   At the time when he undertook this beneficent work, he estimated himself to be worth
about half a million dollars, but the appreciation
of his telegraph interests followed so rapidly that
before he had completed the Library building, he
found himself in the enjoyment of an annual income of more than one hundred thousand dollars,
and the value of his estate more than doubled.

Prosperity came to him in such abundance, and
he had so greatly enjoyed the pleasure of this generous action, that his ambition was aroused to
build a still greater monument, in recognition of

the Divine favor which had fallen upon him. It was just at this time that his attention was called to the failure of the Agricultural College, from lack of adequate endowment for its support and development. Heartily sympathizing with the project of establishing an educational institution which should afford facilities for instruction in sciences relating to agriculture and the mechanical arts, he determined to devote a portion of his then ample fortune to the accomplishment of this worthy purpose. It was the conjunction of these circumstances which culminated in the endowment and organization of the Cornell University.

CHAPTER XIV.

ADDRESS OF DEDICATION.—CORNELL LIBRARY.

Appreciative Co-operation.—Address of Dedication by Hon. Francis Miles Finch.—An Eloquent and Impressive Discourse.—Educational Influence of Libraries.—Duty of Grateful Appreciation.—Useful Lessons.—Neglected Opportunities.—Unhealthy Excitement.

FOREMOST among the citizens of Ithaca in evincing cordial and loyal appreciation of the good work so generously tendered, was one who from the beginning was zealous in endeavor to aid in promoting it; whose rich culture and valuable but unobtrusive services were freely rendered to the founder of the Library in carrying out his admirable purpose. This was the HON. FRANCIS MILES FINCH, now a distinguished Judge of the Court of Appeals of the State of New York, whose eminent abilities, great learning, and high character contribute much to elevate and strengthen that august tribunal. For many years he gave cheerful and valuable assistance to the organization and management both of the Cornell Library, and University. With manifest propriety, this estimable co-laborer in all of the munificent projects of Mr. Cornell, had been designated to pronounce the address of dedication on the occasion of the inaugural ceremonies of the Cornell Library. This extremely interesting production is here inserted, despite its considerable length, not only as an appropriate element of this record, but also as a grateful tribute to the faithful, appreciative, and confidential friend of the founder.

DEDICATION ADDRESS.

By Hon. Francis M. Finch.

Ladies and Gentlemen : When the dream of a lifetime has been suddenly realized, it is difficult to believe that it is not a dream. Especially when this is effected by some unusual agency, whose creative force and energy operated with a power and certainty akin almost to enchantment, it is hard to grasp and master the wide range of results.

We who are assembled here in this completed and perfected edifice, containing within itself the elements of its own support and the power of independent action, free from the domination of the partisan, either in politics or in religion, with the rich columns and still alcoves, and waiting shelves of a library, where already rest the germs of a broad and liberal culture, and many rare triumphs of art and of literature, whose doors are open, whose privileges are promised, whose encouraging care belongs to all alike— to the child of want and weary poverty as well as him whose head is sheltered from the chill of every wind ; we, who are gathered here, amid all these results of one clear brain, one generous heart, one lavish hand, can hardly estimate the value and grandeur of the gift. The receding waves of influence spread their widening circles to such distant shores that none can measure the endless arc or tell the radius of the departing curve. A good deed done to-day repeats itself in the tireless repetitions of the years. A life of good deeds grows more beautiful as it nears its close, as the autumn woods gather a mellow splendor that does not belong to the brilliance of their June ; and far along the summers that garland, and the winters that whiten, this changing world, that life, though ended, will still repeat its work, and nearer with the chime of every advancing hour, will approach the completion of its aims.

One such deed of broad beneficence begins its mission to-day. For the gift we receive we owe a debt of gratitude not to be paid by words. The world is full of hollow thanks ; the forms of politeness flash like crystals, and are as cold ; only as the warmth of grateful words is fed by the fire of grateful deeds are they worthy the giver or the gift. I do not, therefore, indulge in the flattering phrases of eulogy. The coinage is too cheap and easy. The pale dull notes that fluttered in the streets of burning Richmond were not more plenty nor more worthless. There is a way, however, to lift the load of obligation this day imposed, to pour back upon the heart that has made us rich the wealth of cheerful gratitude, to make the memory of our gift a daily happiness to the giver, and that way is to thoroughly appreciate what is bestowed. Neglect, misuse, destroy it, and the good becomes bad, the sweet grows bitter, the pleasure is a pain. Cherish and protect it, enjoy its beauty, thrive upon its benefits, keep it alive and busy with daily and earnest use, and the blessing it proves to us will add an hourly joy, a happiness sincere and unalloyed, to the life that has crowned its years of honest labor, of persistent faith and undaunted courage with this costly and generous gift.

The cavalier of days gone past, the hero of old romance, odd mixture of robber and gentleman, who, in the quaint pages of Froissart or Monstrelet, gives choice flowers to her whose colors adorn his helmet, is poorly repaid by the ready smile and phrase of courteous compliment, if, in an hour, he finds the faded petals crushed and thrown away, but is rewarded beyond desert if they bloom in the dark locks, or blossom in the castle window, watched and watered with patient care. The generous friend who gives some work of art, some choicely selected triumph of the chisel, or the brush, some gem of Rome or Florence, has but slender thanks, if, after courtesy is done, and novelty is gone, the picture glooms in cobwebs, or in the dark, and the marble bust is broken or defaced ; but is richly paid if, over the student's desk, or in the firelight of a cheerful home, his gifts are kept and prized. We can bear that toys and playthings should be first forgotten and then destroyed. The child's new happiness is so fresh and earnest that we feel at once repaid, and, knowing well the fitfulness of the little heart, the curious turns of the little mind, the sure destructiveness of the little hand, we expect, when the novelty has worn away, to see the doll bleeding sawdust from gaping wounds, the tin engine ruined in collision, the playhouse splintered by an earthquake.

But it is not a toy or a plaything with which we have to do. It is a broad and substantial good. And we are not children to be judged by the child's years and weakness. If, therefore, this great gift of ours, when every room has grown familiar, and every quaint old volume has lost its charms, and the rare birds of the hunter artist, and the bold illustrations of Dante's verse, and perfect etching of all art and science have ceased to be new and strange, if then we neglect them all, and shadows only occupy the quiet alcoves, and the neglected books gather dust upon their shelves, and the pleasant reading-rooms are dim and vacant, and the grand purpose of the gift fails of its aim, no flattering words of ours, however softly phrased or deftly framed, will soothe the painful convictions that the costly effort is but a waste and a failure.

Just here, and in the light of these reflections, we get clear views of our duty and our grave responsibility. The gratitude we owe for the princely gift whose keys and title-deeds have just been given us, demands that we appreciate the boon. Our own personal interests, the good that but awaits our will to take it, the long and endless train of benefits that are ours, if we will but have them—these, too, demand that we appreciate the gift. If you ask me how, you furnish me a theme hard to compress within the

moments granted me, and yet the one most needing thought, and
of gravest consequence to us all. · Let us, at least, frame some
brief and general answer.

One cannot appreciate what he does not thoroughly understand.   A man may see the expansive energy of steam, and even
understand the engine mechanism—here opens, here shuts a valve,
and the piston-rod moves, and the wheels revolve ; but until he
sees the giant power at work, beholds it linking with an iron chain
the commerce of hemispheres, cutting the ocean into roads and
grand avenues of trade, weaving the faintest fibre into glossy silk
and spotless lawn, grinding the grain of continents, and proving
itself the great world artisan, he utterly fails to appreciate the
magnitude and grandeur of the tireless force.   We must thoroughly
comprehend the gift we have received, or we shall fail to appreciate its value.   We have a costly edifice, a place for books, and
rooms in which to read them.   So much is on the surface.   Set
this simple machinery at work, and what is it then?   An educating force, an aid and a stimulant to intelligence, the refining element of social life, the means and the guide of advancing civilization, the safeguard of freedom, the sure foundation of the
Republic.

But just emerged from a sad and terrible war, let us not be
blinded by the splendors of victory to the truth that underlies
that victory.   Brave as were our citizen soldiers, bravery alone
would never have won success.   Bravery, led by intelligence, sustained by intelligence, armed and supplied and stimulated by intelligence, that planted the stars upon every fortress, that turned
the batteries of fate, that made the Republic iron-clad against its
enemies.   And if, in the future, we are to reap the promise of our
youth, if the last great storm has been encountered, and the last
deadly peril escaped, and the nation is to march steadily in the
van of civilization, it will be because intelligence keeps pace with
prosperity, because just such agencies as that we organize to-day
crown the hillsides and crowd the valleys of the land.   Commerce
will not save us, wealth will not save us, armies will not save us.
Only as every door is opened to that knowledge which is power,

as every mind is flooded with the sunlight of intelligence, as every avenue of civilization is swept of the barriers which ignorance builds, and crime arms and mans, can we hope to round the history of the world with that world's crowning triumph. A key to one such door, a ray of that golden sunlight, a battery to breach these barriers—that is the kind and the character of the gift we have received to-night. Thus grasping the expansive and pervading force with which we work, we shall better appreciate the wisdom which has framed it to our hands.

Men little appreciate what they do not need, but always, and greatly, that which supplies a want and fills an evident void. The folly of giving what is not needed, of heaping coals on the mine of original supply, has crystallized into the sarcasm of a proverb ; and unless we know and feel that this generous gift of ours is a needed one, that the harvest is ripe for the sickle, but the reapers are indeed few, we shall not half appreciate the importance of our trust. Deeming this village home of ours no worse, if not better than the average of her sisters in the land, there are yet some truths to be plainly said, some wounds to be probed, not poulticed. And I declare to you as the result of careful observation, of thought not hasty, but deliberate through the years, that no one thing has been more needed in our intellectual social and business life than the very institution now organized. It is needed by us as individuals. We have suffered—none rightly appreciate to what painful extent—for the want of means of fair and accurate investigation. We have been guided by old standards. We have travelled in the deep ruts cut by the venerable wheels of habit, and only wondered at the daring horsemen scaling fences and fields far in our advance. Our very business energies have thus been dwarfed. The vision habitually limited in time grows hopelessly narrow. The mechanic builds and forges, molds and completes, as his father or his master did, because, without chart or pilot, he dares not brave the storms of bold experiment. The laborer and his children settle down into the treadmill round of daily toil, sad-eyed, and weary, and unambitious, without temptation, because without the means of living a broader or more intelligent

life.   The men of the professions save and lose, succeed and fail,
preach and pray, successful within the range of some narrow horizon, but themselves conscious of the need of some broader culture, and the means of wider study.

But, if needed by individuals, this institution, which we dedi-
cate to-day, is more needed by the community.   Is our American
intelligence diffused as it should be among all, or largely limited
within narrow ranges?   I do not like to speak as strongly as I
think, but some facts are palpable and tangible.   We can put a
tambourine upon one corner of the public platform, clattering
bones upon the other, and blackened faces all along the curve,
and fill audience seats almost to suffocation.   Or, we can place
there unrivalled eloquence, thought clear as the spring, yet deep
and grand as the ocean, learning boundless though unassuming,
logic forged red-hot upon the anvil of intellect, brilliant beauty
inwove with compacted reason, and be chilled with the solitude
that fringes the few who are assembled, and bear our losses with
the hopeless calm that comes of long experience.

What are the masses reading?   I think it would shock you to
know accurately and in detail.   Newspapers that pander to the
worst passions of human nature ; weeklies that systematically cor-
rupt the public taste ; novels that are stimulating and fiery ;
poems rank and luxuriant with vicious fascination ; magazines
literally framed of silliness and folly—these, and worse than these,
too largely engross the public mind, and too surely deprave the
public taste.   Love of excitement—the American fault—which
makes our pulses throb savagely and our hearts beat swift and
hard ; which heats the machinery of our activity, and burns out
our lives at middle age—this hot, hurried, eager temperament
craves and is fed by an ephemeral literature both stimulating
and dangerous ; while the books of solid merit, the volumes
rich in ennobling thought, the pages fruitful of eternal truth,
lie silent upon the shelves, or shed their light only within narrow
bounds.

What are our young men doing?   Dare we write the history
of the street ?   Idle evenings, vacant thoughts, restless longings,

grow, by inevitable law, into folly or into vice, and that culminates into crime. And those who safely run these terrible risks—and the wrecks are more than the saved—gradually dwarfed by daily drudgery, brain starved by lack of mental food, sad and despairing for want of wise encouragement and intelligent aid, plead with their sad eyes and beg with their mute lips for the very assistance it is now possible for us to give. Do you know their number? More than you think or dream. The need is great, the want is terrible ; and, if we feel it as we should, realize it as we may, we shall better appreciate the gift that has been bestowed, and the grave responsibility that rests upon us all, of so wielding its advantages and guiding its energies that the evil we see may at least be lessened, if not destroyed.

A thing made for use is never properly appreciated unless used. If the deft machine, marvel of modern ingenuity, whose needle clicks through tiresome hem and weary seam with happy speed, stands idle and unused, the giver is pained, for the good intended has failed of its purpose. If the clattering teeth made to level the golden grain and reap with bite of steel the autumn harvest, lie silent in the field, weather-stained and gnawed with rust, and perishing with neglect, the giver grieves, for the gift is a waste and a pain. Our gift, therefore, we must steadily use, both for the sake of him who gave and of those who receive. Not a few, but all. The artisan must come to improve his work and lighten his toil ; the man of business, to better mold and more surely shape his plans ; he of the professions, to elevate and adorn his art ; she who graces our homes and firesides, to add the charm of high culture and intelligence to the beauty of womanhood ; and all, that knowledge may be diffused, industry stimulated, greater attainments won, and the doors of honorable ambition thrown wide to each who chooses to enter for the struggle. That it be used by all, that is the important thing. This is not the library of an Astor, fit home for the scholar and man of letters, rich in its grand collections, but not to be profaned by common feet, and close and surly to the nameless crowd ; not a British Museum, out of whose half million of volumes but twenty thousand are free to all comers, and useful access to the rest is clogged and hindered by exclusive rules and tedious forms ; not an Imperial Library, with more than its million of books, whose very vastness bewilders and daunts the poor and lowly ; nothing too great, nothing too grand for daily and common use, to which it invites and urges all.

It belongs to all. Let that be remembered. Not to a chosen few to monopolize its benefits ; not to a narrow circle to frown on all the rest ; but to all, to every one as equal with every other. The poorest boy, barefooted in the street, if he but come to read and learn, may climb yon solid staircase with the confidence of title, with the step of a master, joint owner with us all ; he has a right to demand, and shall surely receive, from those of us who hold this gift in trust, a kindly reception, all needed aid and assistance, not as a favor, but as a right, for which he holds our founder's title-deed.

It is yours, this welcome gift. Treat it, therefore, as your own, use it as your own. I hope to see its alcoves filled with quiet students, its reading-rooms each evening occupied with earnest youth, its volumes circulating in every home, its peaceful influence everywhere. Let that result be attained, and we shall indeed have thanked the giver ; the fact alone, better than parchment-written flatteries, or a city's freedom in a box of gold, will crown his gift with gratitude.

Men never appreciate justly what they hate, and seldom what they do not truthfully love. This institution, therefore, must have no enemies ; if any, those alone whom vice and crime have made the brutal foes of all intelligence. I know that in every community there are sour and envious natures, of bilious tone and acid tongue, whose words are sharp and acrid, whose opinions are rank and rasping, whose theory of climbing high is hurling others low, who grow tired of hearing Aristides called " the Just," and whose friendship it may be a hopeless task to win. But these natures, preyed upon by canker and gangrene, are simply diseased, to be pitied and passed by. From all the rest, their love, their care, their watchful regard is due to this enterprise, which is their own.

It will make mistakes, perhaps ; let the error be shown only to be forgiven. It may, sometimes, give offence ; not purposely, you may be sure ; if so, let pardon at once wipe out the pain. Difficulties will often obstruct its management : tastes will differ, judgments will collide, dangers perplex ; but all these troubles will be light as foam if only the gift be strongly anchored in the love and trust of those to whom it is given. To justify that confidence it has, we think, been wisely planned. Creeds differ. It will respect all, but ally itself with none. If theologians grow belligerent, and preach the gospel from the back of a war-horse clothed in thunder, and with fierce flashings of battle-axe and cleaver, the fight shall not come here to divide and distract our quiet work. Men disagree in politics. It is their right. We shall treat them fairly and alike, but side with none. With however much of storm or fury the battle may rage, peace alone shall be the conqueror here. Society is cut into classes ; invisible lines divide ; arbitrary divisions sever. We must recognize none of them. For us there can be but one class, and that the entire community. In all these respects this institution will be neutral ground, and belligerents are warned to leave their arms at the gates. Not that opinion shall be muzzled, or free thought manacled, or reason chained ; but that all shall have equal favor, equal rights ; not less, not one grain more.

So much is due to those for whose benefit this gift is made. And may not we, who hold this trust, expect from them that sympathy with and regard for the interests in our charge which will insure their successful working ? Then no vandal hand will mar and deface the purity of these walls ; no envious word or spiteful sneer will sow the seeds of discord ; no cold neglect will chill and freeze ; no hostile blow be aimed ; but many a rare volume, placed where all may read, will prove its owner's interest in our work ; and in the end, by gradual growth and fostering care, will come a public good, a public blessing, honorable alike to the hand that framed and the hearts that cherished it.

But one word more. The example of which this gift to-day is the first fruit ; of which a proof more rich and costly is fast rising,

with massive walls and graceful arches, upon the heights that overlook our homes—that example I commend to each in his own degree.   It shames the miser's clutch upon that, which hoarded, is
but cankering dross ; it shames the selfish instinct that bars out
the world from all it has and hopes ; it shames the vicious reason-
ing that all can starve and yet each one thrive ; it brings to light
the rusted links of the forgotten chain that binds our interests in
one ; it bids us bear our part in generous deeds and manly efforts
for the good of all.   Intelligent public spirit, that is what we
need, and of which we shall never have too much.   Let us catch
the spirit of the age.   Washed from the blood and dust of war,
conscious now of a strength we knew not of, roused by the pressure of magnificent debt to a new prosperity, the Nation moves
with speed redoubled—breathless.   The bars of iron stretch
toward the Pacific, the lightning traverses the ocean's bed ; great
stormy lakes are tamed to fill the goblets of a city; a buried
wealth is reached to light the hamlets of the world ; mountains of
surly rock are tunnelled out to make a road for steam ; invention
knows no sleep, and genius dares not rest.

Something of this spirit should be ours.   So many lights are
being set upon our hills, so wondering a gaze is turning hither, so
grand and grave is becoming our position, that more of thought,
more of labor, more of energy will become us all.   If we cannot
beat the drums of the advance, at least let us not sleep in the am-
bulance at the rear ; if we cannot reach the mountain top, at least
let us not slumber in the valley.   Above all let those who lead in
every good and noble work receive our sympathy and gratitude.
Let them see and feel that every possible aid of ours is at their
service ; and, as the first important step of such grateful action,
let us take this generous gift which has been made to-night, with
thankful and appreciating hearts ; let us enfold it in our love and
care ; let it be our pride as citizens, our blessing as individuals ;
let us firmly resolve its success ; forever make impossible the burning shame and bitter disgrace of accepting a costly gift only to
bury it in neglect and failure.

It is now a noble and generous boon ; the passing years will make it sacred. The day will come which must come once to all—and, Oh, may it be far and dim in the distant years—when the unwearied giver shall give no more on earth, and this gift will become a monument. Let us love it now, that we may better give it reverence then, and from its silent influence learn anew the lesson that

> Only the actions of the just
> Smell sweet and blossom in the dust.

CHAPTER XV.

THE CORNELL UNIVERSITY.—CHARTER AND ORGAN-IZATION.

Demand for Scientific Education.—The Agricultural College.—Its Failure.—Congressional Appropriation of Public Lands for Agricultural and Mechanical Education.—Acceptance by the State.—Appropriation to People's College.—Inadequate Vitality and Withdrawal of Appropriation.—Mr. Cornell's Offer of $500,000.—Animated Contest.—Charter of Cornell University.—Offensive Proviso.—Location of the University.—Additional Contributions by the Founder.—Erection of College Edifices.—President White.—University Faculty and Equipment.—Liberal Attendance of Students.

THE importance and desirability of providing special facilities for advanced education in the sciences relating to agriculture, were for many years subjects of earnest discussion in agricultural journals of the country, and more especially in those of this State. The cause was warmly espoused by the New York State Agricultural Society, and found many earnest advocates among the more intelligent farmers of the State, as well as among the active friends of education. The agitation of the subject finally resulted in the passage by the

Legislature, in 1853, of an act incorporating the " New York State Agricultural College."

The act provided that the State should loan the institution forty thousand dollars for a period of twenty-one years, without interest, on condition that an equal amount should be raised by private contributions. The trustees, named in the bill, fixed the location of the institution in the town of Ovid, Seneca County, and selected for its site a magnificent estate of six hundred and eighty acres of fertile land, overlooking the Seneca Lake. It was not, however, until the year 1858 that the necessary subscriptions had been secured to render the State loan available, when the trustees began the erection of a college edifice on the site designated. The funds at the disposal of the trustees were exhausted before the building was completed, and the liberality of the friends of the enterprise was strained to the utmost to provide for finishing the building, and fitting it for active operations.

The College was finally opened for the reception of students in the autumn of 1860, and instruction was begun with a class of between forty and fifty students, and a faculty consisting of the president and four professors. Unfortunately, however, no adequate endowment had been provided for the support of the College; nothing, indeed, had been furnished beyond the land and building, a very limited equipment of furniture, and a quite insignificant apparatus. The institution had no income for its support beyond that derived from tuition fees, which were wholly inadequate for the payment of current expenses.

Upon the outbreak of the great rebellion, in April, 1861, the President of the College, who was a graduate of the West Point Military Academy, was called to Albany by the Governor to aid in the military preparations of the State, returning occasionally to the College as his duties permitted, during the remainder of the school year. Under all of the discouraging circumstances attending the early experience of the College, it was not strange that before the close of the first year a considerable number of the students had abandoned the pursuit of agricultural science, and responded to the call of President Lincoln for volunteers to suppress the rebellion.

As it became apparent that the war was to be of considerable duration, the trustees of the Agricultural College decided not to open it for instruction in the fall of 1861, but to await more fortuitous circumstances. This closing of the College, however, proved to be permanent, in default of any provision for its support, and the property was afterward taken by the State in satisfaction of its claim, and devoted to the purposes of the Willard Asylum for the chronic insane.

At the most critical period of the great struggle for national existence, responding to a general sentiment in favor of some practical provision for agricultural education, the Congress of the United States illustrated the unwavering faith of the loyal people in the complete restoration of national unity by the enactment, in July, 1862, of Chapter 130, General Statutes, entitled, " An act donating public lands to the several States and Territories which may provide colleges for the benefit of agriculture and the mechanic arts."

This act conceived in far-reaching wisdom, granted to each State a quantity of public land equal to thirty thousand acres for each senator and representative in Congress under the census of 1860, and provided for the sale of the lands and investment of the proceeds in permanent funds, the income of which should by each State be appropriated " to the endowment, support, and maintenance of at least one college, where the leading object shall be, without excluding other scientific and classical studies, and including military tactics, to teach such branches of learning as are related to agriculture and the mechanic arts, in such manner as the Legislatures of the States may respectively prescribe, in order to promote the liberal and

practical education of the industrial classes in the
several pursuits and professions of life."

Under the provisions of this act the State of
New York became entitled to receive 990,000
acres of public lands, and by the enactment of
Chapter 460, of the laws of 1863, the State accepted the trust, and made preliminary provision
for the receipt and custody of the scrip, and authorized the Comptroller to sell the land and invest the proceeds in conformity with the law of
Congress.   A subsequent act, Chapter 511, laws
of 1863, appropriated the income of the Land
Grant Fund to an undeveloped institution, known
as the " People's College," at Havana, Schuyler
County, thus completely ignoring the State Agricultural College, which, by all fair means, should
have been selected by the Legislature as the recipient of this federal bounty.   Although the passage of this measure was earnestly opposed by
the friends of the Agricultural College, it was
promoted by some invisible power, and became a
law.

That the partisans of the People's College
proved to be more effective as promoters of legislation than in building up a real college, was
demonstrated by the report of the Regents of the
State University under an investigation made,
pursuant to the direction of the State Senate, in

the month of February, 1865. This report exposed the ridiculous pretence which had been made in reference to the People's College, and clearly demonstrated that no adequate steps had been taken to create such an institution as the statutes contemplated. The earnestly devoted friends of agricultural education were fully aroused by this exposure, and urgently demanded legislation which should make proper amends for the injustice done to their cause by the wrongful appropriation of the Land Grant Fund to the so-called People's College.

At this juncture of affairs, Mr. Cornell offered the trustees of the Agricultural College a personal endowment of $300,000, on condition that the institution should be removed from Ovid and located at Ithaca, and provided further that the Legislature should appropriate to it one-half of the income of the Land Grant Fund. Finding, among the more intelligent champions of higher education, a very decided expression against dividing and frittering away the federal income, Mr. Cornell subsequently increased his offer of endowment to $500,000, if the entire Land Grant income were permanently appropriated to the institution.

This proposition aroused the enthusiasm of the friends of agricultural education to a high pitch, and stimulated their ambition to still higher aims than they had ever before entertained. Mr. Cornell's proposition was very cordially accepted, and, after careful consultation, it was decided to abandon the Agricultural College entirely, and take steps to secure the necessary legislation for the organization of a general university, which should also embrace the special features required by the congressional act. In pursuance of this policy a carefully prepared bill was presented to the Legislature for the incorporation of the " Cornell University," and embracing the conditions named.

The measure was very bitterly opposed by the adherents of the People's College, and zealously advocated by the friends of the Agricultural College and other leading friends of higher education. The passage of the bill was earnestly contested at every step of progress, from its introduction to its final enactment. The controversy attracted general attention throughout the State, and the antagonists of the measure were reinforced by the friends of several of the minor colleges, who loudly clamored for a division of the fund among all of the existing colleges. This policy was, however, successfully combated, on the ground that it would be an idle dispersion of the fund, which would practically defeat the objects of its creation.

The contest over the University bill was so evenly balanced that its friends found themselves obliged, as a preliminary to final success, to accept an amendment providing that "*within six months from the passage of this act, said Ezra Cornell, of Ithaca, shall pay over to the trustees of Genesee College, located at Lima, in this State, the sum of twenty-five thousand dollars for the purpose of establishing in said Genesee College a professorship of agricultural chemistry.*" Thus, as a condition of being permitted to contribute the sum of $500,000 to endow the Cornell University, a public institution for the benefit of the people of the entire State, Mr. Cornell was required, by legislative enactment, to first give $25,-000 to another institution. Many friends were so indignant at this provision, that they strongly urged him to reject it; but he overlooked the indignity, and duly paid the money to Genesee College.

This monstrous abuse of philanthropic generosity was, however, by the Legislature, in 1867, so far corrected as was possible, by appropriating, out of the general fund of the State, $25,000 to the Cornell University for its sole and exclusive use, "being the amount which Ezra Cornell has paid to the Genesee College, pursuant to the requirements of Chapter 585, of the laws of 1865." The

Cornell University charter also contained a proviso, giving the trustees of the People's College three months' time within which to deposit such sum of money as the Regents of the State University might designate as sufficient to enable said trustees fully to comply with the requirements of the law appropriating to that institution the income of the Land Grant Fund. This essential was not met by the authorities of the People's College, which practically repealed the appropriation of the federal bounty for its benefit.

Upon the fulfilment, therefore, of the conditions of the act of its incorporation, the Cornell University became entitled to receive the income of the Land Grant Fund for its exclusive maintenance. The sale by many States of their land scrip had, however, depreciated its value from more than one dollar an acre in 1862 to about fifty cents an acre in 1865, with a downward tendency. At these figures even the princely domain granted to the State of New York would produce but an insignificant sum to meet the necessities of a great educational establishment, and one of the first questions which engaged the attention of Mr. Cornell was the possibility of realizing a more adequate price for the land grant. This branch of the general subject is worthy of more elaborate treatment than it can properly receive in this connection, and will therefore be reserved for subsequent observation.

The charter of the Cornell University fixed its location " in the town of Ithaca," thus leaving to the trustees only the discretion of selecting a site within that town. This question was speedily solved by Mr. Cornell's tender of two hundred acres of his homestead farm as a free contribution added to his original endowment. This magnificent site was unanimously regarded as the most appropriate location in the town, and was therefore gratefully accepted by the board.

Situated on the brow of East hill, within a mile of the village, and about four hundred feet above the valley level, a landscape of marvellous beauty is spread out before the observer. In one direction the beautiful Cayuga Lake is visible for thirty-five miles, while to the southwest the eye wanders over the valley and hills for a distance of nearly twenty miles, making altogether a line of vision more than fifty miles in extent. One who has chanced to gaze upon this grand view, especially on a bright and cloudless day, will long remember it as a privilege to be highly regarded.

At the outset of their administration the trustees of the Cornell University determined upon the preservation of Mr. Cornell's endowment as a capital for revenue, and to proceed with the

13

erection of buildings only so fast as their surplus
income and other contributions might provide
means for the purpose. The erection of the first
building, now known as " Morrill Hall," was begun in the spring of 1866, and was followed by
a large frame building designed for the temporary
uses of the departments of chemistry and kindred
purposes.

The organization of the University faculty received its first formal impulse in 1866, by the appointment by the board of trustees of the HON.
ANDREW DICKSON WHITE as president of the University.   President White was a distinguished
graduate of Yale who had also pursued a post-
graduate course at the University of Berlin. He
was for some years professor of history in the
University of Michigan, and was a member of the
New York State Senate, serving four years as a
colleague with Mr. Cornell, where they had become warmly attached as personal friends. Senator White was the author of the bill incorporating the Cornell University, and was ardent in his
support of that measure. The defeat of the proposition to divide and disperse the Land Grant
income was due more to his arguments and influence than to any other cause.

Senator White was, with complete unanimity,
chosen one of the trustees of the University at

the first meeting of the incorporators, and was unremitting in his efforts to promote the interests of the institution. He was selected as president of the University by the trustees upon the earnest recommendation of the founder, who, by long observation of his personal characteristics, had become convinced of his peculiar fitness for the extremely onerous duties which would devolve upon the executive head of the great institution, which, it was fondly hoped, might grow from the undertaking then just initiated. After a lapse of nearly twenty years the declaration is here made with entire deliberation, that no wiser selection could have been made for this important position.

President White entered upon the discharge of his duties with an earnest purpose to plant the foundations of the infant University broad and deep, to insure its ultimate development into a grand and useful institution, which should be worthy of the imperial Commonwealth which had given it corporate life, and of the noble-hearted FOUNDER whose generous endowment had first given it vitality, and whose unselfish labors contributed so much to its subsequent growth. He declined farther service in the Senate, and visited most of the great colleges in America and Europe for observation as to the best methods of advanced education, and embraced every opportunity to

gather materials for the library and equipment of
the University.   President White was entrusted
with the unrestricted choice of his associates in
the faculty, the appointments having been formally
made by the trustees wholly upon his recommendation.   He selected for the regular force of
resident professorships, almost exclusively, young
men of high attainments and of especial adaptation to the particular duties for which they were
respectively designed.

It was President White's theory that he could
secure better results for the permanent usefulness of the institution, by entrusting the hard
work of the administration to young men who,
with their reputations yet to make, would have
more ambition to distinguish themselves, than
perhaps would ensue from the labors of others
who, having achieved a name, might be more disposed to rest contented with less exertion.   He
supplemented these selections by securing as non-
resident professors, several gentlemen of wide repute who were engaged to spend a few weeks at
the University each year, in delivering before the
advanced classes elaborate and carefully prepared
lectures in their respective spheres of observation
and study.   The President's policy has proved admirable in practice, and has been followed in many
of the older institutions, with like good results.

At the formal opening of the University the faculty embraced the following members: Six non-resident Professors, nineteen resident Professors, four Assistant Professors, and five Instructors. This general University faculty was divided into nine special faculties, each constituting a college or department, designated as follows: 1, College of Agriculture; 2, College of Chemistry and Physics; 3, College of History and Political Science; 4, College of Languages; 5, College of Literature and Philosophy; 6, College of Mathematics and Engineering; 7, College of Mechanic Arts; 8, College of Military Science; 9, College of Natural Science.

The University Library at that time comprised about twenty-five thousand volumes, which had been selected under the direct supervision of the President. The Museums embraced very complete collections in Geology and Mineralogy; Botany and Agriculture; Zoology and Physiology; Technology and Civil Engineering; Chemistry and Physics; and the Fine Arts. There were enrolled and entered in the different departments of study nearly four hundred students, coming from fifty different counties of the State of New York, and twenty-seven States of the Union, besides several foreign countries.

CHAPTER XVI.

THE CORNELL UNIVERSITY.—INAUGURAL CERE-MONIES.

THE CORNELL UNIVERSITY was formally opened for
the reception of students in the autumn of 1868,
and the event marked an era in the history of Ithaca, long to be remembered by her citizens. The
village was thronged with visiting strangers, and
everything betokened a joyous holiday. Many
prominent citizens were present from distant
sections of the State, as well, indeed, as from
many different States. Prominent officers of the
State government, and educators of eminence in
their profession, were present in large numbers,
and the occasion altogether was one of exceptional interest in the educational annals of the

State. A large concourse of people were in attendance at the lecture room of the Cornell Library, where, on Wednesday, October 7th, the formal exercises of the inauguration occurred. The address of the FOUNDER, and some extracts from that of PRESIDENT WHITE, are here inserted as pertinent to a review of the history of the University.

MR. CORNELL'S REMARKS.

Mr. Chairman, Citizens, and Friends : I fear that many of you have visited Ithaca at this time to meet with disappointment. If you came as did a friend recently from Pennsylvania, " expecting to find a finished institution," you will look around, be disappointed with what you see, and report on your return to your home, as he did, " I did not find one single thing finished."

Such, my friends, is not the entertainment we invite you to. We did not expect to have " a single thing finished," we did not desire it, and we have not directed our energies to that end. It is the commencement that we have now in hand. We did expect to have commenced an institution of learning, which will mature in the future to a great degree of usefulness, which will place at the disposal of the industrial and productive classes of society the best facilities for the acquirement of practical knowledge and mental culture, on such terms as the limited means of the most humble can command.

I hope we have laid the foundation of an institution which shall combine practical with liberal education, which shall fit the youth of our country for the professions, the farms, the mines, the manufactories, for the investigations of science, and for mastering all the practical questions of life with success and honor.

I believe that we have made the beginning of an institution which will prove highly beneficial to the poor young men and the poor young women of our country. This is one thing which we have not finished, but in the course of time we hope to reach such a state of perfection as will enable any one, by honest efforts and earnest labor, to secure a thorough, practical, scientific or classical education. The individual is better, society is better, and the State is better for the culture of the citizen; therefore, we desire to extend the means for the culture of all.

I trust that we have made the beginning of an institution which shall bring science more directly to the aid of agriculture, and other branches of productive labor. Chemistry has the same great stores of wealth in reserve for agriculture that it has lavished so profusely upon the arts. We must instruct the young farmer how to avail himself of this hidden treasure.

The veterinarian will shield him against many of the losses which are frequent in his flocks and herds, losses which are now submitted to as matters of course by the uneducated farmer, and which, in the aggregate, amount to millions of dollars every year in our own State alone.

The entomologist must arm him for more successful warfare in defence of his growing crops, as the ravages of insects upon both grain and fruit have become enormous, resulting also in the loss of many millions of dollars each year.

Thus, in whatever direction we turn, we find ample opportunity for the applications of science in aid of the toiling millions. May we not hope that we have made the beginning of an institution which will strengthen the arm of the mechanic and multiply his powers of production through the agency of a better cultivated brain? Any person who visits our Patent Office, at Washington, and contemplates the long halls stored with rejected models, will realize that our mechanics have great need of this aid.

The farmer is also enriched by increasing the knowledge and power of the mechanic. Mechanism, as applied to agriculture, was the great motive power which enabled the American farmers to feed the nation while it was struggling for existence against the late wicked rebellion, and it will enable them to pay the vast debts incurred by the nation while crushing that rebellion. This is an inviting field in which we must labor most earnestly. The mechanic should cease the fruitless effort " to bore an auger hole with a gimlet."

I desire that this shall prove to be the beginning of an institution which shall furnish better means for the culture of all men, of every calling, of every aim ; which shall make men more truthful, more honest, more virtuous, more noble, more manly ; which shall give them higher purposes, and more lofty aims, qualifying them to serve their fellow-men better, preparing them to serve society better, training them to be more useful in their relations to the State, and to better comprehend their higher and holier relations to their families and their God. It shall be our aim and our constant effort to make true Christian men, without dwarfing, or paring them down to fit the narrow gauge of any sect.

Finally, I trust we have laid the foundation of an University— " an institution where any person can find instruction in any study."

Such have been our purposes. In that direction we have put forth our efforts, and on the future of such an institution we rest our hopes. If we have been successful in our beginning, to that extent and no further may we hope to be encouraged by the award of your approval. We have purposed that the finishing shall be the work of the future, and we ask that its approval or condemnation shall rest upon the quality of its maturing fruit.

To take the leadership of this great work, we have selected a gentleman and a scholar, who, though young in years, we present before you to-day for inauguration, with entire confidence that the " right man is in the right place."

We have also selected a faculty which, I trust, will very soon convince you that we have not thus early in the enterprise commenced blundering. They are in the main young men, and they are quite content to be judged by their works.

Invoking the blessing of Heaven upon our undertaking, we commend our cause to the scrutiny and the judgment of the American people.

INAUGURAL ADDRESS OF PRESIDENT WHITE.

Six years ago, in the most bitter hour of the Republic, in her last hour, as many thought, amid most desperate measures of war, the councils of the United States gave thought and work to a far-reaching measure of peace. They made provision for a new system of advanced education; they cut this system loose from some old ideas under which education had been groaning; they grafted into it some new ideas for which education had been longing; they so arranged it that every State might enjoy it; they imposed but few general conditions, and these grounded in right reason; they fettered it with no unworthy special conditions; they planned it broadly; they endowed it munificently.

This is one of the great things in American history—nay, one of the great things in the world history. In all the annals of republics, there is no more significant utterance of confidence in · national destiny out from the midst of national calamity.

Four years ago, war still raging, a citizen of this State, an artisan who had wrought his way to wealth, but who, in wealth, forgot not the labors and longings of poverty, offered to supplement this public gift with a private gift no less munificent. He alloyed it with no whimseys, he fettered it with no crotchets; he simply asked that his bounty might carry out a plan large and fair.

Three years ago the State of New York, after some groping, accepted these gifts, refused to scatter and waste them, concentrated them in a single effort for higher education, and fixed on a system of competitive examinations to bring under the direct advantages of this education the most worthy students in every corner of her domain. Six months afterward the authorities to whom the new effort was entrusted met in this pleasant village. Among them were the highest officers of the State. He who had offered the private endowment appeared before them. He not only redeemed his promise—he did more—he added to it princely gifts which he had not promised; more than that, his earnest manner showed that he was about to give something more precious by far —his whole life. So was founded the Cornell University.

Months followed, and this same man did for the State what she could not do for herself; he applied all his shrewdness and energy to placing the endowment from the United States on a better footing. Other States had sold the scrip with which they were endowed at rates ruinously low ; the founder of this University aided the State to make such an investment that its endowment developed in far larger measure than the most sanguine ever dared hope.

Such, gentlemen of the Board of Trustees and fellow-citizens, are the simple landmarks in the progress of this institution hitherto—not to weary you with a long detail of minor labors and trials ; such is the history in the chronological order, the order of facts.

.   .   .   .   .   .

Proceeding thence to review the work thus far accomplished, and discussing at considerable length the theory of organization and the plans of operation which were to direct and govern the conduct of the institution, the President concluded as follows :

Gentlemen of the Faculty : After this imperfect suggestion of the ideas underlying, forming, permeating our work, I appeal to you. The task before us is difficult. It demands hard thought, hard work. You will be called upon to exercise skill, energy, and forbearance. The faculty of this institution is the last place in the world for a man of mere dignity or of elegant ease.

But if the toil be great, the reward also is great. It is the reward which the successful professor so prizes—the sight of men made strong for the true, the beautiful, and the good through your help. The petty vanity of official station too often corrodes what is best in man ; the pride of wealth is poverty indeed for heart, or soul, or mind ; but the honest pride of the university instructor, seeing his treasures in noble scholars within the university and noble men outside its halls, is something far more worthy.

Said St. Felippo Neri as he, day after day, came to the door of the college at Rome at the time when the English scholars passed out, young men who were to be persecuted and put to death under the cruel laws of Elizabeth of England, "I am come to feast my eyes on those martyrs yonder."

So may each of us feast our eyes on scholars, writers, revealers of nature, leaders in art, statesmen, who shall go in and out of yonder halls.

Let us labor in this spirit. The work of every one of us, even of those who deal with material forces, is a moral work. Henry Thomas Buckley was doubtless wrong in the small weight he ascribed to moral forces, but he was doubtless right in his high estimate of the moral value of material forces. He found but half the truth; let us recognize the whole truth; let it be full-orbed. Every professor who works to increase material welfare acts to increase moral welfare.

I ask your aid as advisers, as friends. Let us hold ourselves in firm phalanx for truth and against error.

To you also, who appear in the first classes of students of the Cornell University :—You have had the faith and courage to cast in your lot with a new institution ; you have preferred its roughness to the smoothness of more venerable organizations ; you have not feared to aid in an experiment, knowing that there must be some groping and some stumbling. I will not ask you to be true to us. I will ask you to be true to yourselves. In Heaven's name, be men. Is it not time that some poor student traditions be supplanted by better ? You are not here to be made ; you are here to make yourselves. You are not here to hang upon an University ; you are here to help build an University. This is no place for children's tricks and toys, for exploits which only excite the wonderment of boarding-school misses. You are here to begin a man's work in the greatest time and land the world has yet known. I bid you take hold, take hold with the National Congress, with the State authorities, with Ezra Cornell, with the trustees, with the faculty, to build here, by manly conduct and by study, an University which shall be your pride. You are part of it. From your midst are to come its trustees, professors. Look to it that you be ready for your responsibilities.

Gentlemen of the Trustees : In accepting to-day, formally, the trust which for two years I have discharged really, I desire to thank you for your steady co-operation and support in the past, and ask its continuance.

You well know the trust was not sought by me. You well know with what misgivings it was accepted. In the utmost sincerity I say that it will be the greatest happiness of my life to be able, at some day not remote, to honorably resign it into hands worthier and stronger than my own.

Not a shadow of discord has ever disturbed our relations. Permit me to ask for my brothers in the faculty the same cordiality which you have extended to me.

You have been pleased to express satisfaction with my administration thus far ; I trust that with this aid the work may be better.

And, in conclusion, to you, our honored Founder : I may not intrude here my own private gratitude for kindnesses innumerable. Sturdily and steadily you have pressed on this enterprise, often against discouragement, sometimes against obloquy. But the people of this great commonwealth have stood by you. Evidences of it are seen in a thousand forms, but at this moment most of all in the number of their sons who have come to enjoy your bounty.

You were once publicly charged with a high crime. It was declared that you " sought to erect a great monument" for yourself.

Sir, would to heaven that more of our citizens might seek to rear monuments such as this of yours. They are, indeed, lasting. The names chiselled in granite in the days of Elihu Yale and John Harvard have been effaced, but Yale and Harvard bear aloft forever the names of their founders. The ordinary great men of days gone by, the holders of high office, the leaders of rank—who remembers their names now ? Who does not remember the names of founders or benefactors of our universities ? Harvard

and Yale, Dartmouth and Bowdoin, Brown and Amherst, all answer this question.

The names of Packer, Vassar, Cooper, Wells, Cornell, they
are solidly rooted in what shall stand longest in this nation. They
shall see a vast expanse of mushroom names go down, but theirs
shall remain forever. Their benefactions lift them into the view
of all men.

But, sir, I will bear testimony here that your name was never
thrust forward by yourself. You care little, indeed, what any man
thinks of you or of your actions, but I feel it a duty to state that you
were preparing to deal munificently with the institution under a
different name, when another insisted that your own name should
be given it.

It has happened to me to see your persistence, your energy, and
your sincerity tested. We have been too much together for me to
flatter you now, but I will say to your fellow-citizens that no man
ever showed greater energy in piling up a fortune for himself than
you have shown to heap up this benefaction for your countrymen.
You have given yourself to it.

Therefore, in the name of this commonwealth, and this nation,
I thank you. I know that I am as really empowered to do so in
their behalf as if I held their most formal credentials. I thank
you for those present, for those to come. May you be long spared
to us. May this be a monument which shall make earnest men
more earnest, and despondent men take heart. May there ever
rest upon it the approval of good men. Above all, may it have
the blessing of God.

The generous example of the founder of the
Cornell University speedily promoted in others an
ambition to assist in the great work of building
up and developing the institution which he loved
so well. John McGraw, of Ithaca, one of the original trustees, erected at his individual expense

the McGraw Building. This noble edifice, which accommodates the library and museum of the University, cost about one hundred thousand dollars. Hiram Sibley, of Rochester, also an original trustee, provided the handsome building and equipment for the college of mechanic arts, at an expense of more than fifty thousand dollars. President White built out of his own private fortune, at the cost of more than sixty thousand dollars, a very elegant residence for the President of the University. May it be many long years before he shall feel constrained to surrender it to his successor. Henry W. Sage, now chairman of the board of trustees of the University, has contributed more than three hundred thousand dollars for the building and endowment of Sage College, and for the erection of the beautiful chapel on the campus, as well as the extensive conservatories for the botanical department.

These gentlemen have also at different times advanced large sums for various important necessities of the institution. Dean Sage, of Albany, furnished a permanent endowment for the Sage Chapel, from the income of which the most eminent clergymen in the entire country, of all denominations, are engaged to conduct religious services each sabbath during the school term. Thus the students have the extraordinary privilege, quite unequalled elsewhere, of having presented before them, each year, twenty or more of the most distinguished pulpit orators of America. These services are largely attended, not only by students, but also by citizens of Ithaca.

Miss Jennie McGraw presented a chime of bells, which were placed in the tower of the McGraw Building. She also made large bequests to the University, in her will, but at the present time the right to receive these bequests is being contested before the Surrogate by the person to whom she was married in the last year of her life. Other contributions, large and small, have also been made by many other persons. The combined offerings of all these generous benefactors, added to the other revenues of the institution, have enabled the management to make many valuable improvements.

Within the past year a physical laboratory has been completed and brought into use, which, for superior excellence in all of its details and for the completeness of its equipments is claimed to be equal to any in this country or Europe. A large and handsome building, serving the double purpose of an armory and drill-room for the military department, and for general assemblies and commencement exercises, has also recently been completed, and adds very much to the necessary conveniences of the institution. In connection with the last-named building there has also been provided a very complete gymnasium, with every appliance for physical culture and healthful exercise.

THE SAGE COLLEGE.

From the very beginning of the enterprise for the establishment of the Cornell University, it was the hope and expectation of Mr. Cornell that provision should be made for the education of women on a perfect equality with the male students. President White was also in full sympathy with this idea, but it was his opinion that some special facilities should be provided before this condition could be properly announced. Conforming to his judgment in this respect, no reference was made to the subject of co-education in the report of the plan of organization, nor in the official prospectus of the University.

The founder, however, made reference to his own anticipation and desire in this direction, in his address at the opening of the University. The unexpectedly large attendance of male students at the very outset, however, taxed to the utmost all of the facilities which had been provided, or that the financial resources of the institution were sufficient to furnish, and the subject of pro-

14

viding for female students was allowed to lie dormant for the first two years of practical operations.

At the annual meeting of the trustees of the University, in June, 1871, a proposition was received from the Hon. Henry W. Sage, offering to contribute $250,000, one-half to be used for the erection of an edifice for the accommodation of female students, and the other half to be invested as a special endowment for the maintenance of the building, on condition that women should be admitted to all of the departments of the University on equal terms with the male students.

Some of the trustees were outspoken in their opposition to the admission of women on any terms whatever, but the offer of Mr. Sage was referred to a special committee for consideration and report. After a thorough investigation of the subject, President White, on behalf of a majority of the committee, submitted to the board of trustees, in February, 1872, an elaborate and exhaustive report recommending "that Mr. Sage's gift be accepted on the conditions named by him, and that the establishment created under it be known as the Sage College of Cornell University."

This report was adopted by the board of trustees by nearly an unanimous vote. A plan of the building was perfected, and preparations for its erection were instituted during the ensuing year. The corner stone was laid with interesting ceremonies, May 15, 1873, including addresses by President White, Mr. Sage, Mr. Cornell, Chancellor Winchell, of Syracuse University, Professor Tyler, Professor Goldwin Smith, Professor Sprague, and President Angell, of the University of Michigan. The edifice, which was completed the following year, is one of the most elegant and imposing college buildings in the country, and is in every respect most admirably adapted to the purposes for which it is designed. It forms a noble addition to the grand collection of buildings which have been erected for the use of the University, and is a monument which does great credit to the generous instincts of its liberal hearted patron.

In each succeeding year of the progress of the University its standard of scholarship has been constantly raised. The qualifications requisite for admission have been placed higher and higher each year, in order that only those should be accepted who could give reasonable promise of successfully completing the University course and reaching their degrees. The departments, or special courses of instruction have been augmented from nine to fourteen, and the faculty now embraces more than fifty persons, as follows : Non-resident Professors, five; Resident Professors, twenty-five; Associate Professors, four; Assistant Professors, twelve; Instructors, six; Curators, Foremen, and other subordinate officers, nine. The library has advanced until it now contains about forty-six thousand volumes, besides fourteen thousand pamphlets. The various collections have also largely increased, and now embrace the necessary material for illustration in almost every branch of study and research.

Probably no college or university ever attained such prominence and standing among the established institutions of the whole country in such short time as the Cornell University. In some respects, perhaps, this was unfortunate, as it aroused expectations beyond the facilities of a new and undeveloped institution. With all of the wealth that has been so generously lavished upon it, the trustees have never yet, in any year, been able to respond to nearly all the calls made upon them for means to provide the facilities which have been demanded. Despite every embarrassment, however, the progress in nearly every important department has certainly been most gratifying. In every competition with the chosen representatives of other colleges, whether in intellectual contests or in athletic sports, the

Cornell University has carried away its full share of honors. In every field of professional and scientific activity the graduates of Cornell are achieving honorable repute and adding lustre to the name of their Alma Mater.

Although only now in the fifteenth year of practical operation, Cornell University has already sent forth about one thousand graduates, who are taking high rank in the communities in which they have located. This is especially true in reference to those graduating from the departments of civil engineering and architecture. While, perhaps, students in other departments are equally well equipped in their specialties, the demand for services in these particular vocations seems to offer better opportunities for graduates than other professions. In public life the graduates of Cornell have already made gratifying progress. Since the year 1876 no Legislature of the State of New York has assembled which did not contain on its list of members from one to four of the graduates of the University; while in other representative capacities they are found to occupy a fair share of public favor.

The purpose of the founder of Cornell University was expressed by himself on one occasion in these words: " I would found an institution where any person can find instruction in any study."

This comprehensive declaration, terse in words and pregnant with ideas, was chosen by the trustees as the motto of the institution, and placed on the official seal of the University, there to remain as a constant reminder of the noble aims and high hopes of him who gave the best labors of his life to the successful establishment of this beneficent institution. May these simple but expressive words inspire all who are or may hereafter be responsible for the administration of its affairs, to the highest possible endeavors toward the attainment of the object which was so dear to their revered and honored founder. The work which he planned with so much wisdom, and which he labored so diligently and unselfishly to promote, remains for them to carry forward toward ultimate success. May his example be emulated by those who follow in the course marked out by him.

CHAPTER XVII.

THE CORNELL UNIVERSITY.—THE LAND GRANT FUND.

Conditions of the Appropriation.—Depreciation in Value of Land Scrip —Prospects of Meagre Endowment.—Mr. Cornell Volunteers to Locate Public Lands for Benefit of the University. —Contract with the Comptroller.—Immense Labors.—Large Advances.—Gratuitous Services.—Serious Illness.—Contract Transferred to University Authorities.—Successful Realization.—Traducers.—Vilification.—Cruel Misrepresentations.— Official Investigation.—Complete Vindication.

THE donation of public lands made by the Congress of the United States to the several States and Territories of the Union was explicitly dedicated, by the terms of the enactment, " to the endowment, support, and maintenance of at least one college, where the leading object shall be, without excluding other scientific and classical studies, and including military tactics, to teach such branches of learning as are related to agriculture and the mechanic arts, in such manner as the Legislatures of the States may respectively prescribe, in order to promote the liberal and practical education of the industrial classes in the several pursuits and professions of life." This measure, introduced by the Hon. Justin S. Morrill, of Vermont, and approved by President Lincoln July 2, 1862, granted to each State a quantity of public land equal to thirty thousand acres for each Senator and Representative in Congress to which the States were respectively entitled by the apportionment under the census of 1860. The total amount of land required to meet this appropriation was nine million four hundred and twenty thousand acres, of which the proportion belonging to the State of New York was nine hundred and ninety thousand acres.

The nominal valuation of the public lands, fixed by the United States, is one dollar and a quarter per acre, but, unfortunately, in this act, while the States were required to sell their scrip, there was no price named in any way limiting the sum to be realized for such sales. The inevitable consequence of this oversight was to speedily depreciate the value of land scrip, and the large quantities offering by the several States continued to depress current quotations. The Comptroller of New York received the share to which the State was entitled, in 1864. The market value of the land at that time was about eighty-five cents per acre, which was the price fixed by the State officers for its sale. At that price seventy-six thousand acres were sold in 1864, the avails of which had been received by the Comptroller, and by him invested for the trust designated, prior to the enactment of the charter of the Cornell University, April 27, 1865. At that date the selling price of land warrants had fallen to about fifty cents per acre, with the prospect that the offering of any considerable amount would still further reduce the current value.

It was apparent, therefore, that if the remainder were to be sold at the best available market rate, the entire proceeds of the Land Grant Fund would amount to only about $500,000. It was Mr. Cornell's belief that if the warrants could be located on well-selected timber lands in some of the Western States, a much larger sum could be realized from the advance in the value of lands so secured. He found, as the result of careful inquiry, that the location of desirable public lands well covered with pine timber, had been uniformly successful.

By the terms of the Congressional act, no State could itself locate public lands within another State, and as there were no federal lands within this State, no disposition of the grant was available but the actual sale of the scrip. Mr. Cornell endeavored to induce the trustees of the University to purchase it from the State, and locate the lands directly for the benefit of the institution, offering himself to advance the money necessary to defray the expenses of the examination and location of the lands.

The University, however, had no revenue beyond the requirements for its current necessary expenditures, and the trustees felt unwilling to encumber themselves with the burden of annual expenses and local taxation which would be involved by that course. This was probably a wise decision, in view of the subsequent history of the enterprise, as it is more than probable that they would have been induced to sell the lands to relieve themselves from their financial burden too soon to realize the full measure of benefit which, under other circumstances, finally accrued to the University from this source.

Finding, at last, that there was no other available mode of saving to the cause of education the great value which he felt sure could be realized from the Land Grant by its proper treatment, Mr. Cornell made a proposition to the Comptroller, offering to purchase the scrip at sixty cents per acre, (payable one-half down, and the balance when realized from sales,) locate the land at his own expense, pay the local taxes and other necessary expenses, and obligate himself to pay into the State treasury, for the benefit of the

Cornell University, the entire profits to be realized
from the sale of the lands thus located. In his letter to the Comptroller, under date June 9, 1866,
tendering this proposition, Mr. Cornell estimated
that a clear profit could be realized, for the benefit of the University, of at least $1,600,000 above
and beyond the sixty cents per acre to be paid
into the State Treasury to the credit of the College Land Scrip Fund. With the concurrence of
the Commissioners of the Land Office of the State
of New York, the Comptroller accepted the proposition, and entered into a formal contract with
Mr. Cornell on the basis stated, which was duly
executed in the month of September, 1866.

To those familiar with the details of selecting
and locating public lands, the magnitude of the
undertaking of thus handling eight hundred thousand acres will be readily understood. For the
information of others not thus familiar, it may
briefly be stated that it was first necessary to inspect, by the personal examination of a trusted
agent, each section of land available for location,
and estimate the quantity of standing timber contained thereon, in order to secure the selection of
lands of desirable value. Within the first year of
these operations, Mr. Cornell disbursed more
than $200,000 on account of the expenses inci-
dent to the location of the land scrip, and on Sep-

tember 30, 1874, he had advanced for the purchase of warrants and expense of location, for
local taxes and other expenditures for the necessary protection of the lands from depredation, beyond what was received for lands and timber
sold, the large amount of $525,082.77. Of the
lands selected for location much the largest portion, probably seven-eighths of the whole amount,
consisted of the pine timber lands of Wisconsin,
and the balance was superior farming land in
Minnesota and Kansas.

In the spring of 1874 Mr. Cornell was suddenly
prostrated with severe illness, in consequence of
which he was for many months confined to his
room, and wholly incapacitated from giving attention to business affairs. He had overtaxed his
usually robust constitution by the extraordinary
labors with which he had for years burdened himself in the interests of the University, and when
exhausted by the effects of a protracted and painful illness, he lacked the necessary vitality for restoration to health and strength. His physician
imperatively urged that he must be relieved from
the cares of business as a condition of possible
recovery.

He was, therefore, finally constrained to ask
the trustees of the University to relieve him from
further service in the Land Grant enterprise, and to

take upon themselves the responsibility of carrying out the provisions of the contract with the State. Mr. Cornell had borne the weight of this great undertaking, taxing both his financial resources and his physical strength for a period of eight long years, and it only now remained for the trustees to patiently await the fruition of his wise foresight and unselfish labors. The lands were rapidly appreciating in value, and there was every promise of abundant reward in the ultimate profits to be realized by the University. The commissioners of the Land Office approved the proposed transfer of the contract to the board of trustees, which was finally accomplished in the month of November, 1874, a few weeks prior to the lamented death of the founder. The same general policy of management which had been pursued by Mr. Cornell in the administration of the trust was continued by the University authorities.

The derangement and prostration of business affairs following the great financial crisis of 1873 was wide-spread and long-continued. In no other branch of business was it more severely felt, probably, than in the lumber trade. The cessation of building operations curtailed the demand for lumber, and reduced its value below the cost of manufacture. Owing to this serious and protracted depression in the condition of the lumber business, the demand for timber lands was limited, thus checking the advance in the value of this class of property, which had been very marked prior to the transfer of the Land Grant contract to the University.

For some years subsequent to that event, sales of the lands were slow, but sufficient to furnish means with which to provide for the expenses of carrying the lands without resort to other resources. The final exhaustion of other sources of timber supply, however, soon brought the valuable lands of Wisconsin more especially to the attention of buyers, and when renewed prosperity of the country began to manifest itself, as it did in 1880, the demand for the University lands became active and strong, and large sales were effected at prices which were very gratifying. The aggregate sales of these lands, which had been effected down to the close of 1882, amounted to about three million seven hundred thousand dollars. The total expenses for location, local taxes, interest, and care of lands, including the cost of the land scrip, were in the vicinity of one million five hundred thousand dollars, thus showing profits accruing to the University of about two million two hundred thousand dollars; while there still remain unsold, lands which will yield several hundred thousand dollars to be added thereto.

Too much praise cannot be given to the Hon. Henry W. Sage, who succeeded Mr. Cornell as the chairman of the board of trustees, and upon whom, since the death of the founder, the great responsibility of this good work has fallen. He was peculiarly qualified for the intelligent and sagacious discharge of these duties, by reason of his previous successful experience in this particular line of business, extending over a long period of years. The successful administration of this great trust, and the gratifying results produced by it, vindicate in the highest manner the wisdom and foresight of Mr. Cornell in projecting the policy of locating the lands for the benefit of the University.

Every dollar of profit realized for the endowment of the University, from the location and sale of public lands, was just as positively contributed by Mr. Cornell as though it had been paid out of his private fortune. He foresaw the advantages to be secured as the result of that policy, and he had the courage as well as the disposition to undertake it unaided. He furnished the capital, amounting to half a million of dollars, which was indispensably necessary to carry the enterprise through to a successful termination. Others were solicited to render assistance, but none were found willing to make the venture. With him it was a work of

love, in which he enlisted with all of the characteristic determination of his personality. He is,
therefore, to be credited, including his direct contributions, with an aggregate benefaction in behalf of the University of at least three and a half
millions of dollars. This magnificent endowment
will place the Cornell University among the two
or three wealthiest educational establishments in
America, and wisely administered, there can
hardly be a limit to the extent of usefulness which
will flow from its operations.

This great work was undertaken by Mr. Cornell without fee or reward. Neither he nor any
member of his family was to be benefited to the extent of a single dollar. It was his original proposition, and it was so stipulated in his contract with
the Comptroller, that every dollar of profit should
inure to the exclusive benefit of the Cornell
University. His services were rendered without
compensation, and he was almost exclusively engaged in the conduct of the enterprise for a period of nearly eight years. Members of his family
also rendered valuable service in the details of the
business, for which no charge was ever made nor
compensation rendered in any form. Never was
a work taken up and carried forward from higher
motives, nor with more devoted regard to the interests involved.

Reviewing these circumstances from this distance, it is extremely difficult to realize how malignantly Mr. Cornell was libelled and misrepresented in reference to the philanthropic labors which he had taken upon himself with such unselfish devotion to the public good. He was with coarse brutality assailed in the public press and in the halls of the Legislature by the partisans of petty institutions which had endeavored, but failed, to secure the whole or a portion of the Land Grant income. He was denounced as a land grabber and a corruptionist of the worst kind. No terms of obloquy were too vile to apply to him, and yet his only offence, in thought or deed, was to contribute his own money, with lavish hand, to build up a great college for the people of the State of New York, and to save, for its exclusive use, every possible dollar of the intrinsic value of the princely domain granted by Congress, for the benefit of agricultural and mechanical education in the State.

These vile insinuations, which, though repeatedly demonstrated to be absolutely without foundation, were reiterated year after year, in one form or another, until finally, in 1873, the Legislature ordered an investigation of the entire subject of the Land Grant contract and its administration, and authorized the appointment of a commission for that

15

purpose, which was directed to report to the next Legislature. Governor Dix named as the members of that commission Governor Horatio Seymour, Vice-President William A. Wheeler, and Colonel John D. Van Buren. They devoted several months to the investigation, giving the assailants of Mr. Cornell the widest possible latitude to enable them to substantiate their charges. The result of the investigation and the unanimous report of the commission to the Legislature was in all respects a complete vindication of Mr. Cornell and of his administration of the trust which had been committed to him by the officers of the State. The result of this proceeding effectually silenced the slanderers, and the generous founder of the University was thereafter permitted to devote himself to his philanthropic labors without farther molestation.

CHAPTER XVIII.

RAILROADS.

THE peculiar geographical location of Ithaca has
at different periods of its history exercised a material influence upon its prosperity and development as a business centre. In the early days of
the navigation of the canal system of the State,
the situation of Ithaca at the head of Cayuga
Lake, through which connection with the Erie
Canal was secured, made it a point of shipment
for the products of a large section of country, embracing the southern tier from Binghamton to
Elmira and the adjacent northern counties in
Pennsylvania.

Supplies of merchandize received by canal and

lake at Ithaca were distributed through this extensive region by teams which had brought lumber, grain, and coal for shipment. In view of the
magnitude of this traffic, a railway—one of the
first built in this State, and indeed in this country
—was projected and constructed between Ithaca
and Owego. This road—the first for which
ground was broken within the State—with its
celebrated inclined planes, worked by stationary
power, to overcome the high elevation near Ithaca,
was completed and put in operation about the
year 1832. Like many similar enterprises, the
road found inadequate business for its support, and
· proved a failure financially. After a few years of
languishing business, it was abandoned by its
owners, and finally ceased its operations for a
number of years, until rebuilt by a new company.

So long as Ithaca commanded the trade of this
extensive interior country, it continued to prosper,
but the ultimate extension of the Chemung Canal
from the head of Seneca Lake to Elmira, and the
Chenango Canal from Utica to Binghamton, diverted much of the commercial traffic which had
formerly found its outlet by way of Ithaca and
the Cayuga Lake. Later, when the New York
& Erie Railroad was extended along the southern tier, and branches were constructed from
Binghamton to Syracuse, and from Elmira to Ca-

nandaigua, the territory tributary to the business interests of Ithaca was substantially confined to the County of Tompkins. In 1849 the railroad between Ithaca and Owego was rebuilt, thus placing Ithaca in railway connection with the Erie road at Owego, as it was also connected by steamboat navigation with the New York Central road at Cayuga Bridge. Thus the situation of Ithaca was changed from a point of commercial importance, commanding an extensive trade from a wide range of territory, to that of a mere local village, isolated from the great lines of travel and connected with them by transportation of very limited character. It was no wonder, therefore, that the growth of the village was checked and the ambition of its residents substantially culminated.

Such was the condition of Ithaca when Mr. Cornell projected the establishment there of a great educational institution. One of the first, and really the most serious embarrassment that was realized as to the location of the University, was the lack of adequate facilities for travel. Four months in each year the lake was closed with ice, and communication with the Central road depended upon stages, or, if by rail, by the circuitous route via Owego and Binghamton to Syracuse. All felt that this condition of things must be overcome, or the University would fail to accomplish its proper mission on account of its isolated situation.

The development of the Pennsylvania coal fields had already given new life to the Susquehanna Valley, and the people of that locality were seeking railway facilities to connect them with the canal system of New York, as an outlet for their coal product. To meet this necessity, the Ithaca & Athens Railroad Company was organized in 1866, with Mr. Cornell as president. This company constructed a railroad from Ithaca to Athens, where it connected with the Lehigh Valley Railway via Wilkesbarre to New York and Philadelphia.

The new road, while developing important business interests and connections for Ithaca, failed to remedy in any important degree the lack of railway facilities requisite to accommodate the University travel. The result of greatest importance to be accomplished was some direct communication with the Central road, but no progress was made in this direction until the enactment of the law authorizing the bonding of towns and villages to provide for railroad building. Under the unhealthy stimulus of this profligate measure several lines of railroad were projected to connect Ithaca with the outer world. Three of these projects finally gained the requisite vitality to undertake the building of roads: one from Ithaca to Geneva, another from Ithaca to Cayuga Bridge along the east side of Cayuga Lake, and the third from Ithaca to Cortland—which latter was afterward merged into the Utica, Ithaca & Elmira Railroad Company. The town of Ithaca bonded herself $200,000 for the Ithaca & Athens road; $300,000 for the Geneva & Ithaca; and the village of Ithaca was bonded to the extent of $100,000 for the Ithaca & Cortland enterprise.

Other towns on these various routes were also bonded for different sums, varying in amount according to the ability of the towns or the extent of their active interest in the proposed roads. Unfortunately, the easy process of issuing town bonds encouraged the commencement of roads for which no adequate warrant of business existed. Besides, the great stimulation in railway building advanced the market value of iron and other supplies to an extravagant price. In some instances the cost of iron rails for these roads was more than one hundred dollars per ton, and other materials in proportion. Thus the double mistake was inevitable, of building roads which would starve each other in competing for business inadequate for all, and at the same time making the roads cost one-quarter or one-third more than they would if but half as many roads had been constructed.

The town subscriptions and those of individuals were generally sufficient to provide the right of way and grade the lines, leaving the bridges, superstructure, and equipment to be provided by the bonds of the companies secured by mortgage on the roads.   Mr. Cornell, as was his custom in regard to all local enterprises, subscribed liberally to the stock of the several roads leading from Ithaca, but his constant occupation in the conduct of the business of the Land Grant contract, prevented his taking an active part in the preliminary work of the later organized roads.   Inability of the managers of the Geneva & Ithaca road to place their bonds at any satisfactory rate, led them to appeal to Mr. Cornell for assistance, and he was finally induced to take the $800,000 of bonds in order to provide for the completion of the road, which seemed likely to fail of accomplishment without his aid.   Under similar circumstances the Utica, Ithaca & Elmira Company appealed to him for assistance, without which it was apparent that the road must be abandoned—and this he considered would be extremely unfortunate for the interests of Ithaca, and especially for the University.   He finally added this last burden to his already heavy load of undertakings.   His loyalty to Ithaca and the University, and his anxiety to promote their prosperity, overcame his good judgment, and induced him to take upon himself obligations too great even for his extensive means.

The financial crisis of 1873, which shook the country from centre to circumference, was essentially a railroad panic. The extraordinary development in the building of railroads during the several years after the close of the war had absorbed enormous amounts of capital, for which there was nothing to show but vast quantities of depreciated stocks and bonds. Europe had enriched herself on our extravagancies, and had been gorged with an endless supply of corporate securities. One after another, enterprises which should never have been built, began to default in the payment of interest on their bonds, and it was not long before these securities, which had so recently been the favorite of all investments, came into a general disrepute. Often the good were condemned with the bad, for, aside from roads of exceptional merit, there was an indiscriminate discredit of all such securities.

It was just at this crisis that Mr. Cornell had taken these new complications upon himself. He had already given the University three-quarters of a million dollars, and had advanced half a million in the operations of the Land Grant contract. The two railroads which he had undertaken to complete required a million and a half. By the conversion of the remainder of his telegraph interests, he raised two-thirds of this amount, and the other third he was obliged to borrow. The railroad bonds were absolutely discredited, and could not be used for the purpose of raising funds, so he was forced to pledge his personal credit for these necessities. His courage, however, never faltered, and he went on with all of his old-time energy and perseverance, determined to carry his undertakings to a successful issue.

In the midst of these struggles, however, Mr. Cornell was suddenly, in June, 1874, incapacitated from personal attention to business by a severe illness, which kept him indoors for several months. This misfortune, superadded to his financial embarrassments, was a severe blow to his operations. The knowledge of his serious illness, at an advanced age, with his large liabilities, and encumbered with two new railway enterprises yet unfinished, quickly impaired his credit, and rendered the conduct of his business all the more difficult.

While his illness greatly enhanced the embarrassments of his business, it is undoubtedly true that the anxieties and discouraging circumstances which surrounded him materially aggravated the effects of the disease which prostrated him. His medical attendant advised absolute relief from business cares and removal to a milder climate for the approaching. winter. Neither of these conditions could possibly be complied with, and the sufferer was released from farther struggle by death, after an illness of about six months' duration.

It is of course superfluous to say that the death of Mr. Cornell, under the circumstances which preceded it, left the affairs of his estate in a most deplorable condition. With extended liabilities and the necessity of large additional investments to complete the unfinished roads, the situation was indeed alarming. Fortunately, however, the administrator of the estate was equal to the occasion, and by heroic treatment was enabled to save something from the threatened wreck. Realizing that a large actual loss had already been made, he decided that it was useless to attempt to recover what had originally been invested in the roads, but that it was his duty to rescue what value then remained. He, therefore, sold the Geneva & Ithaca road to the Lehigh Valley interests for the best price he could obtain, which was about two hundred thousand dollars, or less than one-third of the original investment. This great sacrifice proved to be extremely wise, as subsequent events demonstrated that the entire sum realized would have been lost to the estate had the road been retained a few months longer.

The condition of the Utica, Ithaca & Elmira enterprise, at the period of Mr. Cornell's death, was still more embarrassing than that of the Geneva road. Sections of the road had been so far advanced as to be put in operation between Ithaca and Cortland, and also between Van Ettenville and Horseheads. Between these separated portions, a distance of twenty miles, the grading had been substantially completed, and seven or eight miles of track was laid. Under the operations of a contract concluded by Mr. Cornell a few weeks prior to his death, means were provided during the following year to connect these sections, and to discharge some three hundred thousand dollars of his personal liabilities which had been incurred in the enterprise. This arrangement saved the estate from absolute confiscation which menaced it for several months, but, down to the present time, not one dollar of the half million invested in the road by him has ever been realized.

Though these railroad enterprises proved exceedingly disastrous to the financial resources of Mr. Cornell's estate—depleting it to the extent of a million dollars—they proved extremely advantageous to the prosperity of the village of Ithaca, and furnished ample and convenient access to the University from every section of the State. Aside from principal stations on the great through lines of travel, probably no town in the State now enjoys better facilities for travel and transportation than Ithaca. Direct lines of railway communica· tion connect that village with Elmira, Waverly, Owego, and Binghamton, on the Erie road, and with Geneva, Cayuga, Auburn, Lyons, Syracuse, and Canastota, on the Central, as well as with the main lines of the Lehigh Valley, the Delaware, Lackawanna & Western, and the New York, West Shore & Buffalo railways.

Viewed from the present standpoint, the action of Mr. Cornell, in taking upon himself the burden of completing these roads, can only be regarded as a hazardous and unwarrantable undertaking. There are, however, many mitigating circumstances to be considered before passing censure upon him as a man lacking prudent judgment. In the first place, the investment by the town and village of Ithaca amounting to $600,000, and of individuals, his friends and neighbors, to a considerable amount in addition, had already been made. These interests were imperilled by the inability to complete the roads, and the threatened suspension of efforts in that direction would apparently leave the locality more destitute than ever of the hoped-for facilities. It was the fond expectation of Mr. Cornell that he might avert these unwelcome results, and his efforts were enlisted purely from motives of public spirit and loyalty to local interests. Governed by these motives, he was more likely to overlook the merits of the venture as an investment of his own means, than he would have been under other circumstances.

The special causes of the disastrous consequences which ensued, were of a character not to be apparent when Mr. Cornell enlisted in the undertakings. These were the unprecedented financial revulsion, and the loss of his own health. Although it was true that railway securities had, for the time being, ceased to be considered desirable investments, there was no reason visible at that period to anticipate the utter collapse which so suddenly burst upon the country. That occurrence was in important respects aggravated by numerous collateral circumstances which were wholly invisible and could not have been estimated in advance. It was like the explosion of an extraordinary electric storm from an apparently clear atmosphere, which carried ruin and devastation in its track. So, too, in reference to the prostrating illness which came upon him without warning. Though advanced in years, the firmness of his general health, and the long life of his father, gave promise of many years of activity and usefulness.

CHAPTER XIX.

PUBLIC ENTERPRISE.—LOCAL IMPROVEMENTS.

COMMENDABLE as is the disposition to foster and promote public improvements, most men, as a general rule, are too much absorbed in devotion to individual interests to think of, or care much for, the common welfare; and it seldom happens that those who are endowed with public spirit are at the same time possessed of the requisite means to gratify their patriotic impulses. The combination of these important conditions for public advancement in the same person is a fortunate contingency for any community. More especially was it fortunate for Ithaca that circumstances favored her with a citizen both able and willing to render the necessary service to overcome the barriers which checked her progress. Her peculiar topographical situation and the results which attended the development of the great railway lines of the State, had combined to narrow the field of her former patronage and arrest her material growth. Only the interposition of powerful and energetic influences could have rescued her from the insignificant position to which adverse fate had consigned.her.

Whatever may have been the considerations which first attracted Mr. Cornell's attention to Ithaca, and induced him to choose it as the location of his home, it was certainly an incident of the utmost importance to its subsequent development. He had but just attained his majority when it became the home of his adoption, and through the remainder of his life his loyalty to the welfare of the town was continually manifested by efforts to promote its material prosperity. During all the years of his engrossing engagement in the telegraph enterprise, he continued the residence of his family at Ithaca at great personal inconvenience, owing to its inaccessible location and the difficulty of getting to and from his business. That he did not determine to change the residence of his family to a more convenient point was another fortunate circumstance for Ithaca, as it would probably have resulted in his permanent location elsewhere.

Throughout his entire career Mr. Cornell evinced an especial interest in the promotion of all such public enterprises as promised advantageous results for Ithaca. The successive steps taken by him for the erection of the Cornell Library and the establishment of the Cornell University, and finally for the completion of the railways to connect Ithaca with the outer world, were evidences of the highest ambition to serve the public weal. The extent of his contributions for the public benefit, supplemented by so much laborious personal effort to insure the most useful results, exhibited a patriotic devotion which can probably be found in no other instance. Not only was the great bulk of his fortune—considerably more than three-fourths of it—given in furtherance of these objects ; his very life was probably not a little shortened in consequence of his efforts to advance these interests so vital to the locality. No man ever died more clearly a martyr to the cause of his devotion, than did Ezra Cornell as the result of his efforts to develop the interests which were so essential to insure the continued prosperity of Ithaca.

Long before he had acquired a competence, when he was a simple mechanic, employed in the service of Colonel Beebe at Fall Creek, Mr. Cornell was an early and persistent advocate of

16

the development of additional manufacturing interests at Ithaca.   He devoted much effort to call·
ing the attention of citizens and strangers to the
manifest advantages to be derived from the improvement of the unoccupied water power of the
Fall Creek stream.   Though of extremely limited
means at the time, he contributed with characteristic liberality to the capital stock of the Ithaca
Falls Woolen Company, and was largely influential in securing the necessary capital for the estab·
lishment of that important enterprise.   That the
company ended its career in insolvency after several years of languishing business, was due to the
eccentricities of its administration, with which Mr.
Cornell was in no way connected, and for which
he was in no wise responsible.

The project for the connection of Cayuga Lake
with Lake Ontario by a ship canal, in order to
place Ithaca in direct navigable communication
with the great lakes of the northwest, was a favorite subject of Mr. Cornell's advocacy.   He devoted much attention and effort in this direction
prior to 1840, and again renewed attention to the
subject during his service in the Legislature,
where he introduced a bill to promote the enterprise.   The topographical features of the section of
country between the two lakes were extremely favorable to the economical construction of the pro·

posed work, and there can be no doubt that its construction would have concentrated at Ithaca commercial activities and manufactures of great importance. Mr. Cornell was greatly impressed with the possibilities which might follow the successful inauguration of this proposed improvement.

As early as 1846, Ithaca was placed in instantaneous communication with the principal cities of the country, by the construction of a line of telegraph to Auburn, which was done almost wholly at the expense of Mr. Cornell. He also made earnest efforts to induce his neighbors and friends to participate in the advantageous opportunities which this novel enterprise at that day offered. Unfortunately, however, they were discouraged by the disappointment which awaited their small investments in the New York & Erie Telegraph Company, and they could not be induced to take further risks. Could they have been enabled to comprehend the cause of that disappointment, and continue their ventures in the subsequent opportunities which were offered to them, some of the many millions realized as profits on the investments of citizens of Rochester and Utica, might have been brought to Ithaca in addition to the realizations of the pioneer. In the early days of the telegraph development, a large number of

young men of Tompkins County entered into
that service by the assistance of Mr. Cornell,
many of whom have, in consequence of the opportunities thus secured, become men of large wealth
and influence. They have, however, almost uniformly failed to return to their early homes, having permanently settled in other localities.

The establishment of the manufacture of glass
at Ithaca must be credited to the sagacious fore-
thought and the persistent efforts, as well as the
generous encouragement, of Mr. Cornell. The
remarkable prosperity which now attends the development of that important industry by the extensive works now in operation in the village, is a
marked vindication of the wisdom of his judgment
in this respect. It is an especially gratifying feature
that the quality of glass produced at Ithaca, is
much superior to other glass of American manufacture, and that it commands a higher price in the
market. This important fact is attributed to the
peculiar influence of the movements of the air-cur-
rents in giving a strong and steady natural draft
in the furnaces. It is supposed that this particular effect is produced in consequence of the location of the works at a point between the lake
and the great ravines, which have been cut in the
faces of the surrounding hills by the flow of the
large streams of water seeking the level of Ca-

yuga Lake. If this shall become an established fact as it is now a generally accepted theory, there can be little doubt that Ithaca will become at no distant period a still more important seat for the production of this valuable staple.

It was a favorite idea with Mr. Cornell that the manufacture of iron could be located at Ithaca with great advantage. He made careful investigation of this subject, and satisfied himself that the necessary ingredients for the production of a superior quality of iron could be more economically and advantageously brought together at this point than at any other locality. Based upon this investigation, he subscribed a large sum toward the organization of a company for this purpose, and at his solicitation the requisite amount of capital was provided; but the enterprise was finally abandoned after having broken ground for the erection of works, on account of the depressed condition of the iron industry, consequent upon the financial disturbances of 1873.

The Ithaca Savings Bank, which has become one of the most prosperous financial institutions in that section of the State, owes its organization to the wise conception and urgent endeavor of Mr. Cornell. Its charter was enacted under his procurement as a member of the Legislature, and the eminent degree of success which has at-

tended its management, has been due in no slight
measure to the confidence inspired by his acceptance of the presidency of the institution in its
initiatory stage. He was impressed with the belief that a highly beneficial influence would follow
the substantial establishment of a sound and well-
managed institution of this character, in promoting
habits of increased frugality among the industrial
classes of the community. The accumulation of
more than half a million of dollars in the custody
of this organization, in the few years of its existence, attests not only the wisdom of the project,
but also the confidence which its administration
has inspired. Mr. Cornell took great pride in the
development of the institution, and continued to
serve as its presiding officer until the close of his
life. He was also one of the originators of the
First National Bank of Ithaca, of which he was a
director for ten years. The marked success of
this organization is highly creditable to the management which has so advantageously directed its
affairs.

The advancement of Ithaca, from the condition
of a finished, and indeed superannuated, country
village, into a thrifty and ambitious town, with
every reasonable promise of becoming at no distant period a city of growing importance, was due,
unquestionably, to the successful efforts of Mr.

Cornell in the projection and development of the great University, and in the completion of the admirable system of railway facilities which cost him so dearly. He took a deep interest and was a leading spirit in every project for the advancement and improvement of the village, not only in its material, but as well in its moral progress. For the erection of churches of all denominations he was ever an open-handed contributor, and it is quite safe to assert that every place of worship in the village was indebted to him for benefactions of greater or less degree. There is not a village lot in Ithaca which does not bear an increased value, and in many instances doubled and even quadrupled value, in consequence of the philanthropic and unselfish efforts of Ezra Cornell. May the residents of the beautiful and prosperous town long remember the debt of gratitude which they owe to his memory.

Without some little reflection it is impossible to appreciate with much intelligence the magnitude of advantage which the people of Ithaca enjoy in a business way, from the location in their midst of an institution like the Cornell University. In the first place, it now has a fixed annual income of more than two hundred thousand dollars, nearly all of which must be disbursed for its current working expenses in the immediate vicinity.

Next, it brings from a wide expanse of territory more than four hundred students, who spend nine months of each year at Ithaca. Assuming that they expend only the small sum of two hundred and fifty dollars each for their maintenance, it will amount to one hundred thousand dollars, which, added to the University expenditures, aggregate nearly one thousand dollars contributed to the material interests of Ithaca every business day of the year from these sources alone. Then there must be credited a very considerable sum expended by the thousands of visitors who are every year brought to the village by the University. Added to these advantages are many residents, who have been, and are continually being induced to locate at Ithaca, on account of its superior educational opportunities. The extensive and growing manufactures of the village, also, find many advantageous circumstances for the introduction and sale of their products, growing out of the good fame attaching to the name of Ithaca as the seat of a great University.

Another subject of local significance for which Mr. Cornell evinced an especial interest and made liberal contributions to render more accessible, was the romantic, and indeed extraordinary, natural scenery of the region about Ithaca, which he felt was worthy of attracting a large concourse of summer tourists. Clustered within two or three miles of the village, on the half-dozen considerable streams which pour their water over the rocky and precipitous hill-sides, on their way to the level of the beautiful Cayuga Lake, are nearly one hundred waterfalls of such magnitude as to be worthy of especial notice. Some of these cataracts and cascades are wonderfully interesting. The Fall Creek gorge, within a few rods of the University campus, affords a day's stroll of thrilling interest and excitement. Taghanic Falls, throwing an unbroken stream two hundred and fifteen feet, is the highest waterfall in any of the Northern States east of the Rocky Mountains. Taken altogether for extent and variety of scenery, this region has few rivals in the United States, while numerous other localities, with comparatively nothing like the attractions of Ithaca, enjoy a patronage from tourists, many fold greater. With the added advantages of the extensive buildings, museums, and library of the Cornell University, the repute of this neighborhood should be infinitely greater than it now enjoys.

Nor was Ithaca alone the beneficiary of Mr. Cornell's enterprising public spirit. His activity was ceaseless, and he never tired in the promotion of meritorious projects. The wonderful development which has in late years been made in producing illustrated publications, is due in no small degree to results following the establishment of the American Photo-Lithograph Company, of which Mr. Cornell was a large stockholder and for many years held the office of president. The great advance which was made by this organization in the art of lithography, by combining with it the use of photography, has completely revolutionized this important and useful branch of illustrative publication. Through the inadequacy of the patent laws to protect inventors in the enjoyment of the fruits of their labors, Mr. Cornell failed to realize profit from his ventures in this direction, but the benefits accruing to the public, as the result of the efforts of the organization, which was effected under his patronage, cannot be estimated. They are indeed inestimable, and are of constantly increasing value. Mr. Cornell was extensively interested in the manufacture of agricultural implements at Albany, and was also the patron, promoter, and proprietor of a variety of meritorious enterprises, not only in the State of New York, but likewise in Ohio, Michigan, Wisconsin, Kansas, Colorado, and other States.

CHAPTER XX.

HABITUALLY reserved in manner, with a prevalent appearance of mental preoccupation, having
but slight inclination to the usual modes of recreation, there was little in the ordinary intercourse of
Mr. Cornell to denote the depth of earnest affection with which he was in a large degree endowed.
While remarkably exempt from impulsive or emo-
tional tendencies, he was peculiarly devoted in
attachment to his kindred. Despite a quiet and
undemonstrative nature, there was in his organization a development of filial and fraternal love
which was apparently inexhaustible. This admirable trait of his character grew stronger and
became more marked with advancing years, and
was altogether a charming feature of his life. The

uniformly cheerful obedience of his youth, and the respectful and affectionate bearing of his subsequent years, were frequently the subjects of grateful commendation on the part of his venerable parents ; while his tender solicitude for their welfare and his delicate attention to the comfort of their declining age were characteristic of him and most interesting to observe.

Ambitious of securing for himself an independent and self-reliant maintenance, while yet but eighteen years of age, Mr. Cornell voluntarily departed from the paternal roof in quest of employment. Successful in his purpose of self-support, he thenceforth returned to the family home only in the capacity of an occasional, but ever welcome, visitor. At the period of his leaving the home of his youth, his parents were just in the mature prime of life, surrounded by a bevy of young children ; but as the years rolled by in constant succession, one child after another reached the age of independence and sallied forth into the great world, each thus leaving a vacant chair at the family board. Occasionally returning in deference to the promptings of filial devotion, he could not fail to be impressed with the advancing age of the parents, and the depleted household, continually increasing in loneliness with the departure of each succeeding child. Though this touching

feature of domestic life is but the repetition of ordinary family experience, it cannot fail to revive
tender memories in the hearts of all, who observe
and reflect upon the changes which are constantly
attending us here.

Animated by an intense desire to render more
cheerful the lonely pathway of his aged parents,
and to make good so far as possible his own
departure from the family circle, Mr. Cornell
appealed to them to change their location to the
vicinity of his home. Conforming to his solicitation, the family in 1841 abandoned their residence
in De Ruyter, and accepted a home at Ithaca
provided for them by their eldest son in his own
immediate neighborhood. Several of their other
children had also previously established themselves at Ithaca and in that vicinity, so that at the
time of their removal, it was a most eligible and
convenient situation for them on this account.
Here they continued to reside, for a period of
about fifteen years, in the calm enjoyment of
serene old age, surrounded by the children of
their love, from whom they received the most
tender and respectful attention. Their greatest
privation, and one which they greatly missed and
regretted, was their church association, from
which they were so distantly separated.

During much of the time of the residence of

his parents at Ithaca, Mr. Cornell was necessarily
away from home in the pursuit of his telegraph
engagements, but when thus absent, he was a
faithful correspondent, and always upon his return
home, he took early and frequent occasion to pay
respectful devotion to them, and evinced in many
ways the depth of his abiding affection for them.
The final location of several of their daughters
near together in the State of Michigan, naturally
created a desire on the part of the parents to reside near them. Though reluctant to have them
leave his neighborhood, he recognized the rea-
sonableness of their wish to be near his sisters ;
he personally attended them on their journey, and
arranged for their comfortable establishment in
their new home. His mother, however, did not
long survive this change of residence, as she was
suddenly called to her final rest in the spring of
1857, at the age of seventy. This bereavement
was sadly distressing to Mr. Cornell, whose affection for his mother was entwined in every fibre of
his nature. Notwithstanding his apparently composed demeanor, those familiar with him could not
fail to observe the intense suffering which this
irreparable affliction caused him. Mr. Cornell's
father subsequently returned to Ithaca, and spent
a considerable time as a member of his family,
but finally returned to Michigan, where he was

domiciled with one of his daughters. Here his long life was brought to a tranquil ending from the effects of old age, having attained the remarkable measure of ninety-one years.

If the evidences of Mr. Cornell's sincere and devoted affection for his parents were unusual, and the subject of particular observation, his fraternal relations were none the less so. Through all of his life his bearing toward his brothers and sisters partook much of the peculiarities noted with reference to his parental devotion, ever seeking when opportunity offered to render them some useful or valuable service. When separated from them by distant residence, he was assiduous in the duty of correspondence, and whenever chance brought him within the vicinity of their residences he was accustomed to visit them. Each and every one of his brothers and sisters, was in some form, to greater or less extent, as circumstances and necessities dictated, the recipients of his favor, and realized in some measure the benefits of his material prosperity.

In the relation of husband Mr. Cornell was in all respects worthy of the highest commendation. Faithful in observing the duties imposed by wedded vows, respectfully considerate of the feelings and wishes of his life partner, tenderly devoted to her in affection, patient and forbearing under

all circumstances, abstemious in habits, circum-
spect in conduct and unimpeachable in all the
ways of life, his married life was one continual
source of satisfaction.   Assuming the responsibilities of matrimony at the age of twenty-four,
though in extremely modest financial circumstances, he was enabled to provide a home which
was the abode of happiness, refinement, and contentment; in which his nine children were born,
and from which four of them were buried.   Ten
years of domestic tranquillity were marked by the
loss of accustomed employment, incident to the
change of the business in which he had been engaged.   Failing to secure occupation near home,
he was forced to seek it abroad.   Circumstances,
elsewhere related in detail, connected him with
the development of the electric telegraph, and in
the prosecution of this business he was for a dozen
years necessarily much absent from home.   The
entire discipline of the children was thus left to
the judicious discretion of their mother, who performed her duty with painstaking fidelity.   He
was an industrious and prolific correspondent, and
the home which was so much of the time lonely
because of his absence, was brightened by the
arrival of frequent and always interesting letters,
which were sure to break the tedium of each
week.

In the later years of Mr. Cornell's telegraph service, when the children required less exacting attention from their mother, she frequently accompanied him on his journeys, especially at such times as he would be likely to remain long in any particular neighborhood. As they advanced in years, and home cares were still more relaxed, they travelled much together, and it was his delight always to be accompanied by her, as if to make amends for the years of absence which the exigencies of business requirements had rendered necessary. Thus they journeyed together to Europe, and in many trips undertaken for pleasure through the Canadian provinces, and the eastern and southern as well as many of the far western States. In all of his legislative career Mrs. Cornell was his constant companion, and for the last two years in the Senate, they maintained an independent household in Albany; and they were the recipients of many social attentions from the leading families of the capital city.

In personal intercourse with his children Mr. Cornell was affectionate and considerate, and in return was loved and respected by them in more than an ordinary degree. If he was firm in enforcing his authority in opposition to the desires of a child, it was in such manner as to avoid any appearance of harshness. He was especially ambitious for the thorough education of his children, in which he was to a considerable degree disappointed, more especially with his sons. This was owing, probably, to the fact that his absence from home so much of the time, during the years of their school attendance, prevented the necessary control of their movements in this regard. While their mother exerted every possible effort to keep them in school, and their minds absorbed in study, the establishment in Ithaca of a telegraph office proved too great an attraction for the older son, who at the age of fourteen had acquired the art of telegraphy without the knowledge of his parents. Between the attractions of a telegraph office and those of an academy for a boy at the witching age of fourteen, it may be safely calculated that the former will carry the palm three times out of four, and thus it was in this case. This defection of the older son from school life proved demoralizing upon the younger brothers, and although they were kept in school as long as possible, the second son completed only a portion of his academical education, while the younger one finished his preparatory studies, and devoted two years to a University course. With the daughters there were no such counter-attractions, and they more kindly followed and availed themselves of the educational facilities which were placed at their disposal, having both been educated at the Vassar Female College.

In both the projection and development of his plans for the establishment, first of the Cornell Library, and afterward of the Cornell University, Mr. 'Cornell had in every particular the cordial co-operation of his wife and children. They realized that his great fortune had come to him as the result of his own exertions and privations, and they did not desire to interfere with such disposition of it as should best gratify him. No word of objection or disapproval was ever expressed by the members of his family in reference to any of the schemes of benefaction which he entered into. They saw him dispersing with lavish hand the princely inheritance which, but for his philanthropic plans, might have enriched them; but they uttered no complaint nor gave expression to feelings of dissatisfaction.

In the several relations of domestic life, it cannot be denied that Mr. Cornell was in many respects a person of marked and impressive individuality. Far beyond the commonalty of men, he was a loving, dutiful son, considerate of the pleasure of his parents, the pride and hope of their earlier years, the prudent counsellor of middle life, and the ever faithful comforter of their declining age. To all of his numerous brothers and sisters he was ever the cheering, helpful, and generous brother, always quite willing to aid in promoting their interests, and not infrequently at the expense of his own. As a husband, he was affectionate, considerate, and faithful, with a strict and delicate sense of the obligations which the marriage vows imposed on him; while in the parental relation he was always impartial, requiring obedience as necessary to wholesome discipline, and animated with commendable ambition that his children might attain by good conduct respected standing in community.

Tender and devoted as was his affection for those with whom he was connected by the nearer ties of kinship, it by no means limited the interest of Mr. Cornell in the more distant lines of consanguinity. With him persons of any degree of blood relationship were certain to find cordial welcome. He was greatly interested and devoted much personal effort to the investigation and perfection of his genealogical record. For many years, and amid other laborious occupations of absorbing interest, he conducted a voluminous correspondence for the purpose of extending and completing this work. Especially was he interested in the name of CORNELL, and he spared no reasonable effort to trace out and identify the pedigree of each person bearing it, to determine whether any direct relationship could be established, however distant in degree. Genealogical investigation was a work which possessed peculiar attraction for him, and increased in interest as the weight of years rested upon him. He had accumulated a vast mass of information bearing on this subject, which, owing to the engrossing labors of his later years, was left by him in an unfinished condition. It is, therefore, to be hoped that some of his descendants may in the future feel disposed to take up and complete this work which so greatly interested him.

With all of his affectionate regard for his family relatives, Mr. Cornell always had a warm place in his heart for the old friends and neighbors of his family whom he had known in early years. Whenever opportunity permitted, he took great delight in visiting the localities where his parents had formerly resided, and looking up the old friends with whom they had been familiar. Neither age nor condition in life was a bar to his interest in their welfare and prosperity, and if it so happened that fortune had changed to their prejudice, they had no cause to regret the continued acquaintance of the son of their old friends; while it sometimes happened that circumstances permitted him to do something to smooth the path of those who had fallen into distress. So, too, the friends of his own humble early life were never changed in his regard, by the great prosperity which came to him. Once a friend always a friend was his rule, unless sundered by some unworthy act.

Necessary absence from home a considerable portion of the time for several years, in the projection and management of his telegraph interests, naturally made Mr. Cornell appreciate all the more, when permitted to enjoy, the comforts and pleasures of home. It was no cause of surprise, therefore, that with his exceptional prosperity came the ambition to build a dwelling which should be an ornament to the locality. Having procured the necessary plans, he began, in 1868, the erection of a tasteful and elegant gothic villa of stone, which was designed as a permanent residence for his family. Several expert carvers in stone were imported directly from Europe, and employed on the work. "TRUE AND FIRM,"— the motto which surmounts the principal entrance —is indeed characteristic of the building in all of its details. The elaborate design of architecture and the elegance of the interior finish, necessarily made the process of construction extremely slow. Nearly eight years were consumed in building the house, which was not entirely finished until about a year after the death of its projector.

This unique and beautiful edifice, which is the admiration of all who have the opportunity of viewing it, has been, since the spring of 1876, the home of Mrs. Cornell, with whom her two daughters have resided. There are certainly but few residences in the State, outside of the great metropolis, which can compare with " Villa Cornell" in beauty of design or perfection of workmanship. The house, completed and ready for occupancy, cost about one hundred thousand dollars, exclusive of the value of the plot of nine acres on which it is located. The place is charmingly situated on the eastern bluff, overlooking the village of Ithaca and the ever beautiful Cayuga Lake. It commands an extended and superb view of the surrounding country, which, from this particular spot, presents a diversity of scenery rarely observed. Just out of the village, and yet within a short walk of the business centre, it is thus sufficiently retired to avoid the dust and noise of the town, and still within convenient distance of all of its variety of privileges. A little farther up the hill and within half a mile, is the Campus of the University, with its grand collection of buildings, always a favorite and accessible resort for recreation or diversion.

CHAPTER XXI.

HOWEVER faithful or impartial the effort, intelligent and appreciative delineation of the personal
characteristics and peculiarities of an individual is
not an easy performance under any circumstances.
When such an undertaking relates to a person
endowed with numerous phases of character unusual, and in many respects extraordinary in
their qualities when compared with those of ordinary development, the difficulty of the task is
materially enhanced. To render justice to the
character under consideration, and present a review acceptable without reserve to those unacquainted with his striking individuality, seem
quite impossible. In a variety of ways, the per-

sonality of Mr. Cornell embraced features of remarkable vigor and the peculiarities of his character in many particulars illustrated his Quaker
origin. From his parents he inherited a combination of characteristics which were especially
marked and easy of recognition by those familiar
with him, prominent among which were frankness,
truth, and sincerity. These qualities with him
were cardinal virtues, and just in proportion as
he valued them, did he despise hypocrisy, pretence, and deception.

Eminently self-contained and exempt from emotion, there was yet in Mr. Cornell's organization
an element of nervous energy which demanded
constant occupation as a requisite for the enjoyment of personal comfort. He was never so un-
happy as when, by circumstances beyond control,
he was the victim of enforced idleness. With him
it could be truthfully said, industry knew no limit.
Work, either mental or physical, was his normal
condition. Strong and vigorous in muscular development, manual labor was to him a source of
positive enjoyment. This was particularly demonstrated by his fondness for walking, which was
ever with him a favorite mode of travel. In this
manner he performed a journey of fifteen hundred
miles, in 1842, through the Southern Atlantic
States, often making forty miles per day. He

frequently described this experience as one of the most interesting episodes in his varied career. When physical activity was not available for him, mental labor was its fixed alternative. Reading, writing, study, and investigation fully occupied his waking hours which were not devoted to other activities. He was a prolific letter writer, and occupied much leisure time in the conduct of a large personal correspondence. In foreign travel he was accustomed, for want of other occupation, to write letters for publication to the Ithaca papers, descriptive of the scenes and incidents of his journeyings.

Perseverance is a valuable quality just in the degree that it is directed by intelligent judgment and wise discretion. Without proper safeguards this commendable qualification may, indeed, become an engine of waste and destruction. With the subject of present consideration, probably no single personal characteristic proved so advantageous as that of persistence, or determination. The great business success achieved by Mr. Cornell was due, not only to the correct judgment which directed his original venture, but in far greater degree to the sturdiness and steadfast energy with which he pursued his chosen purpose, and forced a successful issue through manifold and long-continued embarrassments.

Nothing could better illustrate the unyielding firmness of his character than the patient and unfaltering determination with which he sustained himself in his various telegraph enterprises in the face of impediments which to others seemed absolutely insurmountable. Once he decided upon a line of policy to be pursued, obstacles which would completely discourage ordinary men were brushed aside by him as the merest incidents, while he followed the object of his judgment with all of the untiring vigor of his mental and physical organization. Thus, faith which was unwavering, and energy which never faltered, were finally rewarded by success almost beyond the possibility of belief.

Ability to await with patience the available opportunity when a desired object may be most advantageously accomplished, is a gift with which few are favored. While persistent energy will often achieve great results, it not unfrequently happens that the capacity for " making haste slowly " is a quality of the highest rank. Far beyond the ordinary range of men Mr. Cornell was endowed with patience, which was a direct inheritance from his mother, in whom this beautiful trait was especially developed. With her patience was a virtue which adorned and illumined with its gentle influence an amiable and lovely character, while with him, in the sterner walks of life, it was the strong lever with which he was frequently enabled to successfully remove obstacles which could not be overcome by the use of positive force. He was possessed of this extremely valuable qualification in an eminent degree, and it was an exceedingly potent factor in his mental equipment. This rare gift, often controlling with wise intuition the forcible energies of his nature, was the true secret of much of his exceptional success in life.

The predominant, and especially characteristic features of Mr. Cornell's mental endowment consisted of vigorous and original practical intelligence, acuteness of perception, resolute self-reliance, calm and even temperament, independent judgment, and positive convictions. With a superior mind, endowed in marked degree with sound common sense, supplemented by habits of careful observation and reflection, he was remarkable for the maturity and accuracy of his judgment on questions of practical utility. Despite the meagre facilities for education which he was permitted to enjoy in early life, few persons were better informed on all general subjects than he was. His studious habits, and peculiar faculty for improvement, enabled him to acquire a degree of cultivation which made him in the maturity of his manhood the welcome associate of the most distinguished scholars in the country. The extent and diversity of his mental acquirements were often the subject of surprise and admiration to those aware of his limited advantages in early life. Doubtless the broad and liberal culture which he thus acquired, exerted potent influence in giving his public benefactions the useful direction which so greatly distinguished them.

The originality and independence of Mr. Cornell's nature rendered him peculiarly adventurous and enterprising in disposition. He was wholly fearless in any venture which secured his confidence or enlisted his sympathies, and the imminence of danger only served to arouse his courage and engage his energies. With a peculiar modesty and gentleness of disposition, he was slow to controversy, but stern and unyielding in a contest forced upon him, especially where the issue involved the defence of unquestioned rights or the maintenance of vital principles. His integrity was unimpeachable, and was never brought in question except through the mouths of vile and wicked slanderers, who hoped by the utterance of falsehood to injure him and diminish his ability to serve the great cause in which he was so thoroughly enlisted, and to which he contributed so much of material aid and valuable personal service. In fidelity he was true as the needle to the pole, to whatever cause he was committed. If the object was worthy of real and earnest support, no divided or half-hearted allegiance satisfied him. With him whatever was worth doing at all was worthy of all requisite effort for its complete success.

Perfect manhood depends not so much on the abnormal illustration of some particular talent, however admirable in itself, as upon the harmonious development of the more important traits of ordinary personal character. Genius, which may command the admiration of the world, is not infrequently marred by combination with inexcusable defects. Considering all features of Mr. Cornell's especial individuality, as recognized by those familiar with the details of his career, the general verdict of impartial observers could not fail to credit him with marked superiority in the complete development of the qualities which adorn human character. Without pretence to any especially attractive or brilliant talent, with no attributes of genius, he was eminently practical in natural ability and acquired attainments. Untiring devotion to useful pursuits, guided by superior intelligence and perfect integrity, enabled him to achieve great results in business enterprises, and in the splendid munificence of his public benefactions.

There was a natural dignity, and manliness of bearing, which, in any presence, could not fail to identify Mr. Cornell as an individual of superior instincts and exceptional personality. Standing about six feet in height in the maturity of physical development, he acquired in later years a habit of stooping forward—more commonly described as round-shouldered—which detracted somewhat from the commanding appearance of his earlier life. His ordinary weight was about one hundred and eighty pounds. His features were rugged and strongly marked with prominent cheek-bones. When in repose there was an apparent hardness of expression, which quickly melted into a winning and attractive smile upon a friendly approach. Though habitually reticent in speech and ordinarily reserved in manner, he was of a peculiarly cheerful disposition, and when engaged in social discourse was a most agreeable and instructive companion. In conversation which interested him he was animated, while, as a friendly disputant in the discussion of a definite subject, he was accustomed to maintain an argument with fervor and effectiveness. Temperate in his usual habit, almost to total abstinence, moderation and sobriety were the inflexible rules of his life. His tastes were simple, and his personal expenses inconsiderable. Economical in useless expenditures, his generous liberality found expression in what he considered ways of practical usefulness.

Naturally unassuming in manner and personal bearing, with a friendly but undemonstrative cordiality which was especially characteristic of his Quaker descent, there was a quiet self-possessed dignity in Mr. Cornell's ordinary demeanor, which was well calculated to put strangers quite at ease in approaching him. The modest, unaffected simplicity of character which was particularly noticeable in him, continued without change through all of the evolutions and vicissitudes of his extraordinary career. The unpretending, laborious mechanic, striving to establish himself in a new community, was the same self-possessed and unostentatious individual, as the opulent millionaire, whose munificent liberality had rendered his name familiar to the entire civilized world. The generous patron of higher education, laboring to develop and render available the inherent value of the Land Grant, was the same earnest, hard working man, as the enterprising telegraph pioneer devoting all of the energies of his vigorous personality to the pursuit of successful fortune. Neither prosperity, nor the exacting cares of advancing years, effected any visible change in the cordiality with which he was accustomed to meet the humble associates of early life.

Pertinent and very convincing evidence of the impression made upon the students of the University by the simple, unpretending appearance of the honored Founder, was recently given by an intelligent and observing member of an early class, who has since achieved enviable distinction in one of the chief cities of the State. The occasion of his remarks was the annual social gathering of an alumni association, when reminiscences of college life were the subject of comment. Speaking of the crude condition and unfinished appearance of the University establishment in its early years, and the disposition of many students to find fault therewith, he said, " Nothing quieted the discontent so effectively as the earnest and devoted labors of Mr. Cornell in striving to push the unfinished buildings and grounds to completion, and to remove every just cause of complaint. Many of us had never seen a millionaire before, and when we saw him in modest garb, giving attention to our comfort and contentment with the simplicity of an ordinary man, we were filled with amazement." He also attributed much of the spirit and success of the early graduates of the University to the wholesome influence of this very impressive example.

The very magnitude of his public contributions tends to obscure, and by comparison to dwarf, the

18

private benefactions which Mr. Cornell was constantly bestowing in response to innumerable appeals to his unfailing generosity. The story of misfortune was sure to find a sympathetic listener in him, and to secure prompt and practical assistance at his hands. He delighted especially in helping those who were striving to help themselves, and a long list could be given of those whose success in life was due to his kindly patronage and encouragement. Nor would the list be complete, without embracing the names of several individuals, who have become millionaires from the initiatory aid rendered them by Mr. Cornell. The poor boy ambitious of acquiring a liberal education, but without means to gratify his worthy aspiration, never appealed to him in vain. As a general rule, this class of beneficiaries rewarded their patron and his memory with grateful appreciation of his timely assistance. Due regard for the truth of history, however, compels the statement, discreditable as it must appear to every instinct of manhood, that this result did not in every instance follow his generous patronage. A single exception, however, perfidious though it may seem, is perhaps valuable in demonstrating the general uniformity of the prevailing appreciation.

In the usual intercourse of every-day life, Mr. Cornell was reserved in expression far beyond the ordinary range of individuals. This was caused by neither austerity nor the lack of a genial disposition, but was the result of his peculiar organization. He was more of a thinker than a talker. Naturally a man of few words, as he matured in years this tendency was increased in consequence of his habitual mental occupation. While this was his custom in reference to matters of worldly interest, it was still more so in regard to spiritual affairs. This habitual reticence cannot, however, be interpreted as an evidence of his indifference as to religious questions. On the contrary, there were many indications that he was a person of more than ordinary religious feeling. Though these were incidental in character, they were sufficient to demonstrate beyond question the nature of the impulses which prompted them. He was frequently accustomed to quote in reverent manner, expressions from the Great Book of Life, which indicated much familiarity with its contents. To him the word of God was indeed a higher law, which he believed, if faithfully accepted and relied upon, would shield the humble follower of the cross from all harm. "Do unto others as ye would that they do unto you," was with him a favorite maxim, and observed with great fidelity.

Although there is probably no existing means of demonstrating the fact, there can be little if any reasonable doubt, that the action of the Friends' Society at De Ruyter, in expelling Mr. Cornell from membership therein as a penalty for marrying out of the Church, exerted a continued influence over him through all of his subsequent life. His distant residence, away from any society of Friends, rendered it impossible for him to contest the action of those who undertook to administer the discipline. He vigorously disputed their right to take such action, but there was no earthly tribunal available to take jurisdiction of his appeal. His only practical remedy was in direct, silent communion with his Heavenly Father, and this mode of worship was ever after the form which he observed. He held himself aloof from connection with other churches, as an evidence of his faithfulness to the form of worship from which he felt that he had been unjustly and wrongfully excluded. He refused to recognize the right of any church organization to place themselves between him and the Divine Master, and attempt to exclude him from the right of worship. Beyond this he felt that the condition attached to his expulsion, of reinstatement upon his rendering an apology and expressing regret for his action, was wholly inconsistent, to comply with which would be to dishonor himself. He, therefore, firmly and persistently refused.

CHAPTER XXII.

LAST ILLNESS.

Vigorous Constitution.—General Good Health.—Promised Lon-
gevity.—Fatal Exposure.—Sudden Attack of Pneumonia.—
Extreme Prostration.—-Languishing Weakness.—Financial
Burdens.—Physicians plead for Exemption from Business
Cares.—Attempted Relief.—Menaced by Rigorous Weather.
—Relapse.—Final Rest.

WITH the inheritance of a superb constitution,
developed by vigorous, industrious habits, and
sustained by temperate practices, it was as a
general rule Mr. Cornell's good fortune, through
all of his life, to be favored with more than an ordinary degree of health and strength.   Though in
a few instances subjected to brief illness, his recovery was always prompt and complete.   His father
lived to the good old age of more than ninety years,
in the enjoyment of excellent health, and blessed
by a kind Providence with the possession of un-
impaired faculties.   With this remarkable longev-
ity as the basis of expectation, it was not strange
that the friends of Mr. Cornell fondly hoped for
the continuance of his useful, philanthropic life

through many years of gently declining maturity, that he might be permitted with them to enjoy the development of the great work of higher education which his generous beneficence had done so much to establish and endow. This cherished hope, however, was destined to suffer cruel disappointment, for while still in the enjoyment of apparent good health, and considerably within the limit of three score and ten, he was suddenly stricken with disease, which, after a languishing sickness of six months' duration, closed his earthly career, and plunged an entire community into the depths of mourning.

The fatal illness sounded its first dreaded note of alarm on the ninth day of June, 1874. On that day, Mr. Cornell was prostrated by an attack of pneumonia, of such severity as to confine him to the bed. The disease was supposed to have been the result of a severe cold, contracted by his unconscious exposure, while sleeping without adequate protection, to an extraordinary change of temperature, which occurred during the night, in travelling by the Erie Railway from New York to Elmira. Before the dangerous character of the disease had made itself clearly apparent, it had made serious progress in its course, and had become thoroughly seated on the lungs. From the very beginning, the skill of his medical attendants was completely baffled, and their efforts to check the ravages of the malady were quite ineffectual.

The patient was extremely debilitated, and unable to leave his bed for several weeks. Slowly the weeks succeeded each other, and lengthened into months, and still the tiresome cough continued, and the prostrating weakness remained, to hold him a helpless prisoner within the house. Finally, as the summer waned, a slightly improved condition enabled him to visit New York and the sea shore, with the hope that a change of air and surroundings might prove beneficial. This, however, turned out to be delusive, as no material improvement was manifested in the appearance of his symptoms, and he returned to his home at Ithaca, after an absence of several weeks, in much the same state of debility as before. If there was any improvement, it was so slight as not to be apparent to the kind friends who so fondly watched and prayed for his recovery.

Earnestly, but in vain, did the medical attendants demand the seclusion of their patient from the pressing anxieties of business. This they declared to be indispensable to recovery, and that without this precaution their efforts in his behalf must prove futile. Such a course seemed, however, quite impossible in consequence of the peculiar circumstances which surrounded him. While he was relieved from every possible annoyance, there were certain details of business which could only be solved by Mr. Cornell's personal consideration and direction. Even the attempt to keep the less important matters from his attention, failed in great measure to accomplish the desired result, as it was inevitably known to him that many interests were suffering for his personal supervision, and thus the exciting cause of apprehension was ever present, and weighing on his mind. As the autumn was approaching, it became more than ever manifest that he could not safely encounter the rigors of the coming winter, and much consideration was given to the practicability of his seeking a more genial climate for the winter months. The emergencies of his business affairs, however, forbade his absence from the vicinity of his home, and hence the plan was reluctantly abandoned.

Never before, perhaps, in the course of his entire career, had there been a period when ability to devote personal attention to business affairs had been so necessary, and, indeed, so vital to Mr. Cornell's material interests, as at the particular time of his sudden prostration. A peculiar combination of circumstances seemed to designate it as the crisis of his notable career. The self-assumed burdens of the land grant contract, and the uncompleted railroads, were bearing their cruel weights upon him, and he had need of every facility and every faculty at his command. Confronted by financial complications of great magnitude, at a period of serious monetary derangement, the successful solution of his plans of operation, depended, of course, largely on the stability of his personal credit, already so seriously disturbed. It can, therefore, easily be appreciated how extremely embarrassing must have been a severe and long-continued illness under such circumstances. There can be no reasonable doubt that the peculiar situation in which he was then placed, contributed greatly to aggravate the malady under which he was suffering, and to prevent the recovery of strength which might otherwise have been restored to him. The unavoidable mental depression incident to an occasion of such perilous anxiety, could not fail to produce that result.

Continued weakness and inability to resume active personal attention to business, rendered imperative the necessity of relief from every burden which could possibly be avoided. Yielding to this necessity, Mr. Cornell was finally, but reluctantly, induced to request the trustees of the University to assume the independent management of the business under the land grant contract, and thus relieve him from this great responsibility.

This proposition was promptly and very commendably accepted by the board, and, upon the approval of the Commissioners of the Land Office of the State, the contract, together with all of the business incident to it, was formally transferred to the custody of the University authorities, in the month of November. A contract was also concluded about the same time, under which other parties undertook to make arrangements for the necessary funds for finishing the Utica, Ithaca, & Elmira road, and connecting its hitherto separate sections ready for complete operation, thus relieving Mr. Cornell from the necessity of making further provision for this great work. Although these arrangements were highly important in the extent of relief which was thus afforded in a financial direction, he was still left with the care of the Geneva road, which yet required a large investment to complete its adequate equipment, and to successfully place it on a prosperous, self-sustaining basis.

Despite the extraordinary business embarrassments, incident to the wearisome months of confinement, there was throughout the entire course of his prolonged, painful illness, an exhibition of patient fortitude and Christian resignation on the part of Mr. Cornell, which was indeed marvellous. Calmly relying on the mercy of his Divine Master, he could await upon His appointed time with perfect repose and hopeful confidence. No word of complaint nor repining was heard to escape his lips during all of the tiresome period of his prostration. Devoutly anxious for recovery, that he might be permitted to complete the labors which interested him so deeply, there was in the composition of his character, an indescribable element of self-control, which enabled him to exercise patient forbearance even in the face of the most depressing discouragement. Familiar to an unusual degree with the conflicts of life, nothing in all his past experience compared in magnitude with these later tribulations.

True to the warnings of his physicians, the approach of winter weather proved too severe for the weakened system of the now confirmed invalid. The painful cough, from which he had never been relieved, increased in its severity, and the general symptoms became more alarming. The years of labor which Mr. Cornell had so generously devoted to the interests of the University and of Ithaca, had exhausted too much of the vitality of his naturally robust constitution, and the powers of recuperation seemed wholly wanting. Relief from a portion of business cares had come too late to be of any practical benefit in the prolongation of his life. A slight cold, resulting from exposure at one of the meetings of the University trustees, aggravated the disease under which he was suffering; his cough increased, and his strength gradually wasted, until, on the ninth day of December, 1874, he was called to his final rest, just six months from the commencement of his illness. To the very end of his life did the wonderful energy of his nature manifest itself. On the last morning, with scarcely strength to stand, he arose from his bed and was dressed, against the protestations of his wife. He had in mind some affairs of business, to which he desired to give attention, and was thus occupied during a portion of the morning. Overcome by weakness, however, he was forced to seek his couch without having fully completed his work, and the final end was reached shortly after noon. He was at the time of his death sixty-seven years, ten months, and twenty-eight days of age, thus lacking more than twenty-two years of reaching the age attained by his father.

Thus, in the shadow of sore trials, and bitter disappointments, closed the life of the generous-hearted and enlightened philanthropist. Would that his useful and laborious career could have been ended, rather, in the mellow twilight of endeavors accomplished and conflicts ended. With what supreme satisfaction he could have watched the gradual but constant advancement of the University, toward that high standard which he had so confidently fixed in his mind as its ultimate achievement. Commencing life without the aid of advantageous circumstances, with only such moderate opportunities for early cultivation as were available to the son of a pioneer farmer, unaided and alone, Mr. Cornell, conquering adverse influences and conditions, achieved great fortune as the recompense of intelligent, praiseworthy enterprise. Without ostentation, or pretentious display, he devoted with unexampled liberality the abundant fruits of his eminent success to the intellectual advancement of the coming generations of mankind, with the modest spirit and grand purpose of a true-hearted public benefactor. The death of such a character, under any circumstances, could not fail to create an impressive sensation. Under the extremely painful conditions which attended the later months of Mr. Cornell's life, there was much to arouse public interest and enlist the earnest sympathies not only of friends and neighbors, but as well of the entire community.

Though by no means an unexpected occurrence, on account of the wide publicity which had attended his prolonged illness, the announcement of Mr. Cornell's lamented death was received with painful emotions and many striking manifestations of grief, not only by the community which claimed him as its especial possession, but as well by a wide circle of sympathizing friends throughout the State, and, indeed, in many portions of the country at large.

This melancholy event was the occasion of much sorrowful comment and unusual observation at Ithaca, as well as in many other places in the State. Expressions of sympathy and testimonials of affectionate attachment were tendered from every quarter. Formal tributes of respectful consideration and appreciation were adopted by many organizations with which the departed had been associated in his life-time, and others with which he had no direct connection. As an appropriate conclusion of this simple record of the devoted labors of this unselfish public benefactor, the final chapters will be reserved for the presentation of some of the many public tributes, and a somewhat detailed account of the funeral observances in honor of his memory.

CHAPTER XXIII.

PUBLIC TRIBUTES.

General Sympathy.—Ithaca "Daily Journal."—Froude's Tribute.—Formal Expressions.—Cornell University.—Cornell Library.—Western Union Telegraph Company.—Village Trustees.—Students.—Ithaca Savings Bank.—Board of Education.—Geneva, Ithaca & Athens Railroad.—Agricultural Society.—Presbyterian Church.—Proclamation of Village President.—Founder's Hymn.

CONSTANTLY advancing in their daily progress toward the eternal world, men become accustomed to the occurrence of death, and only the departure of one held in extraordinary public estimation, will cause an entire community to abandon their ordinary avocations, and stand by an open grave. Beyond any precedent in the history of Ithaca, the death of Mr. Cornell aroused a feeling of sympathy, and brought forth an expression of the sense of public loss which had been sustained. To recall, with the full force of contemporaneous observation, the depth of public feeling which was induced by the sad event, the following expressions and reports of formal proceedings taken in honor of his memory, are reproduced from the columns of the *Ithaca Daily Journal*, of the several dates indicated :

DEATH OF EZRA CORNELL.

[From the Ithaca Daily Journal, December 9th.]

Ezra Cornell is gone. His death occurred at twenty-five minutes past one o'clock this afternoon, after an illness of six months' duration, at the age of sixty-seven years, ten months, and twenty-eight days.

We can hardly realize the magnitude of the loss, not merely to his family, but to this whole community. No citizen has ever left us whose life was so interwoven with all that has created and assured our prosperity.

A generous, large-hearted man ; utterly unselfish in every respect ; ready to make almost any sacrifice to attain some great and general good ; resolute in what he believed to be right and just ; but yielding and sympathetic to every story of misfortune, and to the sufferings and troubles of others ; far-seeing and sagacious, but also hopeful and enthusiastic in the pursuit of noble ends ; he has left behind him a name worthy to be remembered, and, especially, by the citizens of this village, for whose welfare and prosperity he planned so skilfully and labored with so much unflagging energy.

He has built his own monument upon our hills. The great bell of the University he founded is tolling heavily and solemnly as we write. Every heart in our midst feels the bereavement almost as a personal loss. We can write no more to-day. When the sense of grief and sorrow has lost some of its first severity, we hope to do better justice to the memory of Ezra Cornell.

EZRA CORNELL IS DEAD.

[From the Ithaca Daily Journal, December 10th.]

It is difficult to comprehend the full import of these cruel words. The poignancy of the first grief at a great, an irreparable loss, has something of the numbing effect upon the senses of a violent shock to the physical frame. We are at such times stunned and bewildered, and find it almost impossible to realize the fact, much less the extent, of our bereavement. Such is our condition to-day. We know that the emblems of woe on every hand—the tolling bells, the sombre drapings of the whole town, the flags at half mast ; and more than all these, the sorrow-stricken countenances and the subdued voices and manners of his neighbors, attest the painful fact. And yet we cannot realize it. We cannot think of Ithaca without Ezra Cornell ; cannot conceive how one is to go on without the other. They seemed to be at least as closely con- nected as a wise and prudent father and his family. We often see cases in domestic life where a noble and sagacious father seems to be in reality the head of the family—the superior member, to whom all the other members look for advice and guidance, upon whom all depend for support. How frequently we say of such a family : " I don't know what Mr. Blank's family would do if he were to be taken away." Such were, more nearly than any other simile which occurs to us, the relations of Ezra Cornell to Ithaca. In the very few public or private movements, within the past twenty- five years, for the advancement of our interests as a community— pecuniary, moral, social, or educational—which Mr. Cornell did not originate, the first question asked of the projectors was, " Have you seen Ezra Cornell? He will take hold of the work ; and if he is for you, no one will be against you, and success is assured, if success be possible." We do not now speak of his greatest work— the founding of the great University which bears his name. For this he is known and will be lamented by all men wherever noble and generous deeds are held in grateful memory. But *we* mourn, chiefly, Ezra Cornell the MAN. We knew him intimately ; and we know that a more lovable character has seldom appeared among men. He was truly one of Nature's noblemen. His be- nevolence was proverbial, though he judiciously and unostenta- tiously bestowed ; it was peculiarly true of him, if it ever were of any man, that in his good deeds the left hand knew not what the right hand did. His strict probity was another salient point in his character—no man ever held in more utter detestation everything

19

that was mean or dishonorable. And yet, his large, magnanimous heart had no room for malice. No jealousies or rankling hatreds ever clouded his judgment. The unjust and intemperate criticisms of his public or private acts by ill-informed or envious critics; the malignant misrepresentations and assaults of the enemies of his pet scheme—a University " where any person can find instruction in any study "—must have often tortured this patient, tireless worker; but they never wrung from him a bitter word, nor do we believe they aroused any lasting resentment.

The writer of this recalls an instance which came under his own observation, well illustrating this peculiarly rare and admirable trait of character. It chanced that he was coming from New York City in company with Mr. Cornell on the day on which a violent and venomous speech had been made in the Legislature, in which it was charged, in effect, that Mr. Cornell was a scheming speculator in the guise of a generous benefactor. Neither Mr. Cornell nor the writer had heard of this speech. Arriving at Owego at an early hour the following morning, where both had to remain some time awaiting the train for Ithaca, both repaired to a neighboring hotel to pass the intervening time. Here a copy of the *Elmira Advertiser* of that morning, containing a telegraphic report of the speech, was handed us. After glancing over the startling headlines, and the points of the bitter attack which followed, we handed the paper to Mr. Cornell, with the remark: " They have been cutting you up badly down at Albany, I see ; " and then curiously watched his countenance while he carefully perused the whole article. No trace of excitement or unwonted emotion was visible there. After its perusal he remained in a reverie for a moment, when he said, quietly : " Well, time, that sets all things right, will demonstrate the falsity of these charges; I can wait." No excitement, not the faintest tinge of resentment in his manner or in the tones of his voice. That was the manner of man he was, in that view of his character. " True and firm " was his motto ; and never was armorial legend more fairly won. But he might have added another, his greatest quality, we think—" Patient." We never knew a man so patient as he, never knew one who had such an unfaltering, invincible faith in the justice of Time. To his eyes Time was truly the "avenger." He was indifferent to the misconstruction and misrepresentations of the present; but if his faith in the justice of posterity's verdict could have, for a moment, been shaken, that great heart would have burst. We never witnessed so grand a faith in the future—such self-abnegation in the present as this man's hopes, plans, and works evinced.

Of the millions which our departed friend gave to the public, more peculiarly to *us*—the University, the Library, the railroads —some idea can be gained from public records and from an obituary which appears in another place in this issue of the *Journal.* But of his frequent, almost continuous benefactions for the relief of private persons, or for the aid of private institutions, little is known or ever will be known to the general public. The quiet, unobtrusive way in which he gave accounts for this. But hundreds of the recipients of his bounty do not forget and never can forget his generosity. One of these met the writer of this this morning, and related, with a voice tremulous with emotion, how he had been employed with his team in the construction of the "Cornell Library" building, one of Mr. Cornell's gifts to Ithaca, and how one of his horses, by striking his ankle against a rock, received a wound from which he bled to death in a short time; and how, while he was mourning his loss, which he could ill afford, Mr. Cornell called upon him and, after inquiring the value of the horse, drew a check for the amount and handed it to him, remarking, with a smile, " I presume I can better than you afford to lose the horse."

But we cannot continue these reminiscences. If we were to merely notice the instances of his noble generosity which come thronging to our memory, we should require a quarto volume, at least.

Mr. Cornell was a man of marked ability, possessing a remarkably strong, vigorous, active mind. Deprived of early advantages of instruction such as the youth of to-day enjoy, his education was deficient. He was not a cultured man. But he was altogether too large a man to affect any accomplishments which he had not, and hence never appeared awkward or seemed to be in a false position among the learned and refined, with whom he was thrown so much in contact during the latter part of his life. All such soon found that Mr. Cornell's head was a very good match for the books, and he soon came to be the most trusted counsellor in all the practical affairs of the great works with which he was latterly identified. The history of his management of the affairs of the University is a marvel of sagacity, patience, and indefatigable industry.

But after all, it was the qualities of the heart which shone most conspicuously in the character of Ezra Cornell. All good people admired and respected the man who founded our great University, and who brought such singleness of purpose and consummate ability to the work of establishing it upon an immovable, a permanent basis. But those whose good fortune it was to personally know him forgot the public benefactor in the MAN. This was so without an exception. The most eminent and cultured, as well as those in the humbler walks of life, felt this irresistible influence of the moral greatness of the man. Goldwin Smith and the common working man of Ithaca alike were proud to call him friend. Among all the wonderful and admirable works which that illustrious historian, James Anthony Froude, found in his visit here, the man Cornell commanded his greatest respect, his highest veneration. Just on the eve of his departure from among us, Mr. Froude paid a glowing tribute to our deceased friend, with the following extract from which we proudly, gratefully close this crude and hasty sketch :

" Since I landed in America, a few weeks ago, I have had my eyes opened to a great many things, but I must say I have seen nothing which, perhaps, astonished and even startled me more than I have seen in Ithaca. I will not say Cornell University alone ; there is something I admire even more than the University, and that is the quiet, unpretending man by whom the University was founded. (Cheers.) I will not say we wish we had him in England, for if we had him there it would be dangerous to his liberty, as I think we should take him by force and make him Prime Minister.

" We have had such men in old times, and there are men in England who make great fortunes and who make claim to great munificence, but who manifest their greatness in buying great estates and building castles, for the founding of peerages to be handed down from father to son. Mr. Cornell has sought for immortality, and the perpetuity of his name among the people of a free nation. There stands his great University, built upon a rock—built of stone, as solid as a rock, to endure while the American Nation endures, and that, I suppose, will be a tolerably long time.

"This I can say, when the herald's parchment shall have crumbled into dust, and the antiquarians are searching among the tombstones for the records of these departed families, Mr. Cornell's name will be still fresh and green, through generation after generation."

TESTIMONIALS OF RESPECT FOR THE HONORED DEAD.

ACTION OF THE EXECUTIVE COMMITTEE OF THE BOARD OF TRUSTEES OF CORNELL UNIVERSITY.

The Executive Committee of the Trustees of Cornell University having received intelligence of the death of the Hon. Ezra Cornell, ordered that the following Memorandum and Resolutions be entered upon their minutes, and that copies be furnished the family of the deceased, to the various bodies of which he was a member, and to the press for publication.

Mr. Cornell was placed in the relation of the President of this body at the organization of the Board of Trustees in 1865. During the nine years which have elapsed since that time, he has steadily given his best thoughts and efforts to the great work in which we have been associated. Although other enterprises calculated to increase the prosperity of the community and the State in which he dwelt received freely of his self-sacrificing labor and of his fortune, the central point in all his planning and working was the University which he had founded and which bore his name. His labors have been almost without cessation, and entirely without any alloy of selfishness. In addition to many other benefactions, his foresight led him to do for the State of New York what the State could not do for herself, in locating lands for the benefit of the University. Cleverly discerning that this was advantageous to the institution which he had established for his fellow-men, he freely devoted the bulk of his fortune, his best thoughts, his constant labors to carrying out this, of which the only inspiration was the desire to confer a benefit upon young men seeking advanced· instruction. Having decided upon this plan, he consented not only to bear labor, but to brave obloquy. The most bitter opposition, the most chilling indifference, the most cruel calumny, were alike unable to turn him from this noble purpose.

In thoughtful remembrance of his sacrifices for whatever he thought worthy, of his deep devotion to whatever he thought just, of his fearlessness in supporting whatever he thought right, we desire to record for the benefit of a coming generation, which is doubtless to show more gratitude than was given during his lifetime, our deliberate and solemn testimony that, in a retrospect in all these years of intimate association, we can recall not one instance of a procedure on his part actuated by a desire to increase his own fortune, to improve his own position, or to advance his own fame. All our connection with him, close as it has been, has revealed one aim, and that aim the improvement, moral, intellectual, and social, of his fellow-men.

Nor can we close this brief memorial without rendering a tribute of respect to that broadness of view which caused him always to look above and beyond the boundaries of party, and sect, and creed, and to labor simply for man as man. In remembrance of our lamented associate, we add to this memorandum the following resolution :

.Resolved, That a committee be appointed to examine and report concerning the erection of a suitable memorial to our de-

ceased friend at the University which he founded, and that a suitable recognition óf his services be publicly made at such time as
shall be found fitting; and be it further

Resolved, That this Board do in a body attend the approaching
funeral.

ACTION OF THE TRUSTEES OF CORNELL LIBRARY.

The founder of the Cornell Library is dead. His generous hand
scatters bounties no more forever. His large heart beats no
longer in sympathy with his country and his countrymen. Sentiments of humanity, of benevolence, and of material well-being
henceforth will not kindle in his eye, nor stir to new activity the
torpid pulse. His gigantic labors are ended. Let us hope that
the departed spirit may find with God that repose and peace
which a lofty sense of duty to mankind denied the living body.
May the greeting be, " Well done, thou good and faithful ser-
vant, enter thou into the joy of thy Lord."

How utterly unselfish was his life ; how simple his tastes ; how
unostentatious his manners. As for him poverty had no terrors,
so riches begot no pride. He labored to create wealth, but wealth
acquired was but an instrument in his hand for improving the
condition, increasing the happiness, and cultivating the intellect
and morals of the people. Wealth was not a luxury to be enjoyed, but a responsibility to be accounted for—a power to be
used in well doing.

His character was pure as molten silver—loving truth, justice,
purity; hating lies, wrong, and vice. The cold reserve of his
manners was warmed by the hidden charity and kindness of his
heart—that heart as tender as a child's.

His apparent severity of expression, in moments of leisure,
blossomed in geniality and mirth. A mind sagacious in forecast-
ing the future as affected by the conduct of the present ; liberal
in his sentiments ; unyielding in his convictions ; charitable in
his judgments ; he stood a power, self-created, self-confident,
crowned by the respect and admiration of weaker natures

gathered around him for counsel or support. Such was the man.

By his untiring efforts to secure the greatest good for the greatest number, he illustrated the utilitarian philosophy; by his patient endurance of adversity, calumny, and suffering, without wavering in his noble purposes, he becomes entitled to the Stoic's crown.

The institutions and public works born of his benevolence, or sustained by his wealth, are like beacons on the mountain-tops. Their names and fame are world-wide.

Our people owe an unspeakable debt of gratitude for the works of his hands and love. To pay it would bankrupt us all, and yet we would be richer for the payment.

May the Recording Angel write of him in the Book of Life : " He loved his fellow-men."

In view of this sad event, be it

Resolved, That the Trustees and Members of the Cornell Library Association hereby express their deep regret and sense of bereavement in the death of Hon. Ezra Cornell, the founder of the Cornell Library, and the President of this Association from its beginning, and their humble submission to the mysterious but all-wise ordering of Divine Providence.

Resolved, That we will renew our efforts to consummate the purpose which he formed and was seeking to accomplish in the establishment of this Library Association, whose interests are committed to our trusts, by adopting measures to fill its alcoves with books— the best monument our citizens can erect to his memory.

Resolved, That the Secretary of this Association be requested to transmit these Resolutions to the family of our honored President and Founder, now deceased, expressing to them the deep sympathy we feel in their great affliction, and commending them to the tenderness of that merciful God in whose care and goodness he trusted.

Resolved, That these resolutions be entered upon the records of the Board.

THE CITIZENS' MEETING.

[*From the Ithaca Daily Journal.*]

Journal Hall was crowded, last evening, with the business men of Ithaca, met to give fitting and formal expression of their sense of, and their unfeigned sorrow at, the loss they had sustained in the death of Ezra Cornell. Every profession, business, and trade was represented. Men whom the seductive allurements of political meetings, dramatic readings, or social amusements could not entice from their dingy offices and the ceaseless routine of business, seemed to have found an irresistible attraction in the object of this meeting, for those were present, last evening, whom we rarely or never see in public meetings of a secular character, of whatever kind or nature.

The meeting was duly organized, and upon the report of a committee, the following preamble and resolutions were unanimously adopted :

" *Whereas*, The hour has come—all too early, save for the wise purposes of an incomprehensible Providence—when we are called upon to follow to the grave the remains of our beloved friend and esteemed fellow-citizen Ezra Cornell ; and

" *Whereas*, We stand by his bier, powerless to recall the noble life that has gone out, and helpful only to express, in words and by our acts, sympathy with the family of the deceased, and our own deep sorrow on account of the loss that has fallen on our community ; therefore be it

" *Resolved*, by citizens of Ithaca in public meeting assembled, That in the life and works of Ezra Cornell, we recognize a nobility of aim, an earnestness of purpose, a brotherhood of motive, the influence of which has diffused itself through our midst, enlarging our views of manhood and inspiring us with increased desire for greater usefulness to our fellow-men ; that, while the imprint of his ingenious hand is indelibly stamped on one of the most important devices of modern times—or of all time—for the benefit of mankind, the Magnetic Telegraph, we are especially mindful at this sad hour that the most numerous products of his indefatigable industry and business enterprise, belong to the village of Ithaca, and to the county of Tompkins, to have and to hold ; that, by his large foresight, and the unstinted use of his self-acquired means, he planted among us an institution of learning whose fame has already spread throughout the world, rendering the locality of our home really, as its name is traditionally, classical, drawing hither the ripest scholars of the age ; by the influence of his presence and teaching we have been greatly benefited, and our children and our children's children are to be much more abundantly blessed ; that, as we stand beside the coffin of our departed friend and neighbor, to-day, we reflect upon his life-work with divided gratitude—for the legacy he has left us in the way of intellectual advantages, and for the impulse which his business enterprise gave to our material prosperity.

" *Resolved*, That in the death of Ezra Cornell we lose a townsman unselfishly loyal to the welfare of our common village, and a friend whose memory will abide with us, as deeply and warmly cherished as in life his daily walk and counsels were esteemed and respected.

" *Resolved*, That as a token of our respect for the memory of the deceased, we unite in closing our respective places of business between the hours of 12 M. and 3 P. M., on Saturday next.

" *Resolved*, That these resolutions be published in the village papers, and a copy of the same be sent to the family of the deceased."

Upon motion the resolutions were unanimously adopted. After which, Judge Boardman being called by many voices, arose and spoke, with many signs of emotion, substantially as follows :

JUDGE BOARDMAN'S REMARKS.

GENTLEMEN :—As has been suggested, this is not an occasion for eulogy, or for alluding to or summing up the character of the dead. I presume you all feel with me that you have suffered a great loss—the loss of a great man ; a man whose instincts were great, in his love of humanity, in his desire for human progress and human well-being. A man as utterly unselfish as perhaps is compatible with human nature ; whose mind seemed to be centred on the human race, and especially of this locality, of which he has so long been a resident.

For him poverty had no terrors ; and wealth in no instance inspired him with pride. It was a treasure put in his hands—not for his own luxury and for his own advancement, and that he personally might profit by it ; but rather that mankind, that the community in which he lived, might receive those benefits which ought justly to be bestowed on a community. In this way he has lived amongst us ; simple in his habits—unostentatious in his manner—attending carefully to his own business—interfering not at all with the business of others—a man of mark, yet a man of sympathy ; of kindness of heart, yet of resolute purpose.

To such a man we owe a deep debt of gratitude—too deep to be paid by any act or expression of grief ; and it would be strange, indeed, if, now that he is dead and gone, this community should not overlook his faults. He had faults—none of us are free from them—but they were trivial, too trifling to be mentioned—let us throw the mantle of charity over them. Let us not suffer his little foibles to draw our minds from the great deeds of his life—from the grand purposes which he set before himself, and which he so successfully accomplished. As the spots of the sun neither obscure his light, nor prevent his warm and beneficient beams from creating life and beauty for all mankind, so the venial faults of Ezra Cornell did not prevent his life-work from being an honor to his country, and a blessing to his fellow-citizens to the end of time. Gentlemen, need I say more ?

ACTION OF THE BOARD OF DIRECTORS OF THE WESTERN UNION
TELEGRAPH COMPANY.

The Directors of the Western Union Telegraph Company having been officially informed of the death of their late associate, the Hon. Ezra Cornell, adopted the following resolutions as a mark of respect to his memory :

Resolved, That this Board, at this first meeting after the demise of our beloved associate and friend, revert to the sad event to express, so far as words will permit, the hearty tribute of our affection for his memory.

The records of this Board testify to his energy, his faith, and courage in the great struggle to conquer adversity, and achieve success in an enterprise regarded at first as chimerical, but which he foresaw was in the end to triumph and inure to the benefit of his country and the world.

It is meet and eminently proper, therefore, that we, his associates and successors, holding the records of his labors and achievements in telegraphy, and representing the vast interests which have grown mighty and strong in his lifetime, should gratefully acknowledge the obligation, not only of ourselves, but of the country and mankind, to his discernment, fidelity, and perseverance.

Resolved, That we deeply sympathize with the afflicted family of the deceased, and tender to them in their bereavement our sincere condolence.

Resolved, That this note of our respect be entered upon the minutes of the Board, and a copy thereof furnished by the Secretary to the family of Mr. Cornell.

MEETING OF THE STUDENTS.

A meeting of the students of the University was held, according to announcement, at ten o'clock this morning, in Military Hall, to make arrangements for the funeral. Major MacMurray presided. The two Senior companies of cadets were detailed to attend the funeral, fully uniformed and equipped, as an honorary body guard. They are to be followed by the two Freshmen companies, also fully uniformed and armed. The entire body of students, in civilian's dress, will march in procession behind. The different classes are all called upon to meet in Military Hall, at ten o'clock precisely, on Saturday. Eight of the strongest men among the students were appointed to act as pall-bearers in carrying the coffin, at nine o'clock, from the residence to the hall; where they will stand guard over it and return it to the residence at twelve o'clock. A committee of four was appointed to draft appropriate resolutions respecting the death of the honored founder of the University. It was unanimously ordered that the entire body of students wear the usual badge of mourning during the remainder of the term.

ACTION OF THE VILLAGE TRUSTEES.

The Board of Trustees of the village of Ithaca, at their regular meeting, last evening, adopted the following resolutions :

" *Resolved,* That in the death of Ezra Cornell we recognize that this community has been deprived of a public benefactor, that our loss is irreparable, and that his memory will be cherished so long as men know how to honor and revere private and public worth.

" *Resolved,* That his munificence in founding in Ithaca, the Public Free Library and the noble institution of learning that bears his name, and his many self-denying labors to promote and advance the welfare and prosperity of the community with which he has been so long identified, especially entitle him to be held in the highest estimation and warmest gratitude by all persons.

" *Resolved,* That this Board, individually and collectively, ex· tend their sincere sympathy to his bereaved and deeply afflicted family.

" *Resolved,* That this Board attend his funeral in a body.

" *Resolved,* That the Clerk of the Board transmit a copy of these resolutions to the widow of the deceased."

PROCLAMATION OF THE PRESIDENT OF THE VILLAGE.

To the Citizens of Ithaca :

To-morrow (Saturday), the 12th day of December, at one o'clock P. M., having been designated as the time for holding the funeral of our late friend and fellow-citizen, Ezra Cornell, and as all desire to pay due respect to his memory, and give their time to the observance of ceremonies befitting the occasion, without feeling the obligations of business resting upon them, therefore, I, Adam S. Cowdry, President of the village of Ithaca, do respectfully recommend that, so far as it may be practicable, the people of this village forego, for the whole or a part of the day, their ordinary avocations ; and I especially request that all business places be closed between the hours of 12 M. and 3 P.M., in accordance with the action of the public meeting last night.

ADAM S. COWDRY, *President.*

ITHACA, December 11, 1874.

ACTION OF THE DIRECTORS OF THE ITHACA SAVINGS BANK.

At a special meeting of the Board of Trustees of the Ithaca Savings Bank, held December 11, 1874, to take action in regard to its President, Ezra Cornell, it was

Resolved, That the death of our lamented associate and friend, Ezra Cornell, fills our hearts with unfeigned regret and sorrow ; that this institution has lost a wise and judicious counsellor, one whose interest in its affairs has been unremitting from its organization, and who has cheerfully given his valuable time to the advancement of its interests and prosperity.

Resolved, That we desire to record our humble tribute to his worth, and express our sincere condolence with his family in their great affliction.

Resolved, That this bank will be closed for business until after the funeral, and that we will attend in a body.

O. B. CURRAN, *Secretary.*

THE BOARD OF EDUCATION AND TRUSTEES OF THE ACADEMY.

At a meeting of the Board of Education and the Trustees of the Academy, the following resolutions were adopted :

Resolved, That we, as also the friends of education everywhere, owe a lasting debt of gratitude to Ezra Cornell. From early manhood he cherished a deep interest in the great cause ; he established and endowed a public library in Ithaca, and gave it to this town and county ; he founded a university, provided it with facilities for instruction in all knowledge, opened its doors to every race and both sexes, and gave it to this State and to the world ; he freely devoted the ripest fruits and the most active energies of his life to these munificent enterprises. The name and memory of Ezra Cornell will be honored and revered so long as the English language shall be spoken, or written, or read.

On motion, the members of the Board of Education, the Trustees of the Academy, and the principals of the two schools were requested to meet at the office of Judge Boardman on Saturday next, at 1 o'clock P.M., to attend the funeral of Mr. Cornell.

D. BOARDMAN, *Chairman.*

J. STROWBRIDGE, *Secretary.*

ACTION OF THE BOARD OF DIRECTORS OF THE GENEVA,
ITHACA & ATHENS RAILROAD.

At a meeting of the directors and officers of the Geneva, Ithaca & Athens Railroad Company the 12th day of December, 1874, the following resolutions were considered and adopted :

Resolved, That the death of Ezra Cornell impresses upon his surviving associates sentiments of deep grief ; that a great public enterprise has lost its most valuable support, its most intelligent friend, its most intelligent benefactor ; but the material loss is overshadowed and forgotten in that far greater loss which our community and country have suffered, exciting grief in every heart and sympathy in every act.

Resolved, That the patriotism, the integrity, the industry, the purity, and the generosity of the noble dead are and will long continue to be an illustrious guide and example to our people and community, worthy our constant recollection and inviting an humble imitation.

Resolved, That the directors and officers of the Geneva, Ithaca

& Athens Railroad Company, as a mark of respect, attend in a body the funeral services of the deceased.

Resolved, That a copy of these resolutions be conveyed to the family of the deceased, with the expression of the profound sympathy of his surviving associates in their sufferings and sorrow.

ACTION OF THE TOMPKINS COUNTY AGRICULTURAL SOCIETY.

At a special meeting of the Tompkins County Agricultural and Horticultural Society, held at their rooms in Library Building, at 11 o'clock A.M., December 12, 1874, the President stated that the object of the meeting was to make suitable arrangements to attend the funeral of their honored ex-president, Hon. Ezra Cornell. It was unanimously

Resolved, That we attend the funeral in a body and march together to the cemetery.

Resolved, That a committee be appointed to draft a sketch of Mr. Cornell's connection with this Society, and also suitable resolutions to be recorded in the records of the Society, and report the same to the next regular meeting.

Resolved, That this Society invite the farmers of Tompkins and the adjoining counties to unite with them in the tribute of respect for the MAN whose mortal remains are this day committed to the tomb.

The committees appointed from the County Agricultural Society and Farmer's Club to express a proper tribute of respect for the memory of Mr. Cornell, drew up and unanimously agreed to the following resolutions :

Whereas, We are called to mourn the death of our beloved friend and esteemed citizen, Ezra Cornell, and

Whereas, By his liberal donation to the Farmer's Club of a valuable agricultural library and museum, and the use for all time to come of a commodious and ample room in which to store the same, and for the meetings of the Society, and

Whereas, We, as farmers, feel that by his influence, his counsel, his sacrifices, and his many liberal donations in behalf of agriculture, we have been benefited more than any other class, and

Whereas, We desire to express the esteem and veneration in which his memory is held by us, therefore be it

Resolved, By the farmers in Tompkins County in public meeting assembled, that, in the earnest labors of Ezra Cornell for the advancement of agriculture, we recognize a nobleness of purpose worthy of imitation, and in his unfaltering faith in the ultimate success of educating and elevating all tillers of the soil, in common with others, is brought to light a peculiar and beautiful trait of his noble character.

We recognize the vast benefits conferred, not only on the State, but the country at large, by his early importation of the best breeds of domestic animals, by his introduction of many improved farming implements, by his wise counsels in our agricultural societies, and by his earnest endeavors to promote their usefulness. Science and the mechanic arts have received rich and lasting contributions from his fertile brain. The cause of education has been advanced through his efforts more than by any other man of the present age.

While we are mindful of, we can hardly realize all the benefits conferred upon ourselves and posterity ; for what class, what industry, what calling has not felt and will not feel for ages to come the influence of his far-reaching, liberally conceived, and well-executed plans ?

Resolved, That we, in an especial manner, as also do all men of like occupation, and friends of education everywhere, owe a debt of gratitude to Ezra Cornell.

E: L. B. CURTIS,	I. P. ROBERTS,
T. BOARDMAN,	P. B. CRANDALL,
H. BREWER,	W. W. AYRES,
J. ALBRIGHT,	L. C. BEERS,
	Committee.

20

MEETING OF RESPECT AT THE PRESBYTERIAN CHURCH.

At the regular Friday evening prayer-meeting in the Presbyterian Chapel last night, the services, at the request of Dr. White, were entirely devoted to the memory of Mr. Cornell. The Scriptures read, prayers offered, and remarks made were all appropriate. The prayers were especially for the relatives of the illustrious dead and the institutions which he had left.

SIBLEY COLLEGE IN MOURNING.

Among the decorations of mourning for the loss of Mr. Cornell seen on every hand, perhaps none are simpler or more tasteful than those of the Botanical Lecture-room in the Sibley College building. Between the central columns is sprung an arch, which, together with the columns, is heavily draped. From the crown of the arch hangs a Greek cross bordered in black, in the centre of which is the monogram E. C., encircled by a wreath of laurel. Above the arch droop the graceful plumes of the urbim grass of the Amazons. The Mechanical Lecture-room, printing office, and all parts of Sibley College are also appropriately draped.

FOUNDER'S HYMN.

BY HON. FRANCIS M. FINCH.

The " Chimes " are still.   Alone,
  As falls the year's last leaf,
The Great Bell's monotone,
  Slow hymns our helpless grief.
Bountiful heart !—bountiful hand !
  Bountiful heart and hand !
O ! Father and Founder !   O ! Soul so grand !
  Farewell, Cornell !—Farewell !

From Slander's driving sleet,
  From Envy's pitiless rain,
At rest, the aching feet !
  At rest, the weary brain !
Laboring heart !—laboring hand !
Laboring heart and hand !

So calm, and grave, and still,
    Men thought his silence, pride ;
Nor guessed the truth, until
    Death told it—as he died.
Lowly of heart !—Lowly of hand !—
Lowly of heart and hand !

" True " as the steel to star ;
    With eyes whose lifted lid
Let in all Truth—though far
    In clouds and darkness hid.
Confident heart !—confident hand !
Confident heart and hand !

" Firm " as the oak's tough grain,
    Yet pliant to the prayer
Of Poverty, or Pain,   ·
    As leaf to troubled air.
Kindest heart !—kindest hand !
Kindest heart and hand !

Untaught,—and yet he drew
    Best learning out of life,
More than the Scholars knew,
    With all their toil and strife.
Conquering heart !—conquering hand !
Conquering heart and hand !

The spires that crown the hill,
    To Plainest Labor free,
Where all may win who will,
    His monument shall be !
Generous heart !—generous hand !
Generous heart and hand !

Brave, kindly heart, adieu !
    But with us live alway
The patient face we knew,
    And this Memorial Day.
Bountiful heart !—bountiful hand !
Bountiful heart and hand !

CHAPTER XXIV.

FUNERAL OBSEQUIES.

Manifestations of Grief.—Suspension of Business.—Lying in State in Library Hall.—Funeral Ceremonies.—Vast Concourse in Attendance.—Services Conducted by Dr. Wilson, and Dr. Stebbins.—Pall Bearers.—The Procession.—Remains Deposited in Family Vault.—Observances at Syracuse, Auburn, Aurora, Cayuga, Towanda, Syracuse University.—Dr. Stebbins' Address.—"Our Founder."

EVIDENCES of the universal respect entertained by the entire community, and the all-prevailing sorrow which was experienced by all classes of people, in consequence of the lamented death of Mr. Cornell, were everywhere manifested. Public buildings, dwellings, and business houses generally, were draped in mourning, while on the day designated for the observation of the funeral obsequies, all of the public offices, banks, stores, factories, and shops were closed, and there was an entire cessation of the usual avocations and business pursuits throughout the village. The funeral ceremonies were attended by a vast concourse of people, and were impressive beyond any previous demonstration of the locality. Almost the entire population were in attendance, together with thousands from the surrounding towns, while large numbers of prominent citizens from every quarter of the State were present to evidence their respect for the dead, and sympathy for the living. The subjoined account of the funeral, which was published in the *Ithaca Daily Journal*, is herewith presented as an appropriate conclusion of the record of this notable and useful career.

The Funeral Ceremonies.

"EARTH TO EARTH; ASHES TO ASHES."

[From the Ithaca Daily Journal, December 12th.]

This morning broke bright and cold, the threatening appearances of the evening previous having fortunately proved delusive. Somewhat later, grayish, fleecy clouds floated lazily across the sun, though not of sufficient density to entirely obscure his brightness or to create apprehensions of a storm.

But though all nature wore a cheerful aspect, the appearance of the town was gloomy enough. Everywhere the eye rested it saw nothing but the trappings of woe. Every store, hotel, and public building, and many private residences were heavily draped, and every flag hung at half-mast. Those business men who had festooned their store-fronts in black upon the first sad news of our public calamity, had more heavily and elaborately draped them on this day when the last solemn rites were to be paid to their deceased friend, helper and counsellor ; and those who had not hitherto displayed any public evidences of grief, now seemed to vie with each other in appropriate decorations. The result of their combined labors was such as to cast an air of funereal gloom over the town, the like of which had never before been witnessed, not even on that woeful day when the news was received of the " deep damnation of the taking off " of the peerless President—Abraham Lincoln. Portraits of the Founder of Cornell University—most of them very faithful likenesses—were to be seen here and there, surrounded by tasteful black borders, and surmounted by mottoes, expressing the estimate which the various owners of the portraits had of Ezra Cornell. " Humanity has lost a friend," " Our greatest and best friend has fallen," were a few the reporter recalls of the many which he noticed.

Business was not formally suspended until noon, but it may be said to have been suspended, in fact, all day ; little else being done than preparing for the funeral ceremonies, and little else being discussed but Ithaca's irreparable loss. The people from the country came thronging in at an early hour, and trains from every direction brought large numbers to swell the already great multitudes gathered here. The stages and 'buses, which were draped in mourning, as also were the cars, were constantly in requisition to carry the fresh arrivals on the different trains to the already over-crowded hotels. All the forenoon the main streets were thronged with people, their numbers increasing in a sort of geometrical proportion as the time drew nearer and nearer the hour for the final scene.

LIBRARY BUILDING.

The entrances are beautifully and heavily draped, as also all the windows, with rosettes black and white ; from the cornices depend heavy folds of drapery. The residence is without any sign of mourning except the usual simple badge on the door knobs. At half past nine o'clock precisely the corpse was removed from the residence to Library Hall, borne by eight student pall bearers, passing through a line of cadets, armed and uniformed, extending to the door of the Library. Company A, Fiftieth Battalion, National Guard, guarded the entrance and passage-ways to the Hall. A guard of honor, consisting of a company of Cornell cadets, surrounded the bier. The coffin was placed on a catafalque in the centre of the hall, and in viewing the corpse, the crowd passed in at the west door and out through the south door. During the three hours and a half that the remains laid in state, to be viewed by the public, hundreds and hundreds of people, with uncovered heads and solemn step, passed through the hall. By actual count, four thousand people took a last look at the honored dead. The corpse, although bearing evidences of wasting disease, looked very natural and beautiful.

DECORATIONS OF THE HALL.

Library Hall was most beautifully and appropriately decorated. Upon the platform immediately under the arch stood the life-sized portrait of Mr. Cornell, which had been removed thither from its accustomed place in the Library.

The picture never showed to better advantage than as it stands there above the lifeless features from which it was painted. The frame of the portrait is trimmed in mourning, and above it in large evergreen letters is Mr. Cornell's talismanic motto, "True and Firm," the same which is carved upon his new residence. Over the motto is the monogram E. C. on a white shield bordered with flowers. At the foot of the portrait there is a beautiful mourning rosette, and the American flag arranged in the form of a shield. This represents the patriotic side of Mr. Cornell's life. Upon the right are the emblems of the University. There is a vacant Founder's chair, draped in black, with the exception of a medallion of Mr. Cornell on the back, which is surrounded by a wreath of white natural flowers, daisies, bouvardia, Chinese primroses, and other rare flowers, the wreath proper being principally smilax. The chair stands there upon the stage, a sad reminder of the joyous commencement occasions, when it was occupied by the founder. On the left of the portrait, is a small marble-topped stand bearing a cross and crown, which are offerings of the Kappa Alpha society. There are also on this side of the stage, several bunches of cereals, emblems of agriculture, one of the industries promoted by the honored dead. The wall at the back of the stage is completely covered with sombre drapery ; over the stage doors, too, are the emblems of mourning ; also around the front to the floor, and around the front to the gallery. The plate upon the lid of the casket bears the inscription, " Ezra Cornell, died December 9th, 1874 ; aged 67 years, 10 months, and 28 days." At the head of the casket was placed a beautiful floral crown ; at the foot, a floral cone.

THE FUNERAL.

The funeral, which was held at the residence, was considerably delayed owing to the large crowds that thronged to view the remains in the hall. They were not taken to the residence until half past one o'clock, and even then crowds and crowds had not gained entrance to the hall. It was intended to have the funeral proper very private, only admitting the near friends and those officiating ; but a great many others had to be present. There were the trustees and the professors of the University, the trustees of the Cornell Library, the ministers of the village, physicians, and many others—all, indeed, that could be accommodated in the rooms on the first floor, and quite a few were up-stairs. The remains were laid in a large double parlor on the north, where the near relatives were gathered. At the head of the coffin was hung black drapery, in the centre of which was seen a sheaf of wheat fully ripe, and over this depended a wreath of laurels. The floral offerings were many and beautiful. Those conducting the services had a position in the hall, and the trustees, professors, and distinguished strangers, filled the south rooms. The services were begun at a quarter of two o'clock by Dr. W. D. Wilson, who read the impressive burial service of the Episcopal Church, beginning, " I am the Resurrection and the Life." Dr. Stebbins then made the following brief but affecting remarks and prayer :

" ' I heard,' says the revelator, ' a voice from Heaven 'saying unto me, Blessed are the dead who die in the Lord ; Yea, saith the Spirit, for they rest, rest from their labors, and their works do follow them.' ' Mark the perfect man, and behold the upright ; for the end of that man is peace. He goeth to his grave like a shock of corn fully ripe.' ' I go to prepare a place for you, and if I go and prepare a place for you I will come again and receive you unto myself; that where I am, there ye may be also.'

" What could I say more? What is there that we need for our comfort in this hour, dear bereaved friends, but the memory of the life that has closed? What greater consolation can we receive than that these labors were so excellent, so generous, so abundant, so marked with wisdom? These labors, too,—all not finished. How many plans were made so unselfish, for the good of the community; to promote the excellent in every art, in all departments of life ; but more than all, to promote that mature manhood, that true unfolding of the human soul through the influences of the Divine Spirit, which gives to us a perfect stature of manhood, as revealed to us in Jesus Christ, our Lord.

" O! how precious have been the words of wisdom that have fallen from these lips ; how excellent the example of daily life; in purity of speech; in manliness of deportment; in sobriety of act everywhere, bearing the burdens of great disappointments with meekness and serenity; achieving great success with the same meekness and the same calmness, without pride and without boasting ; and yet, ever rejoicing in the greatness of his manly heart when God did bless his endeavors for the good of his fellow men.

" O! how precious to this beloved family now is this inheritance of a noble character. What a rich patrimony have you received! How all your life long you have lived in the sunshine and under the influence of such excellence ! O! how should the heart be moved with gratitude to God that you have been thus cultured ; that you have thus been enabled to cherish the best virtues, and have had ever before you an example of wonderful usefulness ; a life devoted to the accumulation of wealth, devoted also to its dispersion, as the Great Giver of all good delights in scattering the riches of his munificence, rather than in their accumulation. Then when this life, so rich, so full of labor, so full of plans yet to be accomplished, drew to its close, what a serenity gathered around it ! Those of us who saw it, know that he walked as meekly, as calmly, as firmly down into the darkness of the shadow of death as he had walked in his daily life in the streets. O, it was well! The chamber where the good man meets his end is precious above all other places—one very near the gate of Heaven. And but one thing, dear beloved household, was necessary to make these last hours—of which I would not speak if we were not here, a sympathizing company, to shed tears with you out of the abundance of our grief—but one thing was wanting, all the most loving heart could devise, the family link was broken by the absence of one member who was uninformed that the last deep shadow was falling. But the rest, with what love, and fraternal and sisterly sympathy, did they lift the departed spirit with their prayers, to the very threshold of the paternal house of many mansions. And since it must be so, beloved friends and associates of the deceased, that he must depart, how grateful should we be that our prayer was answered, that the life might go out as sweetly as its lamp had burned serenely and steadily before. And so this dear husband and father, this true friend, of such manly resolutions, of such grandness of purpose, of such firmness of will, of such compactness of character, closed his eyes in the last sleep as serenely as his little grandchild was sleeping in the lap of its nurse. For this God be praised. We must all depart some time, and oh, how precious is the memory of such a death! It will be impressed upon my mind as long as I remember anything, and my prayer will be most ardent that I may die the death of the righteous, and that my end may be like his. So wish we all, and so let us pray."

Then followed a very impressive and touching prayer by Dr. Stebbins.

As soon as the prayer was closed the choir of the Congregational church arose in a group and sang the chant, " Thy will be done," with great feeling, adding much to the beautiful solemnity of the occasion. The friends then viewed the remains for the last time, when the coffin was closed and conveyed to the hearse by the pall-bearers as follows : John L. Whiton, William Halsey, Jacob Bates, Joseph McGraw, John Gauntlett, T. D. Wilcox, George McChain, Lewis H. Culver.

The procession for the cemetery was then formed in the following order :

ON THE STREET.

1. Company A, Fiftieth Battalion, N. G. S. N. Y.
2. Carriage with officiating clergy.
3. Carriage with attending physicians.
4. Body-guard of Companies B and E, Corps of Cadets of Cornell University.
5. Hearse with pall-bearers, followed by the family and friends in carriages.
6. On the flanks the body of students.

ON THE WEST SIDE-WALK OF TIOGA STREET, FACING NORTH.

1. Trustees of the Cornell Library Association.
2. Trustees of Cornell University.
3. Faculty of Cornell University.
4. Alumni of the University.
5. Trustees of Ithaca Academy, and members of the Board of Education.
6. Trustees of the Ithaca Savings Bank.
7. Tompkins County Agricultural Society.
8. Employés of Mr. Cornell.
9. Delegates from abroad.
10. Village Trustees.
11. Citizens.

The procession moved along Tioga, Mill, Linn, and University Streets, to the cemetery, where a line of citizens and students was formed on each side of the avenue, between which the casket was borne, covered with the floral offerings, followed by the family and intimate friends, the crowd bareing their heads and bowing in respect. The DeWitt Guard was drawn in line at the right of the family vault, where the remains were deposited at half after three o'clock.

When the casket was placed upon the bier at the door of the tomb, Dr. Stebbins solemnly repeated the following stanza :

> Unveil thy bosom, faithful tomb,
>   Take this new treasure to thy trust ;
> And give the sacred relics room
>   To slumber in the silent dust.

After this stanza was repeated the casket was placed in the tomb. When the bearers withdrew and the family approached and stood by the door, Dr. Stebbins spoke as follows :

" It is finished—the work of our beloved friend and fellow citizen is done ; and we have testified by our tears and our sympathies that ours is now done for him. May his memory linger forevermore in our hearts. Accept, mourning fellow citizens, the gratitude of the bereaved household for this spontaneous, abundant expression of your sympathy with them in this hour of their great trial, and of your respect for your fellow citizen and their husband, father, and brother.

" And now, what wait we for but that the baptism of the Infinite Spirit may rest upon us and fill our hearts ; for, as Christian believers, we have deposited here the earthly remains of our friend, in perfect assurance that the spirit has returned to God who gave it.

BENEDICTION.

" And now may the blessing of the Father Almighty, through Jesus Christ his Son, so work in all our hearts, and be manifested in all our lives, that we shall at last be accepted in the company of the faithful, there to unite with them in ascriptions of praise and thanksgiving to Him that sitteth upon the throne and unto the Lamb forever and ever. AMEN."

———

The body will remain in the vault until its final resting place shall be prepared on the University grounds, where it was the wish of the Founder to be buried.

Thus have we laid all that is mortal of our honored friend in the tomb. All that is left to us of the kind friend, the public-spirited citizen, the unostentatious philanthropist and public benefactor, whom we have known, loved, and honored so long, and whom the idea of losing forever is as unspeakably painful as it is difficult to fully realize, is his fragrant memory—the inspiration of his noble example. *These* may safely defy the corroding, remorseless tooth of time. The luminous pages whereon the world inscribes the names of its benefactors whom it will not suffer to die, will surely be honored by the name of Ezra Cornell. But Ithacans need no such record. To say nothing of the institution which crowns our eastern hills, making them classic, our Ithaca, so long as it has a place and a name among the communities of men, will speak eloquently of Ezra Cornell. We know what it was when he found it. We see what it is as he leaves it. We know the millions he invested in enterprises, which all saw—none more clearly than that sagacious mind—could never bring direct profitable returns, merely because with them present prosperity and future greatness were assured to his beloved Ithaca; without them, this consummation he so devoutly wished must be long delayed, perhaps, by reason of some other locality in our vicinity seizing the opportunity which we neglected, never realized. We trust that others may be found competent to the less difficult task of taking up the work which our departed friend's tired hands have laid down forever, and of conducting these enterprises in such a manner as to realize his cherished hopes and aspirations. Yes, a far less difficult task than was his of originating, projecting, and placing them on sound bases. We trust and believe that both Ithaca and the University are to be what our departed friend designed that they should be. But however this may be, the duty of him, whom loving hands tenderly, sadly deposited in his "narrow home" to-day, was nobly done. His is not the fault if the beneficent plans and aims of his life are not fully accomplished. Let us, then, cease these repinings, selfish as vain. Look at those thin hands—oh, how thin; that pinched face; those gray hairs parted over the care-worn brow! Who would disturb this tranquil rest, and call back to the cares

of life the weary, worn, aged worker? Let us, rather, with resignation yield him to the narrow house; for there all is rest and
peace—peace ineffable.

> No baffled hope can haunt, no doubt perplexes,
> No parted love the deep repose can chafe;
> No petty care can irk, no trouble vexes—
> From misconstruction his hushed heart is safe.
> Freed from the weariness of worldly fretting,
>
> *   *   *   *   *   *
>
> He lies whose course has passed away from life.

> A narrow home, and far beyond it lieth
> The land whereof no mortal lips can tell;
> We strain our sad eyes as the spirit flyeth,
> Our fancy loves on heaven's bright hills to dwell—
> God shuts the door, no angel lip uncloses,
> They whom Christ raised no word of guidance said,
> Only the cross speaks where our dust reposes,
> "Trust Him who calls unto His rest our dead."

STRANGERS ATTENDING THE FUNERAL.

A special train arrived on the Cayuga Lake Railroad about
eleven o'clock, bringing the following party from Syracuse: J. J.
Glass, E. B. Judson, N. F. Graves (mayor), Giles Everson, Ezra
Downer, A. C. Powell (ex-mayor), William Kirkpatrick (alder-
man), E. E. Chapman, Carroll E. Smith, Edgar E. Ewers, G. B.
Kent, M. H. Northrup, Professor Charles W. Bennett, H. Cleveland, S. B. Gifford, and James Terwilliger.

From *Aurora:* E. B. Morgan, H. A. Morgan, A. C. Palmer,
G. B. Morgan, H. Morgan, W. H. Bogart, Edward L. French,
Thos. C. Strong.

From *Cayuga:* J. R. Van Sickle, J. A. Bailey.

From *Auburn:* About the same hour a special train via the

Southern Central and Cortland roads brought a party of some forty of the prominent men of Auburn to attend the funeral. Among them were the following : J. N. Knapp, W. Hollister, C. P. Wood, Henry Richardson, Charles Standart, George I. Lechworth, H. N. Lockwood, H. J. Sartwell, O. F. Knapp, J. T. M. Davie, David P. Wallace, E. R. Fay, A. Fitch, J. G. Knapp, John E. Leonard, James Henderson, E. G. Storke, C. E. Swift, John Brainard, William Searles, E. D. Jackson, S. L. Bradley, E. B. Jones, J. B. Richardson, Charles G. Briggs, M. L. Brown, H. Hughes, G. Rathbun, G. B. Turner.

Among the strangers in attendance were George R. Dusenberre, Fred W. Prince, Langdon Wheat, Geneva ; General Steele, Romulus, and many others.

From *Towanda :* Robert A. Packer, Colonel Victor E. Piolet, Colonel J. F. Means, James W. Ward, A. M. Sanderson, and J. Robinson.

PRESS REPRESENTATIVES.

The neighboring press was represented at the obsequies as follows : *The Elmira Advertiser* by its city editor, A. Towner ; *The Rochester Democrat and Chronicle* by its city editor, J. A. Hockstra ; Mr. Carroll E. Smith, of the *Syracuse Journal ;* M. L. Northrup, of the *Syracuse Courier.*

RESPECT FOR THE DEAD IN SYRACUSE.

At a public meeting of citizens held at Syracuse, Thursday, suitable resolutions were adopted eulogistic of the late Ezra Cornell. The board of supervisors also passed memorial resolutions.

A committee consisting of judges of the county, city officers, and twenty-five leading citizens was appointed to attend the funeral.

IN AUBURN.

There was a large meeting of citizens of Auburn in the Court House, on Friday evening last, called upon short notice, to pay tribute to the memory of Ezra Cornell. General John N. Knapp was chairman, and George W. Peck, secretary. General Knapp, E. D. Johnson, Hon. John L. Parker, Hon. T. M. Pomeroy, General William H. Seward, Charles P. Wood, and George B. Turner made highly eulogistic remarks in respect to Mr. Cornell. A series of resolutions was adopted, and a committee of eighty-five prominent citizens appointed to attend the funeral, which a large number of them did by special train, over the Southern Central Road, on Saturday.

RESOLUTIONS AT SYRACUSE UNIVERSITY.

The students of Syracuse University appointed a committee on Friday, consisting of Professor Bennett, D.D., M. D. Buck, '75, G. Darrow, '76, L. S. Hutchinson, '77, and G. W. Peck, '78, who framed appropriate resolutions expressive of the feeling of the University in regard to the death of the Hon. Ezra Cornell.

DR. STEBBINS'S TRIBUTE TO MR. CORNELL.

[From the Ithaca Daily Journal, December 16th.]

We have obtained from Dr. Stebbins the concluding passage of his sermon, Sunday morning last, on the Discipline of Sorrow, in which he pays a tribute to the memory of Mr. Cornell:

" This meditation is not inappropriate, I trust, to the sorrowful solemnities of the past week. Symbols of mourning have hushed the thoughtless in our streets, and tears of grief have been shed by strong men when they have met each other in their places of business. In all our homes one name has been spoken with hesitating tongue. Such a tribute is seldom paid to a private citizen, so spontaneous, so sincere, so abundant. All felt that they had lost a good citizen, a bountiful benefactor of the town. He was distinguished by a sterling integrity, on which calumny could not cast a shadow, by a marked manliness of character which com manded respect, by a persevering energy which no obstacle could turn aside, by views so comprehensive as to be interested in the construction of a drain or the founding of a University, by an enterprise so daring as to think anything needed could be obtained. He was among the foremost in originating and sustaining all undertakings for the good of the town, by a liberal use of his enlarging fortune and practical wisdom. He was sensitive to his own lack of education, which his narrow opportunities in youth compelled, and he felt the importance of opening to the people, and especially to the young, wider avenues to the sources of knowledge. To this end he lavished his wealth without stint and his strength without measure in founding the two institutions which will merit the gratitude of posterity as well as our own. Nor did he forget, amidst the riches and honors of such princely munificence, the wants of the impoverished and the sorrows of the distressed, but many fires were kindled on cold hearths and many destitute tables furnished with bread by his quiet, private bounty. How marked his simplicity of life amidst abundance! How unassuming his deportment in the midst of highest success! How deep his faith in the capabilities of his fellow-men! How calm when calumny darkened the air around him! How assured he stood in the panoply of conscious integrity! And when the overburdened frame, tasked in the great work he had undertaken even beyond its endurance, began to bend and break under its burden, how serene his patience as life was ebbing away, and how submissive to the great Providence by which he was called to leave his plans unaccomplished, but yet well begun. With what unobtrusive, unspoken, but deep religious trust he closed his days ; no murmur passing his lips, no repining abiding in his heart. What an example he has left behind him as an inspiration to the young of the power of industry, economy, integrity, and benevolence to win competency and honor.

" I need say no more. I hope and believe that soon another occasion will be given to other lips, more capable than mine, to truly and fully delineate before the citizens of the town, a character so full of richest instruction. In expectation of such a tribute from other hands, I lay this token (O, how poor !) of my respect and yours upon the grave of EZRA CORNELL."

OUR FOUNDER.

[From the Ithaca Daily Journal, December 11th.]

Our Founder is dead ! And gone forth from our halls
    Is the sound of mourning and grief.
All hushed is our laughter ; all draped are our walls,
    For the hero whose life was too brief.

" Too brief ! " Ah no ! For ere he had gone,
    Rich fruit had sprung from the seed.
Seed which are symbolled in wood and in stone ;
    Noble marks of his generous deed.

His body may fade, but his works will endure
    Through years that are yet to pass by ;
For the name of a man so honest and pure
    Will never be suffered to die.

When we gather beside him, as we stand at his bier,
    Let us cherish this comforting thought :
That beyond the " dark river " he had nothing to fear,
    For his redemption was gloriously wrought.
                    —S., of '77.

www.ingramcontent.com/pod-product-compliance
Lightning Source LLC
Chambersburg PA
CBHW060531030726
47498CB00004B/1152